Endlessness Again

Horace Belvins Helmick

ISBN 978-0-9895100-3-5

[book title]
O*S*P*O*A*C*L

[intro quip]
"She may have heard herself saying something normal, *normal* as in *commonplace*, a stock comment. But I find the statement curiously deformed."

—Reon, The Silver Star
Monday, December 21, 1992.

(1)

Aye, the two friends are out sitting again at their small table on the sidewalk. Tis another warm sunny day with no wind or smoke noticeable, and from somewhere nearby a bird is singing an adequately complex song. Necky quietly examines his seriously discolored thumbnail while Vogs, who is at present staring down at the tabletop as if the much scarred black metal surface were a mirror, mutters playfully to himself in his remarkably deep voice, "You are one of the few people in this world who I had never laid eyes on. What a pleasure it is to do so now." Down the block, a vigilant dog barks.

And a slinking orange cat passes under the table, between Vogs' legs, just as the brown-bodied, crimson-headed songbird high atop the pole across the all but empty street stops his song cycle and spreads his turquoise wings to fly away. Vogs rears his sizable head. He swallows hard and nods soberly at his chum. "You're wanting to ask me what I'm doing over here right now, aren't you, Necky?"

Necky, as is frequently the case, particularly when he is outside, has been both grinning and silent for some time now. He shines his grin across the little table at Vogs.

Vogs sits up somewhat straighter on his wobbly chair to boom like surf on the rocks, "If you are, my answer is, yep, here I am, Necky, clack-clock-cluck, staring right down the throat of Endlessness again."

Perhaps realizing he had not returned the nod from Vogs, Necky gladly does so now. Still, Necky says not a word.

Vogs nods right back again and continues his answer. "Taking this really close-up gander at Endlessness, I'm finding it no more appealing here today than it was three years ago and a thousand miles from here when and where I started but couldn't finish a lame writing by that name—or nine years ago just fifteen miles from here when Endlessness haunted me so relentlessly that I used it as an excuse to quit the city and take myself into hiding. Away I went, up into the foothills. It followed me, of course. Endlessness has followed me everywhere, all over the continent. Yep, the only times known to me in this foreverness that Endlessness was not lurking near my life was when nothing was lurking near my life—"

Vogs just suddenly stopped talking, cutting his outpour so fast that Necky's chin jumped an inch. Centered on Vogs' forehead is a faint blue question mark. His eyes have descended again to the tabletop. He closes his mouth tightly, bobs his big head.

Necky sits and grins. Necky watches and grins. Necky has demonstrated numerous times in the past that he would be more than content to wait all day if necessary for Vogs to continue with whatever he happened to have been saying.

Other than waiting, and just sitting and grinning, what might Necky be doing during this unexpected break? Could he, despite his totally relaxed face, be making a great effort to unravel Vogs' intended meaning? Or—yes, this is more likely the case—is Necky wondering if this latest gush from Vogs, a mostly familiar minor chronicle, will turn out to be not a bleak memoir at all but the deceptive dawn of another of Vogs' elaborate dry jokes, jokes that sometimes take two and three hours to unfold? Certainly Necky heard the canny perverseness skating around in Vogs' voice right before Vogs abruptly stopped his mouth; but that acoustic hint, if a hint it were, will be of little help to Necky. Why? Vogs is widely known to be both a lover of irony and a frequent, perhaps habitual user of any and all types. He will slide slyly into irony, he will slide slyly out. Vogs can be sliding in when he sounds like he is sliding out. Hence it would or will be tricky indeed for Necky, who has a good and active memory, to distinguish whether Vogs is playing the droll here now for him.

Far less difficult for a friend to discern is that Vogs is not truly as disheartened by this "Endlessness" aspect of his history as his words and quick hand movements and that one nervous swallow may have made him appear.

Vogs' head bobs no more. His hands have calmed. He expounds: "The *nothing* I was referring to when I said '…when nothing was lurking near my life….' is *the void*." Evidently he had interrupted his speechifying about "Endlessness" so that he could explain to Necky (and to himself first?) his use of a particular word, *nothing*. "You know, the great void, the panorama of emptiness, the timeless ultra-reality that deep-sleep so poorly imitates."

While furnishing what he obviously considers a clarification, Vogs had drawn in an extra deep breath of the thick urban air. He now forces all that air out of his lungs while saying, "Over the years I've pretty much just ignored it. Endlessness that is."

He is about to take in another exaggerated breath and speak on of his Endlessness when the sun peeks round the edge of their building at him. Vogs pertly peeks right back at the sun. He arranges a grin on his face.

He grins just like Necky, at Necky. "Hey! You there. You're picturing what I'm going to say next! Aren't you, Necky?

If you're thinking I'm about to say that in order to ignore something so powerful as Endlessness I've had to dumb down much of my perceptual apparatus and pretend that I'm functioning smoothly in society and act out silly-billy roles and acknowledge endlessly and publicly my debt to what little blood and culture I possess, you are certainly correct. Etc. It's the same pooped old poopy story, I know, I know. At least I've never had to do jury duty or attend meetings or suck the famous clonking blue arse." Vogs' delivery will slow a bit, then pick right back up. "And I don't *just have to* follow a curved path to get anywhere, simply *anywhere!*" Vogs slows again. In fact he pauses. He is not altogether pleased with what he just said. He touches the tabletop. "Best you forget that last sentence, Necky; I'll work on it a bit before I try it on you again. —I'm realizing just now something else that I've never had to do. And that's to make promises I knew I'd never keep."

Necky Watershighagain ends another of his sweet interludes of grinning silence by leaning across the tiny table and saying in his habitual whisper, "I'm seeing you as having just made a shaky entry into this gravity field, Vogs, and you're feeling just like a big, black bird disappearing into thick, white fog."

Necky's off words and lucid gestures transform the thin remainder of Vogs' copycat grin, that sun-sparked grin, into a broad smile of pleasure. As always, Vogs particularly delights in hearing Necky conspicuously use a word, like *fog*, that nearly rhymes but doesn't quite rhyme with *his* one and only name. The big smile that grew from a grin lasts but seconds, however. Vogs' smile is obliterated from his colorfully speckled, unevenly tanned kisser when he pensively squinches up his face to propose, "It might be something simple, Necky. I might have this continuing problem with Endlessness because of something real simple, something like, for instance, the fact that I don't see the world as merely mechanical—"

He did it again. Vogs stopped cold again. Does another of his words need defining?

Vogs sighs. Necky silently notes the sigh. And when Vogs then offers up to the sky a lavish, bighearted wave, Necky's eyes calmly record this unsolicited friend-of-the-sky gesture. Still, no fresh reason turns up to explain why Vogs has again suddenly ceased speaking.

Necky practices opening and closing his mouth a couple of times.

Vogs is sitting quiet now.

Necky whispers wryly up at that same sky, "The longest meaningful pause in conventional speech is how long?" Is Necky impatient? That's not likely. Probably he's just having fun.

Raising and lowering his shoulders and clearing his throat, and ignoring Necky's aimed question, Vogs picks up more or less where he had left off and delivers a *nor/or* list of other ways in which he does not see the world. "Nor as elegantly electrical. Nor as filled by faith. Or lopsided with love. Or all puffed up with power."

"Yah, it might be something simple like that." Necky's long-playing grin shifts about on his mouth. "It might and it just might not be. Depends on the attitude."

Vogs leans toward Necky, who is leaning yet toward him. "The attitude? The attitude of who or what?" The men have leaned far enough toward each other that their heads are nearly touching. Their eyes, however, are shooting off in quite opposite directions. Vogs is gazing intently across the street at a lone woman searching her purse. "Huh, Necky? Who or what?"

And Necky is staring in through the giant pane of heavily smudged glass that stands just inches from his elbow. Without focusing his eyes on any one thing, Necky gapes through the wall of glass and into the space that had once housed the infamous, lurid boutique Thesaurus. A number of people had gruesomely met their ends one deadly day in that crazy shop. The business went out of business forthwith, and the building stood empty for nearly three years before Necky Watershighagain and Vogs came to town looking to settle far away from the spotted remnants of

Necky's childhood family. Vogs and Necky have been renting the building and using it as their studios and residences for a couple of years now. "How would I know, Vogs? The attitude is always moving around. And I was just talking hypothetically anyway. No, *hypothetical* is not the word. Anyway!" That was as exclamatory as Necky ever gets.

Vogs' hands and wrists are all but covered with dry or drying paint, of various colors. Wiping one gaudy palm languorously down one side of his not quite so densely color-splattered face, Vogs confesses. "I'm feeling as if I no longer have a self-image."

"Did you ever?" whispers Necky. Necky flicks the tip of his nose with a torn fingernail as he glances down beside the table at the soiled sidewalk between his untied shoe and the low brick wall that supports the tall thick glass. He then resumes his horizontal staring in through the glass. Necky is, of course, still grinning.

"I… Yah." Vogs doesn't quite chuckle. "Well, I was under the impression that I did."

Stopping for a moment to think over what he had just said, Vogs rubs the same painted hand a couple of times across his lips. No…his hand did not quite touch his lips.

"Assuming for a moment that I did once have a self-image, could I have gradually lost it? Could this self-image of mine have just slowly dissolved away? The answer that I'm seeing right this moment is that my image of myself got fainter and fainter because I work in private so much of the time and therefore I don't have anyone to impress."

"Except for me, Vogs."

"Except for you, Necky."

"Except for me too, Vogs."

Vogs jerks bolt upright on his chair.

Necky, however, does not so much as wince. Why? Wasn't he too surprised by the third voice? Wasn't he too taken completely unawares by Corr's phantasmal approach? Or had some freak bending of light on the outside of the window glass allowed him to see a murky reflection of a person drawing near? Naturally, Necky will never say. But he does obediently turn his face from the unwashed window to smile fondly up at the woman, Corr, right after she flicks her index finger at his hair. Corr is now standing as if waiting close beside Necky. She had flicked his hair precisely the way he had flicked the tip of his nose shortly before she spoke.

Having realized who the except-for-me-too is, Vogs slouches purposefully on his chair and assumes an genial sneer. *Everyone knows that Corr can move like a ghost, even in broad daylight.* From the gravel at the bottom of his throat, Vogs intones, "Nice morning, huh, Corr."

And Necky promptly repeats Vogs' salutation. Necky, however, treats the greeting as a catchy jingle with small bells ringing in the voice of the singer. "Nice morning, huh, Corr."

Corr had long ago stopped using her given names, *Correggio* and *Corato*, the supposed birthplaces of her father and mother, because she considers Correggio a male name. In place of *Correggio Corato*, she had taken to calling herself *Corr Cor.* "It is no longer morning, ya'boys." Corr shows them her broken watch, the ruined old-timey watch that she never takes off her wrist.

Vogs corrects himself, willingly. "Nice afternoon, then."

Corr cocks her head at him. "How'd you like your sex last night?"

"Fine. Great. Simply wonderful. Please come again."

When Corr then swings her eyes to direct a keen gaze at Necky, Necky immediately sputters out his take on the night before. "Me too. It was great, Corr. Even greater than great."

Corr softens her face. "Thank you. It is certainly nice to be appreciated. I enjoyed it, too."

"But how come you had to leave while it was still dark?"

Affectionately touching the back of one of her fingers to Necky's stubbly cheek, Corr tells him to just not worry about it. "As you are well aware, my own bed is ever so much more comfortable than either of yours." The skin on Necky's face and the skin on Corr's hand are of the same value but not exactly the same color. She is a painter, too. She lives and works in the building next door. Noisily, one-handedly, Corr drags the remaining chair out from under the table.

She describes her next move as she makes it. "Gingerly Corr lowers her celebrated tail to the failing seat of the empty third chair."

Corr exhales with a hiss of pleasure. Seated between the two men, her place today faces directly across the brief table at the aforesaid big sheet of glass.

"Well then?" Vogs sniffs, snuffles and asks, "Are we ready for today's question? Corr? Necky?"

Vogs proceeds to ask "today's question" when and only when the two addressed heads have been grudgingly nodded. "I've seen dogs run around to the other side of a pond to better bark at something on the pond, a duck perhaps. But I've never noticed a dog at the beach trying to run around to the other side of the ocean. Do dogs know that the ocean is *that* big?"

"Certainly."

"Not a chance."

"Hmm." Forcing his face of many colors into a deep frown, Vogs stands his right pointer-finger on the crown of his large, sparsely haired, fair-haired head. "I shall now interpret the responses. Corr was first to answer. She apparently holds that all dogs are at least as aware as their human counterparts. Necky takes the opposite view and gives no credence at all to the gossip going around that the world's dogs have recently moved into a takeover position."

Corr is first again with a comeback. She retorts, "Though you camouflage them well, I see that you are full of ill humors again this morning, Vogs. Notice, please, sir, that I said *ill humors*, not *chill rumors*."

"Ill humors and not chill rumors?" Emphatically, ambiguously, Vogs ever so innocently shakes his now helplessly grinning head.

Corr spends but two measly seconds wrinkling her noticeable nose at Vogs before she angles her head away from him for a try-on of the not-unfriendly sneer he had used not many moments before to welcome her. The agreeable sneer fits like a glove on her face. So faced, Corr continues her ribbing of Vogs, this time by employing exactly what he likes, his name used in an uncomplicated rhyme. "Why does Vogs ask endlessly of dogs?"

Considerably more effective than Corr's *Vogs/dogs* rhyme was her use of the word *endlessly*. Vogs' head bounced like a soap bubble when she said that word. He makes no attempt to answer her silly question but quickly shades his eyes with his hueful hand.

It is Necky who comes roaring back—a little late—with a reply for Corr, the table's most recent arrival. Note: a roar from Necky is still not much above a whisper. "It's not morning, Corr! Remember? You said so yourself."

Apparently Corr's saying the word *endlessly* had thrown Vogs into a condensed meditation. Done now with his rumination, he comes not roaring but soaring back to the table as an unbelievably perky Vogs, a theatrically vivacious Vogs, who sprightly pushes that pointer-finger of his this time to his temple. "Let us think now! It must be that time again. Time for one of us at this table to ask the question. Who's turn is it?"

The question is the same question every time it is asked by any one of these three cohorts but is not and never the same as *today's question*. Obviously Vogs intends to take this turn himself.

"Are we going to work, lay about, or travel today?"

"Travel." Corr sounded certain of that.

"Work." Necky sounded equally for sure.

"Ok. That is quite fine with me. Yes, it is." Vogs waves his head merrily. "That means I get to lay around all by meself all day."

"No!" That was Corr's *no*. Hoisting a hand high above her head, she points crisply at the heavens. "At an amazing juncture of life and superlife, the woman's head pops through and she can see the land of the simply-living. She sees Vogs and she sees Necky Watershighagain. They are walking beside her. The trio are on their way down to the beach to drown vogs. — Woops, I said *vogs* when I meant to say *dogs*."

Grimacing with an hilariously bogus air of self-satisfied stateliness, Vogs manages the exceedingly difficult task of spitting out words that sound hot-blooded while he is grimacing so stiffly. "If that be true, Corr, I'd be afraid if I were you that it will be *you* who gets drowned today."

Corr wraps her arms across her noticeable chest. "You wouldn't drown me."

"No, but Necky would."

Necky grimaces as weirdly as Vogs and eagerly waggles his head up and down.

Corr does not promptly jab back, as both Vogs and Necky undoubtedly expected she would. As if she is completely unaware that the two men are waiting and watching her, Corr either almost frowns or almost smiles as she slips into utter stillness, where she then abides blank-of-face and as quiet as the long dead while her painter's hand glides gravely through the air and over the edge of the table to slide inside Necky's partially unbuttoned shirt.

Before Necky can change his kinky grimace into a yowling grin, Corr has grabbed a hard fistful of the shiny black hair that has long been growing long on his also noticeable chest.

Vogs snorts and laughs. He slaps the table and barks, "Stop that! Didn't you two get enough of that last night!"

"Shut yourself up, Vogs!" whoops back Corr. "I have to teach this doltish chap here to not ever take sides against me at any cost!"

Vogs shuts himself up. He flies into action. To protect Necky's chest hair? In one blinding thrust Vogs is up, up high on his feet, reaching down and out with two stiff, straight arms. He be the mighty Blackhawk, an unbelievably powerful predator. Bent on grabbing twin clawfuls of Corr's long, dark, straight head of hair, the bird/man dives.

Trapped in the middle, Corr must fend off the hawk's merciless horny talons with one hand while her other hand is being squeezed two-handedly against Necky's hot chest by an eyeless Necky. High, medium, and low: suddenly all three painters at the table are laughing wildly.

Who is the high, who the low, and who the medium? The low would be Necky, for he laughs too at a whisperer's volume. Or Necky could be the medium, if pitch instead of volume be the consideration. Then Vogs would be the low, on account of his exceptionally deep voice. But Corr would be the high in either consideration. She has both the highest pitched and the highest volume laugh.

As unexpectedly as their riotous laugh started, it stops. In the sudden silence Corr and Necky and Vogs snap back to sitting straight up and flat out on their chairs. Their six eyes close as one. In precise and perfect agreement Corr and Necky and Vogs bow their heads and press their foreheads to the scroungy black metal of the tabletop.

Now what was that hush drama about? Are these three plucky people so harmonious that they can act out with exact timing a succinct, wordless, soundless sketch without composing it first? Hmm. A returning-to-neutral ritual has been evolving for the threesome over the past year or so… Could the little show in question here today have been a slippery, quick-witted variant of that shape-shifting ritual?

Who will be the first to speak? Nope, it is Necky. Four full minutes of quiet have elapsed at the table when Necky all of a sudden declares he's hungry. He doesn't lift his head from the table, though, not even when Corr says she is hungry, too. Corr does not raise her head, either.

Vogs does. He springs clear up to his feet and pivots toward the street in search of food.

He all but collapses limply to the sidewalk, for there is someone standing within a foot of him, looking at him without intelligent awareness. Gawking, that is.

It's a woman. Not a woman like Corr, a woman like the ones one sees in certain clothing stores with their heads held high in the air. Vogs' lip rolls up as he inquires of this person, "Are you at all conscious that you are looking at me?" His was not a rhetorical question; no, he really wants to know.

The woman doesn't budge. Had she even heard Vogs?

So Vogs does the supposed suitable thing to do in all such situations: he passes his open hand back and forth before her eyes. The woman does not jerk or shrink back from his hand the way Vogs as like as not had predicted she would.

"Kiss her, Vogs," urges Corr in a hard, rough voice. "That'll wake her up." Corr has lifted her head from the tabletop. Precariously perched on her chair, she is glaring up over her shoulder at Vogs and the mute woman.

Necky strongly disagrees. His head is up from the table now, too. "No! Don't do that!" His forehead still shows the mark of its contact with the table. "Eleven buckets of trouble will rain down on us if you do."

The eyes blink. The face blushes. The woman smiles a tiny smile. "I'm sorry. I thought there was something wrong here. You all had your heads down on the table…as if you were maybe even dead."

Corr is first again, the first one at the table to deliver a tough-toned comeback, puny as it is. "We *are* maybe even dead!"

Next is Necky. He says, "How were or are you planning to determine if we are dead or not?"

Last but not to be the least, Vogs notifies the woman that she has trespassed on their house of worship.

Most of the scarlet drains from the woman's face. "Is that what you were doing? Praying?"

Instead of stepping back a bit to open up the small space between them, Vogs leans slightly forward. "No. I lied. You have a beautiful voice."

He is warned. Fast Corr snaps, "Ease it up, Vogs!"

Corr stands up, faces the woman, and droops her arm over Vogs' shoulder.

Corr and Vogs and the woman remain exactly where they are, not speaking, not moving, standing intimately close, until Necky springs to his feet and tries to duck into the middle of their tight triangle.

The woman recoils.

This staggering-back reaction of the woman startles Corr and almost makes her jump back, too. She, Corr, laughs concavely and haughtily lays her other arm on Necky's shoulder. Hooked together then all in a row, Necky and Corr and Vogs openly defy the woman.

The little smile on the woman's face has grown. And it undergoes a humorous twist as the woman candidly informs her spectators, "If I had the proper device on me right now, I'd take your picture. Three Hams Joined At The Shoulders."

The jaws of two of the three hams-in-a-row drop. Vogs recovers—his jaw is the one that had not dropped—and announces to everyone close and faraway that exhibitionists are not necessarily hams. "A different set of rules apply."

Arrogantly, lazily, Corr lowers her arms from the men's shoulders. "Let's start over." Bluntly she queries the woman. "Were you merely passing by without the proper device attached, or did you come here for the express purpose of staring at us?" Corr's voice has not discernibly un-toughened since she said, "Kiss her, Vogs."

The other woman's voice, however, is wonderfully soft, composed, polished, equitable, and cordial. "I came today to talk to a person named Vogs. My name is Laura."

Vogs cranes his neck at her. "Just Laura?"

"Laura Pepin."

"I am the one you are looking for."

"I guessed that." The woman sounded pleased with herself.

Vogs smirks, but not tellingly. "And is that why you were staring at me, Laura Pepin?"

The woman's face turns (the way a leaf *turns* in the fall) and becomes as beautiful as her voice. "Yes." Her hair is a glistening gold that shows just the slightest touch of red. Her skin is pale yellow-pink ivory. She is as tall as Vogs and thinnish from chin to toes but not skinny.

Vogs still has his neck stretched at her. "Your eyes?"

"Yes. Those are my eyes."

"I am asking what color they are, Laura Pepin, not whether they are truly yours."

"Can you not see their color, Vogs?"

"Most people call me Vogs."

"Ok, Vogs."

Necky swiftly inserts a whisper. "Too quickly and too easily is this yellow-haired interloper dealing with tricky Vogs' penchant for appropriating and sometimes destroying overly familiar verbal constructions."

Vogs could not have not heard Necky, but he gives no sign that he did. "Of course I can see their color."

Laura smiles and keeps her eyes on Vogs' eyes.

Vogs tries again. "Your eyes look, however, like eyes that change their color to fit the situation. What color do you think they *normally* are?"

"Red first thing in the morning, blue at noon, brown after the sun goes down."

Vogs crosses his eyes—no, he cannot cross them any farther than that—and stacks his open hands on the back of his head. "Ok. I asked for that."

Did Vogs' outwardly self-deprecating reply mean that he had or that he had not understood the woman's answer?

"Yep!" Corr nips surly at him. "You did certainly ask for that, Vogs."

Necky laughs brightly and pretends to side with Corr. "Slap him down, Corr. Make Vogs eat concrete."

Yellow Hair reaches out to take Necky's hand. "I am Laura Pepin."

Necky gladly takes her hand. He examines its clear, smooth skin. "I am the humble Necky Watershighagain. At your service. Forever. Might I eat your hand?"

"Sure. In time, Necky. But right now I will talk with Vogs, if he will talk with me."

Not for the first or the last time in her life, Corr plants her fists classically on her hips. "Aren't you going to tell *me* your name?"

"Could you not hear my name?" Was that a barbed remark by Laura? "I have said it twice, and Vogs has said it twice. And neither of us were whispering like Necky here." Or is Laura Pepin merely being coyly friendly with Corr, the way she has been so far with Vogs?

Corr steps up even closer right in front of Laura. "Of course I heard you say your name. Your name, however, sounds like one that changes to fit the situation. What name do you think you *normally* use?" Now it is Corr who sounds like the catty one. Vogs and Necky stare slightly askance at her.

Laura reaches her hand the short distance to take Corr's hand. She examines the paint on the back and front of Corr's hand. "Sometimes I am Laur, like *far*. Some other times I'm simply L, like *dell*. But by far most of the time I am Laura Pepin. At your service. Forever. Sorry, I don't eat the chemicals found in artist's paint." Gently she lets go of Corr's green and puce flecked hand.

Corr immediately retorts with equivalent straight-out insincerity, "I like you, Laura. Maybe we will sleep together tonight. And these other guys too."

Laura cants her head to one side. "Can I believe you?"

Corr tips her head to the same side. "You don't have to wait until nightfall to find out."

As if she had just remembered something, Laura slaps the palm of her hand soundlessly against her temple. "Oh, but first I must talk in private with Vogs."

Corr slaps both of Corr's temples. Not soundlessly. "Oh, but first *I* must talk in private with Vogs."

"No." Vogs breaks up the duel. "Laura and I will saunter across the street for a cup of hot. And you will wait here, Corr, if you indeed must speak with me."

It is Laura's turn to really want to know something. "Is this woman actually going to obey you, Vogs?"

"Naw." Vogs shakes his head and chortles. "Or not unless she wants to, of course. She might be able to figure a way to come out ahead by *pretending* to do what I requested of her."

"Didn't sound much like a request to me," grumbles Corr in a much-lowered voice.

"Never you mind. Never you mind, you poor thingamajig." Necky comforts Corr while petting her hair with much ado. The hair on Corr's head and the hair on Necky's arm are the same color but not exactly of the same value.

"Daddy, might I leave the table now." Corr bows shallowly to all and huffs away.

"Well, Monsieur Vogs, looks like it is a good goodbye again." Necky shakes Vogs' hand heartfully. "And…a good day to you too, Demoiselle Laura." Necky eloquently kisses Laura Pepin's hand and then exits into the building. His and Vogs' building, not Corr's building.

Laura mischievously twirls a lock of her shimmering hair about her index finger. "Your friends?"

"I dink poe."

"I'm ready for that 'cup of hot' you mentioned, Vogs."

Vogs does not answer her but spins swiftly about and dashes across the street to lean against the lamp pole over there, to wait as if impatiently for Laura. What Vogs may be doing here is offering Laura a wide-open opportunity to betray to him a fatal weakness in her seductive armor by pouting and refusing to chase after him.

Laura smiles urbanely and strides handsomely across the macadam to halt in the gutter below Vogs. She stands in the filth and clutter gazing up at him.

Vogs massacres an already decrepit and frequently mistreated bundle. "Gonna be a terrible town in the old time tonight."

"That didn't look much like a saunter across the street to me, Monsieur Vogs." Is Laura going to tastefully pip Vogs right here and now? Could she? Is Laura Pepin a pipper? She just might be. If she is, she coolly refrains from exercising whatever skill she has in the craft of killing people. She refrains for the time being, that is.

"I'm going to live forever." Vogs only sounds as if he is bragging. Lounging now on a café chair decidedly more substantial than any one of the three chairs assigned to the bent black table over on the sidewalk across the street, sipping at a steaming cup of tea, he honestly tells Laura Pepin, "But Necky is facing in the other direction. He plans to die soon as he can. I mean, he's looking for his first real chance. Don't get the idea that he wants to cheat or anything. He's just looking for a good, legitimate chance to die. And he'll take it, he says."

"You two sound very different from each other to be living under the same roof." Laura's marvelous hair dances of its own accord.

"Yeah. I'm much more of a piss-and-vinegar guy than Necky is."

"You don't impress me as being all that disagreeable, Vogs. Where'd you get that name? It mirrors your bottomless voice."

"Don't know." Vogs glances absently out the window. No. He is not looking out the window. A more accurate picture has him looking, not all that attentively, at the window's jamb.

"Don't remember ever having any other name. I think *vog* has something to do with rowing or sailing or vanity. In other words, a single train of consciousness."

Laura quickly sips at her tea before challenging Vogs to defend his last statement. "You will have to pardon me, sir, but I cannot see your paintings flowing out of a single train of consciousness, not even a *massive* yet single train of consciousness."

Vogs holds back. As a rule he would immediately inquire of the forceful woman how and why she is familiar with his paintings, but his eyes remain on the window's edge and his mouth, for the moment, remains shut.

Then he aimlessly points his hand. "People's names don't always fit them their whole life long."

"Meaning you have changed your self but not your name?"

"Maybe, Laura. That might be what I'm meaning."

"Having next to no perspective on your meaning, Vogs, I find it at once a very confusing idea and a very lucid one. Complex, yet truly simple."

"And here I am, not even knowing quite what you're talking about, lady."

Laura pushes the tip of her tongue between her tightly-drawn lips, as if she were tasting something sour or bitter. Did she hear Vogs' *lady* as a rude cheapie? But she opens her mouth and closes it into a charming smile. "Most of the people who I have spoken with about such things insist that the underlying structure of the self cannot be changed appreciably. They hold that a person who is born single-minded remains single-minded for their entire life."

"But you and I know differently? Is that what you are telling me, Laura? I myself cannot remember ever meeting anyone who believes the great mind is so restricted that it is unable to alter its earthly components. Are you perchance using *single-minded* to mean the same as *simpleminded?*"

"No. Yes."

Vogs smirks. "Well, that's certainly good enough for me." His eyes sparkle. "I'd be satisfied with a *no-yes* anytime."

He promptly wipes the smirk off his face and scoots up closer to the table to plant his elbows one on either side of his teacup. "This is a long shot, Laura; so please excuse me if I'm way off. But are you telling me that you suffer from single-mindedness yourself?"

"Daily, Vogs. Sometimes hourly." Laura opens and closes her hands. "In my case, the single-mindedness is not continuous." She sputters and laughs. "At least, I hope it's not. *Appears* to me that it's not, anyway!" She loosely waves her hands and says, "My attacks are intermittent, sometimes periodic. It's a curse laid on me as a fetus by an unknown enemy."

"It doesn't show."

"Ah." To pronounce her next three words the special way she wants them, Laura's lips have to dance through a series of sharp, surprising contortions. "You're too kind."

Two seconds later, as if their strange little performance had been only an illusion, Laura's lips are as smooth and relaxed as lips can be when she says, "But thank you anyway, Vogs."

"Your condition was self-diagnosed, Laura?"

"It was indeed. At an early age."

Vogs shines a big bunch of teeth at Laura and delivers another old saw, essentially unmolested. "Who's putting who on here?"

Laura zips her lips and stands both of her index fingers on the tabletop.

Vogs grins and rolls his head to stretch his neck. "Your *single-mindedness* sounds an awful lot like my *Endlessness*. Except that I don't have any enemies. It's just me, or it's Endlessness, or it's timeless/spaceless emptiness."

"Timeless…spaceless…emptiness?" Laura smiles conspiratorially. "Are we talking now about nonphysical light, light of the spiritual/intellectual order?"

Vogs *O*'s his mouth vividly. Laura rubs the sides of her nose with her index fingers.

Vogs feigns breathlessness. "Go-o-od question, yes, even if it is from out of nowhere. I want to answer your fine question with a *no-yes*."

"Don't force yourself, Vogs." Laura actually giggled. "We'll come back to it later in life."

"What?" Vogs scrunches up his nose. "Oh! You make me swirl, woman. Swirl me, mom, swirl me."

"Calling me *mom* was what kind of slip?"

"My point exactly."

"Oops! Now you're twirling me, Vogs. And much too fast."

"Why did you come to see me? Are you a cunningly camouflaged census taker? A menacing foreign spy? A roaming high-school achievement test? Or is Laur-like-far Pepin an art critic?"

"No." Stretching her lips unsmilingly, Laura watches Vogs closely. "Not one of the above. I'm a lawyer. I represent two people who may be your parents."

She smiles thinly at him. He smiles just as thinly back at her.

"Do you know the people I am talking about, Vogs?" Laura has been surreptitiously checking the spots of paint all over Vogs' head. Is she searching for a pattern?

"Who knows? I could know these people, Laura. I do not, however, know of anyone who could or would think that they are my parents."

Laura watches Vogs' eyes. He watches hers.

"I don't want to appear hard for hard's sake, Vogs." Laura has lost or thrown away the lean smile. And she did certainly cut that last sentence from a stiffer grade of paper. Staring blankly at Vogs' chin, she winds her pinkie in a taut little circle. "These two people are dead."

A grin burgeons on Vogs' face, a giant grin, a simply stupendous grin. "That does make things easier."

Laura's eyes wiggle-wiggle. Her head trembles. "What do you mean by that?"

Vogs shakes his whole beaming head. "If they're dead, I can't be forced to get to know them."

Quickly, Laura looks away. She looks out the window. She does not reply. She sips her tea, she looks out the window.

Vogs' broad toothy smile dissolves with time, yet a thoroughly happy expression remains on his face. "What do you see out there, gal-of-the-law?"

"I see Necky and Corr standing in windows staring across the street and into this window."

"What!" Vogs jumps furiously to his feet and speeds to the window to fire a visceral, universal, full-hand gesture out the glass, twice.

"That wasn't necessary." Laura grins at Vogs as he snarlingly returns to his chair. "I can easily understand their curiosity about me and what I am doing here."

(2) +

"Huh?" he groaned as he strained to raise his weary head from his ageless pillow. Vogs' bedroom is black dark. He was asleep and perhaps having another of what he claims are preternatural dreams when the door to the hall silently opened and then silently closed again. In a weak, wavering voice he calls out, "Is that you, Necky?" If the door's opening and closing made no noise, what was it that woke Vogs?

From somewhere in the soundless boundless dark comes a hesitant, oddly faceted *yes*.

The black of the room had not closed completely around that single cautious word before a jumpy question, its words equally oddly shaped, is heard. "What'd she want?"

Vogs is still deep in the fuzzy passageway leading to and from the land of sleep. "Laura?"

"Of course Laura."

"She wanted what she got."

"What'd she get, Vogs?"

"My permission for her to send me something."

"What?"

"I don't know exactly."

"Oh."

"Good night, Necky."

"OK. Good night, Vogs."

Again the door opens and closes. And silence reigns alongside darkness once more.

It's a strained silence, though, for Vogs has not let his head return to its pillow. Does he sense something? Now... Now his head is gradually dropping. Vogs is almost back to sleep.

His head had all but descended to its crater on the pillow when from the depths of the black came another voice. "You're not going to get rid of me as easily as you did him."

Vogs' head jerks back up. "What!" Surely he can't see a thing. "Corr? Is that you, Corr?" He opens his eyes as wide as they will open. "I didn't know you were even in the building." Why are those little wavy breaks in groggy Vogs' voice? He seems to be finding this second voice-in-the-night more difficult to identify, to positively identify. Is it Corr's voice? Was that Corr speaking? The *almost* unfamiliar voice had a strange quality to it. It could be a bristly Corr, or it could just as easily have been someone else. A simple *yes-it's-me*, or even a *no-it's-blahblah*, would go a long way here toward relieving Vogs' uncertainty.

But no. No help is forthcoming. The mysterious voice offers only, "I've been downstairs lying on the couch." And it has moved. The elusive voice has stilly shifted its apparent point of origin in the room.

When next it's heard, the voice sounds as though it is slowly moving in the darkness. There is, however, no sounds of feet on the bare floor. "I was reading that fat book from your collection." Is there a fat book in Vogs' collection? Has Corr been known to read from it?

Silence, then a soft half-laugh is heard. "I sneaked in here behind Necky. He was so intent on something—most likely what he was going to ask you—that he had no idea I was just inches behind him. Inches!" *If* the source of the voice was in motion before, it has now stopped moving.

Hesitation and a slight warble show yet in Vogs' voice when he says, "I'm trying to sleep, you know." He must still be not totally without doubt as to who he is talking to.

"I'll leave quickly and without raping you first, mister, if you cough up right now what's going on."

Vogs grunts. And sighs. He then whispers like Necky. "From the lengthy scroll of names of all the people personally known to me, one stands out. Your unruly threat, voiced with a vigorous trill, could have only come from Corr Cor."

"What? So? Was who I am a secret of some sort? Was identifying me a problem for someone?"

"No-yes."

"What?"

"Change that to a simple *probably not.*"

"Well? Talk to me, mister! Walk it out your mouth right now."

"You are going to have to help me first, Corr, help me to understand what you are wanting to hear me talk about."

"Oo-wee! Aren't we all nice and considerate tonight."

A moment of silence. No one says anything. In the dark.

Now…faint footsteps can be heard approaching the bed. Is it not perfectly safe by now to assume that they are Corr's footsteps? But would Corr's ghostly steps be hearable? They might, if she intended them to be. Suddenly Vogs shivers. Is the Drowsy Man On His Back entertaining the other possibility, that buddy Corr was not the only person left in the room with him after buddy Necky made his exit? Necky entered Vogs' bedroom thinking he was sliding in alone, but actually Corr slipped in, too. If two people, why not three? If three, why not a full troop of indiscernible armed slinkers in the night ?

Assuming for now that those unfaltering footsteps are indeed Corr's, is Corr Cor seeing where she is going? Moving like a ghost in the day or night is something; but can she actually see in the dark? Or does she merely see in the urban dark a lot better than Vogs? And Necky. And a long roster of others.

Now there is the distinct smell of honey.

Something more weighty than a ghost settles beside Vogs on his bed. He shivers again, more violently this time. A hand starts softly massaging his shoulder. "O-o-h!" he emotes. "Corr's amazing hand!"

Vogs must have recognized the feel of Corr's hand and remembered the pleasure the hand has given him. And the complex, unerring maneuvers of her hand make it undeniable now that she can actually see him.

"All right then." Corr has stopped speaking in the prickly voice. She sounds natural now. She sounds completely like herself again when she says, "*First*, tell me where you and this Laura Pepin went after you had your tea."

"We strolled down to the park and sat on the stone bench under the pig's snout." Vogs' head is still raised, and his shoulders are still flat on the bed. "Why do you ask? Didn't you follow us there?" His neck must be getting pretty tired.

"No need to get all sar-cas-ticky with me, Vogsy." Between her thumb and first finger, Corr delicately squeezes a small patch of skin on Vogs' chest. "And then you two...?"

Four flowers try to bloom in Vogs' speech. "I am not the one artist at any given time who can claim 'only miracles occur to me.' I simply sat there for a while on the simple bench in the simple daylight looking up at the sky, wondering if anyone in history has never seen the sky. I don't know what *she* was doing all the while."

"Can I or can I not assume, VoVo, that after you had pondered the sky to your heart's content, you and she talked some more?"

"You can."

Corr's hand floats invisibly over Vogs' body to touch down briefly at various strategic points. "My next question is more than adequately obvious. Tell me why she came looking for you."

Vogs finally relaxes his neck muscles, and his head plunges to his pillow.

This pillow was once purely white. These days, however, when seen in light bright and true enough to read by, the pillow demonstrates a shocking, arresting irregularity of saturated grays and browns.

"Laura Pepin is a lawyer, a lawyer whose's got something cooking, something that has something to do with me." Here comes the singsong. "But I don't know enough about what that something is to say anything about it to you."

Surprise! Corr is not aggravated by the ding-ding-dong in Vogs' voice. "You weren't lying to Necky then? You truly don't know what's on her agenda?"

"Right." The shifty tone of Vogs' voice says he is totally awake now.

"But she's sending you something?"

"You're right again, Corr," says the same man who, maybe once every two weeks, asks whomever he may happen to be with at the moment, "That a human should have to sleep?"

"Will you tell me what when you get it, Vogs?"

"Will I tell you what when I get it, Corr?"

"Don't play word games with me, Mister Bister Pister. Just a yes or a no."

"Just a yes or a no or you'll take advantage of me sexually?"

"Right now, this very moment, my knows-all female hand is reporting to me that being taken advantage of sexually is precisely what Vogs is wanting to happen here."

"You—and your hand—are right again, Corr. And *you* are not dressed, either."

"Ho!" Corr laughs quickly. "How can you tell that? You haven't even touched me yet—and you're stupidly blind in the dark."

She chuckles at that last thought of hers. "Talk about blind! Your eyes may be the deepest pools on this block, in the daylight; but you didn't even know who I was, here, tonight. Did you, Fig Rig?"

"I'll take only your first question, darling. I know you are not dressed because I can smell your ruddy blossom's sweet nectar unfiltered by clothing."

"Oo-wee! You really are coming a'cruising at me, ya'boy you."

Vogs agrees. "You are right one more time."

"Tell me! Tell me," wails Corr. "What to expect!"

"Yes, I will tell. I will tell you of a hand that is not your 'knows-all female hand.' It is, instead, a hand with a goodly store of male know-how. I will tell you this very instant that this male hand has taken to stroking the very arm that controls your tattling female hand. And he who is the master of the legendary strong-but-gentle male hand makes a promise in the dark that he fully intends to keep: 'I'll cruise gallantly up and down your canals till the cock crows and the cat cries.'"

Corr shivers. "That's so ro-romantic, Vogs. That cock and cat thing. It's from two or three generations back, isn't it?"

"Don't know. Thought I made it up."

"You might have made it up. Although I have definitely heard it before."

The bedroom door opens a third time.

Someone is standing in the doorway in an envelope of feeble light. It is not Necky. This fully clothed person silently stalks straight across the room, directly to the bed. The tall, erect person shoots Corr and then Vogs, blasts them till they're dead.

"Huh? First you granted that I might have made it up, and then you said that you had definitely already heard it. What are you saying, Corr? The two don't exactly mesh. —Or maybe they do! Maybe…they do." Vogs pushes out his lips in the dark. "Then how many people can make up the same thing?"

"Need there be a limit?" Corr has rolled up on top of Vogs and is pinning his shoulders to the bed. "How many gray-speckled, hand-sized stones are taking themselves a vacation along a river's edge?"

"Ah! I get you. Our culture tends to think that each and every describable phenomenon has just one single beginning point. Which is, of course, a ridiculous notion—a childish notion. I wish I could think as clearly as you, Corr. You seem to think freely continually. I just think in spurts."

"Shining like deep water," chants a delighted Corr Cor, "I take advantage of those precious seconds when no one anywhere is aware of my existence." She slips her slick loop over Vogs and sinks deep. "You got me. You're getting me. You will get me." She buries her nose on his chest. "On and on till the cat cries."

If Necky were here and had heard Corr spit out those *You* constructions—one, two, three—he would surely and immediately whisper (something like this) in the ear of his male friend. "Oh, Vogs, you had better say something back to her. And quick."

Vogs either remembers a *b* string or makes one up on the spur (spurt?) of this moment. "The possibility of being! Becoming! Being!"

"Good! Good!" Corr is chewing on what little hair Vogs has on his chest. "Being being being!"

Vogs cuts in a backbeat in *S*'s.

"Slither...slather...slip...slick...slink..."

And on and on like that till the cock crows and the cat cries an infinite number of times. Those cries and those crows do not change anything, however. The stony fact is that (1) Vogs of the deep voice and early thinning hair and (2) Corr Cor of the strongly colored palette are both dead.

Did the intruder pip Necky too? Did Necky get himself shot and thereby make good his plan to die soon? Apparently not. For Necky has just stopped in the doorway to squint into the black room, the room that he might still be thinking of as Vogs' bedroom. Necky doesn't step into the room. He closes the door and returns to his own bedroom.

(3) +

When two *powerful artists* get to mixing their visions of reality, hard facts are of little consequence. Corr jumps to her feet at the first fierce cracking of dawn. Taller than the north sky, she stands on the bed hollering way down south at Vogs. "Get your sleepy bottom up, Mr. Painterlyman!"

Corr starts bouncing on the bed. She's laughing, laughing loudly, laughing joyfully, bouncing nonstop, landing on alternate feet, landing sometimes between Vogs' legs and other times between his arms and the sides of his body. "Up and down! Up and down! Yeah, I'm talking to you, airballs! —Hey! We completely emptied them babies, didn't we!"

Comes a damp report from down on the bed: "Rudug!"

"What you say, sleepyhead?" Corr does not stop laughing. Or bouncing. "Open doze eyes!"

No, the eyes of Vogs do not pop wide open at that *chieftain's command*. Yes, the hand of Vogs grabs Corr's bare ankle on the bounce. And then? The master of this aforementioned strong-but-gentle male hand trumpets in a voice even more compelling than a chieftain's: the voice of an apocalyptic preacher. "Suddenly the ground falls away so fast she thinks she is flying." As Corr's ankle begins its descent, Vogs yanks it out from under her. "So I forget her and talk to myself about...the unevenness of time."

Corr does not panic or even stop her laughing. As her body drops out of control onto the man below her, she declares, "I will not participate in that field of music! I will merely sift down on thee, Jorge Ous-Jorge, like slowly falling rain."

And that she does. One big drop of rain falls on Vogs.

Normally Vogs would love being under Corr, even under the back of her with her feet in his face. This time, however, he wants to be the one on top. He squirms out from under Corr and swiftly rotates his body around head-to-foot before he flips up onto her forever firm belly.

"On and on we will think on and on," confides he to her while he's trying in vain—she is *still* still laughing—to press his nose against her fabulous nose. "But we won't ever even once think about the past. Our pasts. We will then be two very long people, because every place that we have ever been will still be with us."

Suddenly Corr stops laughing and freezes in place. Is she staring up at the Vogs-on-top-of-her? No. Nor is she staring mutely on up at the crumbling ceiling above him.

Vogs' moan is exaggerated, ridiculous. Reluctantly he slides off Corr's body to lie inertly at her side. "Describe it to me," he says without moving his lips. "What is the matter?"

"Did you have a dream last night, Vogs—or a fantasy or a vision or whatever—about someone strutting in here and shooting us dead? And a little while later, Necky came to the door and looked in? Then he closed the door and walked away?"

Vogs gulps hard. "Yes! It's truly true! I did."

His astonishment takes a half-turn into shaky nervousness. "Did I talk in my sleep or something?"

Tears may be forming in Corr's eyes. "No. I had the same dream. Or whatever it was if it weren't a dream. The killer…Necky…you and I dead."

"But we were dead *before* Necky came back to the door. Right, Corr?"

"It seems that way to me too, yes."

Vogs suddenly recognizes the saltwater puddling in Corr's eyes. Corr opens her mouth, and a glistening tear breaks free and slides down the side of her face and into her ear. Her tongue does not move. She closes her mouth.

Again her mouth opens. "What what what what what what…what would it be like to never talk to anyone…to never speak to a person again…any person…to never see another single person…what would that be like?" A second shiny tear falls.

Vogs refrains from answering. He might be clinching his teeth. His lips are definitely quivering.

"I think we had better check on Necky, Vogs."

"I don't understand you, madam, but I'm with you. Let's go."

They are quickly up and quickly to the door. Corr and Vogs run naked down the hall and skate to a halt before the closed door to Necky's room. Vogs grips the old, cracked door's cloudy glass handle as Corr climbs up on his back to ride him piggyback into that bedroom.

The curtains are drawn. That's not like Necky.

Corr wraps her arms round and around Vogs' big head. And she squeezes. And squeezes. There lies Necky. On his bed. Dead. Yes, someone has helped him into death.

(4) +

The long grim choric songs and immoderately poignant commentaries on the nature of sorrow are buried one and all deep in the space break that immediately preceded this sentence. And no discussion, to speak of, of the aftereffects of the tragedy will be found over here on this side of those blank lines.

Onward.

A week later and an hour ago, Corr and Vogs quietly drifted again into the café across the street from their buildings and arranged themselves on their usual choice of chairs at their usual table. That was, again, about an hour ago. Even so, looking ever so much like two tired turkey buzzards roosting in a leafless prehistoric tree, she and he have not got up from those chairs even once since then. What are they doing if not getting up and sitting down? Well, for the past eleven minutes, Corr's head has been hanging gloomily while her eyes stare as if forever at the sleeve of her rumpled T-shirt. And for twice Corr's eleven minutes, Vogs has been sitting with his shoulders sagging like a wilted floret while his eyes silently gaze out the top of the nearby window. No one has demanded of the pair that they account for their droopiness. Maybe someone should.

Hark! After so long a silence at the table, is that Corr saying something?

"We made a great couple, you and I and Necky."

Ten words. All of which were said so softly they could have fallen from Corr's mouth wholly unnoticed by Vogs. Corr's eyes are yet fixed on her sleeve.

Not right away, no, after an indeterminate spell, Vogs ends what is for him an extremely long public silence with what are for him soft words. His body and eyes don't move at all as he speaks. "It seems to me, good goodly woman, that you and a couple of guys total out to three people."

Flat silent again are the subdued pair, Vogs&Corr. Has their tortoise exchange of ideas dried up? If their gradual conversation is to continue beyond that one dictum each, it be Corr's turn now to speak. Still they don't stir. The two sit as inert as gilded stones. These people may have simultaneously forgotten they exist.

Uh-huh, Corr takes significantly longer to respond than Vogs had. Her comeback, when at last it arrives, is minimally packaged in a barren, hollow voice. "No, goof goofy man." Corr's unseeing stare falls from her sleeve to her lap. "There were a couple of guys and me. I was the perceiver. So I didn't count."

A slim possibility does exist that Vogs has been doing something more than just drooping for the past twenty and some minutes. Gazing up and out the window at that angle with his head cocked like that, he could be scrutinizing or even secretly admiring the newly hung sign outside, *WELF et al.* He had been asked if he, "a famous painter," would paint a new shingle for the café. And could he please sign it, too. He had replied that he would be honored. Two days later, when the new blank board was hand-delivered to Vogs' studio for him to paint, the board turned out to be a bit large to be called a shingle. It had been cut to the exact height and shoulder width of Welf Aceicou's standing body. And Welf is not a small man. Vogs had grunted appreciatively to the two delivery chaps. The unexpected size of the board would give him room to work like an artist and not a craftsperson. Deftly he twists Corr's explanation. "Or it was you and a guy and *me*, the perceiver." The safer guess would be that Vogs is not inspecting his handiwork, not at this time; for his unmoving gaze outside is as vacant as Corr's empty stare.

As slow to speak as Corr has been so far, surely not enough time has passed for her to be ready with her next reply for Vogs. Yet her eyes jerk up from her lap to stare at him.

Is she staring at Vogs' eyes? Could be. For his two peepers had not only budged a bit; they are in fact now moving about, seemingly trying to find their way back into the café. When

Vogs' line of vision inevitably reaches Corr and when Vogs soon thereafter recognizes that she is looking at him, he immediately directs his gaze away from her.

Corr smiles broadly at Vogs' ear. For the shortest time she's happy. Or so it seems. She turns the triangle another 120 degrees. "Or it was you and me and *Necky*, the perceiver. From any node that you look at the cluster, Vogs, there were only two actual people. And it seems to me that two friendly people total out to a couple." Like a flower in a dream, Corr's smile lacks significant substance.

Vogs chuckles with little humor from behind a plastic face, a two-days-unshaven face. "You're right, as usual, Corr."

"Vogs?" Corr's voice whined like a siren moving in the distance.

"Yes, Corr Cor? My mind is steeled at attention, awaiting your question." He makes his words true by actually paying attention. He is not exactly looking at Corr though; he is staring at an area of the tabletop in front of her.

"Are we going to find out who destroyed Necky?" Corr's insubstantial smile has expired. It faded like a blur of primeval smoke. Not a trace of it remains.

"What's the use? Necky's dead." Vogs animates his arm and slaps his empty hand down not terribly hard on the tabletop.

Corr, gaping at that familiar hand lying flat on the table, answers in one breath, "The perpetrator might come after you next. Or even after me, for all we know."

Vogs has raised his eyes from the tabletop. "You think it was the lawyer, don't you, Corr?" Someone unfamiliar with Vogs' repertoire of facial expressions could easily get the erroneous idea that he has taken to chivalrously watching over Corr's not-quite-here eyes while they wander purposelessly between his hand and his face.

Independent of her lost eyes, Corr offers, "She did just happen to show up the day of the night of Necky's assisted-death."

What was that first physical movement attributed to Vogs after he had sat with his shoulders sagging for some twenty minutes? Aye, it was the opening of his MOUTH to speak to Corr after she had said ten soft words to him. Then Vogs brought his EYES back into the café. He has since then transfigured his FACE in order to chuckle. And one of his ARMS slapped down its HAND. He will now move his whole package.

Vogs makes a real-big-show of spreading his body on his chair to strike a pose reminiscent of any number of the heroes of yesteryear. "I may look the part, Desolation Doll," he makes known out a twisted corner of his mouth, "but this is not some action-thriller. If you look very closely…and here I am quoting a striped dog I once knew…you will see again that it's just you and me sitting and not drinking our tea."

"And Necky is dead and gone by someone else's hand."

Vogs stops, reflects on that fact. He shakes his head. At nothing. Then he presses all five fingertips of his most-colorful hand against his chest. He blows a practiced please-pardon-me look across his face and admits, "I did tell her about Necky wanting to take leave of life."

Corr's eyelids flutter. "Oh!" And her voice rises sharply. "You did!" Flutter, flutter, flutter.

By the time her eyelids stop all their flapping, Corr's mental state has wholly changed. Hard as nails! Totally pitiless! Bloodthirsty! Vogs must have tripped one or more of Corr's most-hidden switches. She shrieks a question at him, and her utterly unrestrained cry could have come from ten thousand startled starlings all letting out their frantic warnings at the same time. And it is a question. "So now you expect me to believe the dirty, lowdown dame has done Necky a favor?"

Such a precipitate unrolling of a huge emotional load would jar-r-r anyone. Alarm flashes from Vogs' countenance. "Ease up, Corr." He tries to sound unruffled. "Laura Pepin didn't kill Necky. She had no reason to do something that risky."

Corr eases up a little. She does. Yet she does not shut her generous lips about Laura, Laura of the surprisingly acrobatic lips. "Tell me again what *she* was wanting when *she* came here?"

"Laura asked if she could send me some pictures, old faded photos I'm guessing. I was/am to look at them, to examine them. If anything strikes me as familiar in the pictures, she will arrange for tests to be made."

"What kind of tests?" Curiosity tilts Corr's so recently bloodthirsty demeanor. "Tests for what?"

"Tests that would prove or disprove that I am the child of two of her clients, who happen to be dead."

Corr has to think about that. She sips at her tea. The tea is an hour old, yet both of their cups are still very nearly full. "And these two dead people left their long lost child all the money in the western hemisphere?"

"I don't think there is any money involved, Corr. What is involved then? As I told you before, I really don't know enough to say anything."

"Have you received these pictures yet?"

"Nope."

Corr looks skeptical.

With an additional nod of his head, Vogs assures her that the correct answer is no.

Welf passes briskly by their table. If this day be like every other working day, he is leaving right now for his morning break, a snappy walk around the block. Welf had been named Wolf at birth. He strides out the door, stops on the sidewalk, gazes up at his new sign. Beaming in bigly through the window, he shoots Vogs an emphatic A-OK look-and-gesture. Then Welf hangs his head and pulls at the corner of his eye with a lone finger to say he's still sad about Necky. Vogs waves a hand. Welf marches away up the sidewalk.

In walks the lawyer. Corr bristles. Vogs grins.

The grin is looking especially silly on his face.

Laura Pepin meanders lazily across the nearly empty room in her new expensive shoes, her new elegant dress, her latest earth-shattering hairdo. She stops just inches from the edge of Corr and Vogs' table. Bending precisely at the waist, she tips her upper body toward Vogs and asks him, "Are you talking about nonphysical light, light of the spiritual/intellectual order?"

Caught short and thoroughly confused by Laura's question, Vogs stammers something totally unintelligible. When he then completely stops trying to talk and just stares at the lovely woman, the memory light comes on. He's laughing now. He's talking again. "You said to me, 'We'll come back to it later in life,' *it* being that nonphysical light question. And here we are back to it somewhat later in life."

Corr looks as if she is simply going to explode.

Laura stands up very straight and very tall. "I heard about your mate, Vogs. It was tragic, even if he did plan to die early, like you said. Are you still suffering?"

Vogs is not allowed to reply. Corr leaps violently to her feet to fire a tightly clenched extremity across the table. The deadly flight of the granite duke stops just short of Laura's delicate nose. Whispering like Necky used to—except that her voice has a threatening razor-edge—Corr informs Laura Pepin, "That is none of your business!"

Laura lost not a millimeter of her immaculate composure. She coolly overlooks Corr's fist and calmly examines Corr's grimacing face. As a lawyer might examine the face of a juror? Laura apparently decides to ignore Corr altogether. Laura directs the last statement and the last question that she is to make and ask in the café today at Vogs. "I decided to not send the pictures but to deliver them personally." A purse (briefcase?) magically appears from behind Laura. "May I sit down?"

Corr eyes Vogs.

So does Laura.

Vogs is still sitting. He stands up like everyone else. "No."

Corr smirks. Her fist drops light as a feather to her side.

Vogs continues, "Let's, you and me, go on over to my place, Laura."

Corr's hand, her fist, had not yet opened up. It was, therefore, all ready and waiting to punch Vogs hard on his shoulder. Corr's flinty fist does connect with another human body this time.

Vogs swiftly concludes that his friendship with Corr requires that he moan in pain and pitifully rub his shoulder. Which he does. But with that duty taken care of, he instructs Laura to pay Corr no mind. He blatantly grins. "She's in a rough time since Necky."

"Sit down. Sit down, you guys." Welf is back from his walk.

Welf solicitously inquires of Laura, "Can I get you something?" One of Welf's hands is pressing down on Vogs' shoulder while his other hand hovers in the air near Laura's shoulder. Welf is all eyes for Laura.

"Laura Pepin, this is Welf Aceicou." Vogs sweeps his hand at the very room in which the four of them are standing together. "Welf Aceicou of *Welf et al.*"

Next, oozing counterfeit compassion, Vogs softly lays his hand over the hand that is pressing on his shoulder. "And Welf, this is Laura Pepin, a practitioner of law. Or so she has claimed. So don't touch her!"

Welf gasps. His hand jerks away from Laura. He is so shocked by Vogs' insinuation. Then he realizes Vogs was just joshing him. Surely Welf will press down harder on Vogs' shoulder.

Vogs wisely and quickly ducks out from under Welf's mighty mitt. "No. No, but thanks, Welf. Laura and I were just leaving."

Welf's eyes flash to Corr.

Corr is not looking at anyone. She appears to be standing on just one foot. Not so. She reaches down to the tabletop for her teacup. She finishes the tea in one big gulp, turns herself about, and makes an inglorious exit.

Welf shakes a stern finger at Vogs as if to say, "Better watch your step there, Mr."

Vogs deadpans and covers his eyes with his forearm.

Welf curtsies picturesquely to Laura and, as he turns back toward work, winks shrewdly at Vogs.

(5) +

Is one, are both, or is neither of them keeping track of the time? A good ninety minutes have seeped by since either of the room's occupants said a word. The last to speak, more than one-point-five hours ago, was Laura Pepin; she had said to Vogs, thereby locking closed his mouth till she chose to speak to him again, "Let me just take a quick look around." But after Laura had done what she said she wished to do, "just take a quick look around" Vogs' studio, no, she did not then stop her perusing to talk to him, as he must have expected she would. And now she has finished another round, her second complete inspection of Vogs' fabled painting studio. Will she pause even for the slimmest moment to converse with Vogs? No, for she has already begun her third slow, silent circumamblulation of the high-ceilinged space. Is she searching for an understanding, an understanding that continues to elude her; or is she in reality quietly memorizing in detail everything in the big room?

Needed or not, a list will be constructed during this quiet time, a list of what Laura continues to examine in Vogs' work place. This list will necessarily turn out biased and conspicuously incomplete because it will include only the isolable items that Laura's body has come to a full halt to study. The list begins in the best light in the studio.

Here in the good light, three very differently sized, in-process paintings, each mounted on its own easel, unflinchingly persist in readiness. From the best-light area, this list moves to the unwindowed wall, where eight nigh-finished paintings of various sizes lean separately, facing out from that wall, waiting to be varnished. On the adjacent wall, on a rickety table under a sagging window, brushes and tools fritter away this downtime today, while nearby on that same wall, paints and supplies silently overload a second table. Wadded up rags are spotted here and there. A pair of heavily pigmented pants squats in one corner. A shirt, also too caked with paint for anyone to wear, lies strikingly askew on the floor. Also on the floor, a juice cup has been knocked over onto its side and the spilled juice has dried to form a crisp silvery disk that catches the light playfully. The center of the room is utterly owned and occupied by a beat-up couch. The day that this couch was carried into this studio and set down on the very site that it still occupies, Vogs and a few friends, including Necky and Corr, held a short ceremony in which they officially named the couch Sleep and Love and Undifferentiated Awareness. The couch is also referred to by a nickname, the acronym SLUA, pronounced *slew-ah*. No other furniture is to be seen in the room, save those two working tables and perhaps the three easels that are holding up the paintings that began this list: one petite easel, one large easel, one huge double-crank.

"Do you vote?"

That was her. In the course of her third trip around the room, Laura has spoken at last.

"No, Laura. I don't." The perfunctoriness of Vogs' answer suggests he has had to wait, as if serenely, for much too long.

"Do you attend church?"

"No."

"Have you ever either, Vogs?"

Sitting cross-legged on the floor, Vogs starts pulling on his lower lip. He has seated himself again on the spot where he often sits when he chooses to sit on the studio's floor. This good spot is directly under his bed, his bedroom being the room right above his studio. And, yes, the other studio, now unoccupied, is immediately under the bedroom, now unoccupied, that had been Necky's. "Someone once said something sweet and simple when asked questions like your three queries, Laura, something that might be apropos for me to recite here today." Vogs uncrosses his legs. "Sorry for the delay, but I'm trying to remember all the words." Vogs climbs to his feet too quickly and wobbly-legs over to a window that looks out over the blocks and blocks of miscellaneous buildings to the big water. "I don't know if this is exactly what the person said. It probably is; but to be safe we will call it a semi-quote. 'I have no real interest in long-standing organizations; hence, the monsters that they've created over the centuries don't really concern me.'"

Vogs permits a pregnant pause, then asks, "Who said that, do you know, other than me just now?"

Laura halts her stroll to gaze across the room at Vogs' back as he faces out the window. Her answer to his question begins in a deceptively weak voice. "Maybe you made up that 'semi-quote.' Maybe you made it up to look like a memory." Laura smiles at the back of Vogs' faded and paint-streaked pants and then continues her unhurried journey around the room. Her voice sheds the conceit of frailty. "I get the feeling you do that fairly often, Vogs. And vice versa too. A memory turns out to be a creation, a creation turns out to be a memory. Those four points may be the very corners of all your paintings. Realizing this possibility—that those points are your cornerstones—helps me just a smidgen to understand why your paintings *appear* to be too complex for individual souls to comprehend."

"Yah yah yah."

A coarse response like that, that triple-yah, coming from Vogs at a time like this, could well indicate that memory and creativity and painting (and flattery?) are not what he is wanting to talk about at present. Would he rather be still discussing

Laura's from-out-of-the-blue questions and his answers to them, even though he would normally turn up his nose in disgust if someone brought up church-going and the science of government?

Laura stops to contemplate for the third time the smallest of the three paintings biding on easels. Her back is to Vogs' back. She asks him, "Can you see the waves?"

"Only the waves way out. The waves that reach the beach are blocked by the last line of buildings out there."

A tremor shakes Laura's body. "Way out on the ocean!"

"Yes." Vogs agrees. He grins and nods his head. Nods it again. "Wa-a-ay out on the ocean!"

He spins about to face Laura. To face Laura's back, that is. "The world and its people may seem dead to me because I'm dead." Looking quite pleased with his arcane statement, Vogs stretches his arms above his head.

Laura turns around to stare in false wonder straight at Vogs' face. Then she smiles sharply down at his pants again, the front of his pants this time. "Are you thinking that you and Corr died that night instead of Necky?"

Struck dumb, Vogs is struck dumb. He looks ever so much as if he is going to faint.

And Laura will rush over? And scoop him up from the floor? And whisper in his ear? That she had not said that? That he had only imagined it?

Will Vogs ever know whether Laura did in fact ask that devastating question? Couldn't he just ask her if she did? He tries asking. "What… What did you say?"

"What is the matter with you, Vogs? You're looking more than a little peaked."

"Please repeat your question!"

"What is the matter with you, Vogs?"

"No! The question you asked before that!"

"Let me think back. I asked if you could see the waves. After that I said, 'Way out on the ocean!' But that was not a question."

"You didn't ask about Corr and me on the night of Necky's death?"

"I don't even think about you and Corr being together, much less ask you about it."

Vogs, with his eyes swirling round and around in his head like that, probably isn't actually seeing his forearms. Yet he appears to speak to them, one at a time. To his left forearm he says, "Smashable." To the right forearm, he says, "Friable."

Brittlely he strides to SLUA and very carefully lays his now easily broken body down. He covers his eyes with the palms of his hands. Not loudly, as if to himself, he groans, "Am I in trouble? Yes, I am. But is the trouble coming from the inside of me or from the outside of me?"

Laura sweeps up behind SLUA, spreads her hands on the soiled top of the back of the couch, and leans over till her eyes stare straight down at Vogs' head. Her eyes penetrate Vogs' skull. "Do you want to see the pictures now?"

Vogs is still covering his eyes. "Why'd you ask me about voting and going to church, Lady Lawyer?"

"If you had answered yes to any one of that set of three questions, my job here today would be done."

Vogs peeks between his fingers at Laura's face. "You would have been done with me?" His eyes are tracking and focusing reasonably accurately now. "Completely done?"

"Yes. One of the most explicit of my instructions reads: 'Even if the person being interviewed is indeed our child, if he or she answers yes to even one of those questions, without knowing why he or she has been asked them, then you are to abort the interview of that person and leave and never visit that person again. And if that person is indeed our child, you will discontinue the search.'"

Vogs' hands have gradually slipped away from his eyes. He is still in need of a shave. "This couple—these two people don't—er—didn't even know if their child was male or a female?"

"Righto."

Vogs nervously shifts a couple or three of his body parts on the couch. "Hmm. It must have been an exceptionally dark night." Staring up as he is at Laura's very blue eyes, Vogs might well be experiencing considerable difficulty believing that those same eyes were fiery red earlier today. And that they will turn down to brown tonight. That would indeed be hard for anyone to imagine.

"I can't tell you any more about that at this time, Vogs."

Laura leans even farther over the couch and lowers her face almost to Vogs' face. Does she intend to kiss Vogs? Does she kiss Vogs? She does not kiss him. She repeats her last question. "Do you want to look at the pictures now?"

(6) +

"So what'd they look like, these pictures? Were they pictures of you when you were a little Vogs? Or were they pictures of your would-be parents? —When they were *alive*, I hope!"

Corr sucks in her lips and waits. Alone together in Vogs' studio, she and Vogs are lying out long on shabby SLUA with their heads at opposite ends. No answer of any kind comes from Vogs. Wrinkling her nose, Corr prepares to speak again.

Just then Vogs' head jerks spasmodically, as if he had fallen asleep and had, this very instant, awakened from that sleep, which is not the case; for his eyes have been wide open all the while. In a poorhouse version of his Grand Canyon voice he says,

"Working backward up your question list: No. No. It's hard to say." Is Vogs bored? Or is he anything but bored?

"Come on, Vogs! Give me something."

"Which side do you want it on?"

"Later for the sex pickle. Give me some info, you dank scoundrel. Or I'll empty that lovely jar of cadmium red on your head."

Corr had crept into the studio—who knows how long after Laura left—and had found Vogs sprawled on the couch staring ever upward. Vogs is still lying right there on his back, and Corr is lying on her side on the outer edge of the cushions, facing away from Vogs and the security of the couch. SLUA is a tight fit for the two of them, particularly since Vogs is taking up so much of the space himself. Corr's bare heels are not an inch away from touching his cheek.

Needless to say, the poop she had demanded with her red threat to Vogs' head is not delivered here and now. Corr's fellow coucher allows in a soft, lonesome voice that he is all keyed up. He goes on to say/ask, "Why don't we get up from here, Corr?" Where is Vogs headed now? "Maybe we should walk down to the beach."

"*Should?* 'Maybe we *should* walk down to the beach'?" Apparently Corr doesn't know where Vogs is headed either. "What's with you, guy?"

Vogs shoves on Corr's powerhouse of a butt, and she grumbles to her feet. But she makes dead sure that she is standing breasts-to-diaphragm with Vogs when he stands up.

"OK, Corr. I'll tell you everything I know about the lawyer and her search—while we are walking."

Corr crumples to the floor at Vogs' feet. As limp as that, she is surely dead. Vogs whimpers with his mouth wide open.

Corr springs back up to her feet and gives him a peck on the cheek. "Thanks for the whimper, Vogs. I feel much better now knowing that someone will be sad when I'm gone—when she kills me too."

Is that anger?

Yes, tis actually anger. Those are two ireful male hands suddenly and bluntly gripping Corr's bare upper arms and lifting her wholly into the air. (This is not at all like Vogs. It's a good thing Corr doesn't bruise easily.)

Something else is happening now. Is Corr experiencing a need to reciprocate? She has grabbed ahold of Vogs' upper arms and seems to be trying to lift him into the air at the same time that he's lifting her, which is, of course, not possible, not doable. Not here, today anyway. (Corr's trying to lift Vogs into the air while he already has her up gives rise to a digression of arguable relevance here in the middle of the paragraph. Necky Watershighagain, formerly an authority on the matter, once said—whispered—to a woman who had been following him around for days and asking him irrational questions about the mystic talents of developed artists: "The anti-gravity abilities commonly attributed to painters do not have an actual effect on the physical world." But Necky was wearing a dismissive smile while he said those words. And a smile like that on Necky's face could mean just about anything. Perhaps he was denying his own well-turned kinetic genius just to be rid of the woman.) Vogs returns Corr's feet to the dusty floor. She promptly lifts him up into the air, just like he had elevated her. *She is as strong as he.*

How can Vogs not grin? He cannot not grin. He does in fact chuckle chuckle chuckle. Corr laughs as well as she can under the strain of holding Vogs up like a chicken to be sacrificed. She lets him down, and they embrace and kiss tenderly.

They're out of the building, out walking happily side by side down the sidewalk in the late afternoon with a thin band of haze barely rising above the horizon. It's a mild day, not hot, not cool, not windy. But the world's all glary. Corr and Vogs both comment on the glare, yet they are young enough (and not vampires) that the shrill brilliance is no problem for them.

Down the walk in the second block below their buildings they come upon a stick that stops them both. It be Vogs' turn to narrate the trip. "A moss-covered, three foot long stick stands unnaturally upright, reverently pointing at the sky from one end pushed into a deep crack on the sidewalk. No? You think maybe that crooked stick is *not* worshiping the sky? Then maybe, just *maybe*, the purpose of the standing stick is to draw attention to the torn kite thoroughly stuck in the very tree from whence the stick just might have fallen. Oh say there! An edgy, sinister-looking cat steps out of the shadows wanting to be a friend…a friend to one of the humans but not to both of them." Vogs smacks his lips to signal his narration is complete. They, Corr and Vogs, leave off gawking at the stick and cat and stride on in sync towards the sea, their arms swinging like clockwork with each long, weightless step they take.

"He told me, he did. He said it to me, he did." What is Corr rattling on about all of a sudden? "He did." And why is she using such an affected voice?

Vogs merely shrugs and walks on.

Corr continues in that spurious voice. "He said he was working backward up my question list when he answered, 'No *click* No *click* It's hard to say *click*.'"

Those three acrid clicks were made by Corr's tongue and, clearly, were used in place of the periods that Vogs had used back in his studio to end those three terse sentences of his.

Vogs surely knows what Corr is talking about now. He merely shrugs and walks on.

"I am to believe then that the pictures were not of Pepin-the-shyster's defunct pair." Corr has not yet abandoned the gratingly artificial voice. "Just as I am to believe that the pictures were not of Vogs himself. I am also expected to believe, sight unseen, that it's hard to say even what these pictures look like." Corr's use of what only she might label *mordant wit* to pressure Vogs into telling her about the pictures just might backfire on her. "Have I got it right, D-D-Dogs?"

While verbalizing all of that in that unnatural voice, Corr had neither missed nor even blurred a single long step. Neither did Vogs mess up a step. And he looks to be good and ready for his turn to speak. Which is right now.

Absently he kicks his foot at nothing. "It's n-n-not so hard to say what they looked like if I'm willing to be truthful."

Corr hulas her hips in glee. "And willing to be truthful is what you are this very minute. Huh, Vogs?"

"They were pictures of you, Corr. When you were a small child."

"What!" Corr grabs Vogs' shirtsleeve as she skids to a halt.

And Vogs swings a nice ice-skater's arc at the end of her arm before his feet come to a stop. He squints at her out the corners of his eyes.

Corr's eyes are squeezed nearly closed. Her voice is overly loud and clattering. "What does my disgusting childhood have to do with two corpses wanting a live son?"

Vogs just stands there grinning stupidly at her, his hands on the ready to shoot up to shield his head from the blows.

Corr sees what he is doing. Her face melts. She doesn't scream at him again. She doesn't cry. She softly laughs.

They resume their trip to the beach, wandering slowly on down the primitive gray strip of concrete. Slowly? Not for long. Within seconds they have regained their long steps and merry making speed.

Corr and Vogs see themselves approaching a raucous pack of youngs (sic) of mixed gender. It soon appears that the kids are fighting over a red and green scooter. Vogs blurts out, as if those six or seven crazed sons and daughters should hear his decree as pertinent to their own standoff, "They were dead before Laura was hired to represent them."

Corr pretends the inside of her left wrist is a mnemonic device and presses it to her temple. "I think you may have already told me that, Captain Vogs."

Three of the kids have turned to stare belligerently at Corr as she and Vogs pass on by. Corr is the one who gets stared at because she continues to gaze at the kids and Vogs doesn't.

"No, I didn't."

"If you insist, sir," says Corr out the side of her mouth with a clipped crackling elliptical eloquence. "If you did or if you didn't, so what?" She blows a kiss from her hand back at the tallest boy.

The boy gives her the finger but then grins sheepishly at her.

"Best you mind your own business, Corr," advises Vogs from behind his own hand.

Corr twists her torso around so that she can grin wide and wetly back at the kid. "The world is my business!"

While Corr's statement rang good and true and strong, certainly it will not satisfy her for long. She is definitely not done telling Vogs off. Vogs must have realized that *very fact*, for he clutches himself in the safety of his arms as they walk on.

Starting the count there, where Vogs wraps his arms about his middle, C&V have taken six more long paces down the sidewalk before Corr coldly snaps her head to the side to speak over the point of her shoulder to crossly advise Vogs' shoulder, "I did not appreciate your helpful hint. You are a good part of my business, Vogs, but surely not the entirety of it."

Vogs endures. He suffers Corr's subsequent supercilious swaggering without uttering a word of reproach. That is to say he is respectfully silent. And when Corr has finished her messy little performance, he hums. He hums that song about clouds for a while. At long last, in a humdrum voice, in an it's-the-truth timbre, Vogs tells Corr's shoulder, not like Corr had spoken to his shoulder but as if he were talking to Corr's mouth, "I was merely making a suggestion, a recommendation, a warning perhaps, but *not* an admonition."

Corr turns around to walk backward beside Vogs. "Let's go back."

"You walk backwards very nicely. Smoothly."

"Thank you."

"You're wanting to go back to those juveniles? Or back to my studio?"

"Back to *my* studio."

"Why? Why don't we just continue on to the beach, Corr?"

"We can go on to the beach if…"

Vogs waits. And waits for Corr to complete her statement. He shrugs that same way again and says, "I surely recognize the smile that the only woman-of-breeding in my life is presently displaying for me." He megaphones his lips to say to the moving sidewalk out in front of his feet, "So I know far better than to beseech her for the finale of her sentence."

Sliding on by Vogs' provokingly labeling her as a *quality* person, Corr climactically concludes her unfinished sentence. "…if you buckle down to the job and start telling me about those pictures—and I do mean without delay."

"O'lady, you pressure me unmercifully."

Corr must have heard that sentence as an I-will-I-will from Vogs, for she flips back around to be facing in the same direction that she and Vogs are walking, down to the sea.

In the twinkling of an eye, one of the numberless eyes in the sky, Corr and Vogs reach the intersection of 45th and Third Gear. Someone is standing, waiting there on the corner dressed in rags and wearing an antique brown-paper bag over his or her head. This person offers something to Corr. It's a handbill or flyer. Vogs is handed one, too. Vogs and Corr take the bills and nod politely, while the both of them silently check out the inordinately creased paper bag, which seems to have no holes for the covered person to be looking out through. The two painters each in turn say thank you and then pivot away and make it across the medium-busy intersection. The idea that they could stop and gawk back at that singular person must not have occurred to either of them; for when Corr and Vogs reach the far sidewalk, they just walk on toward the beach.

A shout is all but swallowed by its distance from Corr and Vogs. "…rain is you."

Vogs may not have even heard the three words; he shows no attention at all to the pale shout. Corr immediately raises the flyer she was given and started reading out loud from it.

She reads one word at a time, one word for each fresh footstep she takes. "Milk Mandy, in his most tantalizing outfit, will be posing on this corner tonight for all to see. He is, as you all know, attempting to construct a global memory, a memory that anyone can access anywhere at any time with no more equipment than a bare will to know. So, help him! Be here tonight!"

"Given a chance," remarks Vogs as he strokes his chin, "I might agree with that."

Corr screws her face up. "Oh, Vogs! I don't know about the whole idea of making the communal memory *completely* available. Must I withstand memories of you cooking raisin mudpies in your undies?"

Vogs smirks roguishly. Then, as if his smirk weren't already a more amusing face than Corr's, he makes a funnier face and grabs her handbill and wads it and his bill into a ball. "Or me of you making your hundred million immutable pronouncements!"

"The pictures, bad guy! Or I stop and turn around right here."

"Your hundred million *and one* immutable pronouncements!" Vogs neatly lofts the paper ball into what appears to have once been a garbage can.

"I'm stopping!"

"I'm talking!" Vogs thrusts his hands as high above his head as is physically possible if he keeps both of his feet walking on the ground. "I'm going be talking real trash real quick for my demon taskmaster to hear!"

"I *am* your demon! Yes!" Corr pulls one of Vogs' arms down to her side and clutches it under her arm. "I am your demon taskmaster. Tell me now of the photographs."

"They weren't photographs, not real ones. They were constructed on a machine. No doubt about it. They were very clever though. Insidiously realistic."

"Describe them to me, please."

"They were disconcerting." Vogs is turning more serious—both more grave and more earnest—with every word he says. "Quite so." He drops his eyes and his arm, the arm that was still raised. Corr is hanging on tightly yet to his other arm. "They reached into places in my head I'd never visualized before."

Corr is at a loss as to what she should make of the look on Vogs' face. "Can you remember these places, Vogs? Can you see them right now?"

"Yes. I can. I can look in at them at will. It's as if a series of doors has been permanently opened to a new world." Vogs nervously flaps his recently lowered hand. "And...I'm understanding something right now as I'm jabbering to you. It is a coherent world, yet it is a world I could never have conceived of on my own, a world that I am even now having difficulty believing is possible."

"Wow! Wow! And wow! Sounds to me like you went to Painter's Heaven."

"I'm not so sure of that, Amazing Girl."

"Didn't you tell me in the café that you were to see familiar things in these pictures? And if you did, tests would be made?"

"Yes, the *familiar* word bothered me too. And it still is abothering me!"

"What did she, your Laura, have to say about all this?"

"I could tell she was absorbing and processing every move I made, every twitch of my fingers, every wink of my eyelashes. She handed me the last picture; and when I had examined it, Laura said quite simply, 'You are seeing your world.'

She stood up, collected her pictures, and left. Oh yeah! As she was going out the door, she said she would be seeing me soon."

"Did her saying 'You are seeing your world' make any sense to you?"

"No. Not then, not now."

Corr turns her head to the side and whistles three isolated notes. Then her head swings back. "Were these constructed pictures some kind of trick? I mean, were they, just for example, designed to prod long-buried memories of experiences that you had when you were very young or something?"

"What?" Vogs peers at Corr's mouth.

He looks down at the ground and shakes his bowed head. "Naw, I'm a painter. I know all the tricks, the visual tricks, the psychological tricks—well, maybe not *all* the tricks, but I know thousands and thousand of them. I didn't see any. No, it's like I was *really* seeing these places that I'd never seen before even in the preconscious. That's what my experience was."

"Did these pictures or the places that they reached into in your head elicit emotions from you, or drives, like sex or, you know, nausea? Did you have any response to them other than just seeing them?"

"What was my response? No, there were no emotional hits, no pounding drives, particularly not sex. There was awe, but awe is not generally looked upon as a mover. And you were asking about movers, I think, Corr. No, the only thing that happened to me other than my being thoroughly impressed was that I kept repeating to myself an apparently meaningless phrase: 'A dialogue in mono.'"

"Have you come to any understanding yet of what that phrase means? Or meant at that time?"

"No, Corr."

"You said the pictures were 'insidiously realistic.' Realism implies a recognizable image. Don't you agree?"

"But not necessarily an objectively recognizable image."

"We can split hairs forever, Vogs, and I will have learned nothing about what the pictures looked like."

"They were in gray-scale, Corr, on page-sized sheets of some kind of high-quality paper that I didn't recognize. What was the printing medium? I'm sorry, but I couldn't tell that either."

"The images themselves, Vogs. That's what I'm waiting for."

"There were rocks, flowers, grass, trees, cliffs, caves, all objectively recognizable. Lots of details. The light? If the light was from this planet and not merely constructed, it would not be the normal light anywhere on this continent. And the pictures had none of those depends-on-which-way-you-look-at-it effects. None that I could see."

"Was it a sunny day or rainy? Were all of the pictures of the same area or of drastically different areas?"

"There was no sky in any of the pictures…no telling view of the sky." The look now on Vogs' face surely means that the lack of sky is and has been troubling him. "The light sort of looked like the day was cloudy and maybe about to turn rainy. I say that because while there were many lush areas of dark, there were no proper shadows. Even so, the images were as bright and crisp and dry as a sunny day." Vogs nods his head, wiggles his head, shakes his head. "No sky!"

When Corr finally lets go of Vogs' arm, he remembers her other question. "The pictures could have all been of the same area, but there was no repetition of objects in the pictures. None, Corr. So they could just as easily have been scenes a thousand miles apart."

Corr curves away into thoughtfulness. She and Vogs cross the next street in silence. A woman waves at Corr from a high window. Corr doesn't notice. Vogs asks Corr what she is thinking?

In a wearied, offhand manner Corr says, "And she will be seeing you soon."

Vogs is surprised by this new, jaded mode of Corr's. He returns to her, softly, almost at a whisper, "That's what she said."

"That is what she said to you while you repeated to yourself the mantra of the moment."

Vogs grins, slightly embarrassed. "'A dialogue in mono'?"

Suddenly, mysteriously, Corr's eyes brighten and sprightliness returns to her footsteps. "I'm hearing the piano in a night piece." She offers the palms of her raised hands to the missing moon. "Oh, the eternal night!" Corr swirls and twirls and runs headfirst into a post and falls to the ground.

Vogs stops in an instant. He does not whimper this time. He stares. Helplessly he stares down at the pile on the ground.

He hears someone speaking. He spins his head to look. A man is sitting on the sidewalk with his back against a building. This man is watching Corr and Vogs. The man had said, as if he were speaking to Vogs, "I talk like this to myself all day and night."

(7) +

She may have seen the eternal night. She may have seen herself in the eternal night. She was not dead though.

Corr did not die there on the street late that afternoon. She had, however, suffered a severe blow to her head. She spent most of the following week in a dumbing daze. Vogs had to spoon-feed her, had to wash her, dress her. She was like warm, silent, wet putty in his hands. Then one noon Vogs carried Corr to SLUA and carefully propped Corr up so that she was facing the tall easel of the canvas he was presently most involved with. Vogs lovingly stroked Corr's nose and let go of her and turned away to continue his work on the canvas. The studio fell immediately into a silence so long and deep and strained that Vogs started pivoting his head every couple of minutes to peek at the couch to make sure Corr was still sitting upright there and had not flown away. Three-quarters of an hour passed this way. But then Vogs forgot. He forgot and forgot again to take another check on Corr. He was deep in his work, he was totally concentrated on his work, he was stroking a heavily loaded brush on that difficult canvas when all of a sudden Corr said—when suddenly she said her first real words in a week from behind him in a high, ringing voice. "She was trying to kill me! She tried to kill me!" By eventide Corr had come sufficiently to her senses that she could make demands. So she went home, with a little help from Vogs. Corr went home and spent that night alone in her own bed in her own building. And next morning she was dead.

The preceding, fairly long paragraph is set in italics because, again, when two artists (and one sidewalk sitter?) get to mixing their versions of reality, it is often hard to say which is what or why is when. Were Corr and Vogs experiencing a mutual dream/fantasy/vision of death again, like they did that first night of their everlasting separation from Necky? Or was the dumb week that Corr spent in a stupor endured only by her? If so, while Corr was suffering this long period of incapacity that ended with her death, what was Vogs seeing her undergoing? Five minutes of dizziness on the sidewalk?

"I am truly shaken by their lack of conscious reasoning."

"What?" Vogs urgently kneels low and lower beside Corr, frantically hoping he can help her. Either he had not heard what she said, or he didn't understand the meaning of her words—the first words Corr has spoken since she ran into the post.

"We are talking about the generation of personality here, aren't we?"

Vogs instinctively shakes his head and answers Corr's question with a question of his own. "Whose personality?" The verbal half of Vogs' response clearly indicates that, yes, he did hear Corr this time and that, no, he did not fully understand what she had said. While Vogs' overriding concern at the moment is, of course, Corr's health, he cannot help but laugh at her eyes rolling drunkenly in their sockets. "Yours or mine, Corr?"

"Don't know... That seems to be what we are..."

The clouds blow away. Corr's eyes clear up, and she becomes fully conscious of herself and Vogs and of why she is heaped so ungainly on the sidewalk.

She struggles to raise the upper half of her body from the concrete. Vogs helps her, and she flops her head against his chest. "I thought I had died. Then I thought I hadn't died but had become a vegetable. Then the vegetable died. —No! Someone killed it."

"Jonny Facemoral."

Vogs cranks his head around fast to see who said that.

Indeed, even the littlest events of life are not isolated and fortuitous. To turn his head around that far, Vogs had to swing his shoulders and chest too, with the result being that Corr is now looking straight at the man sitting on the sidewalk.

The man had moved from sitting with his back against the wall to sitting just five feet from Corr and Vogs. To all appearances he had made this move without the slightest change in his sitting posture. His eyes are fixed on Corr's.

Corr stares back at the man. She is not hawking belligerently at him, the way that group of kids had stared at her. No, her eyes are friendly.

Only the man's jaw, mouth, and cheeks move as he says in a perfect voice, "Resist...the inability to acknowledge the flexibilities within your self; therefore you might learn who you actually are...or something like that—whew!"

The man's perfect voice was not absolutely perfect. A little something in the voice apparently caught in Vogs and Corr's hearing and became the aspect of primary note to them. In other words, the man's voice further upsets Corr and Vogs. And. The man's eyes are on Corr, but is he actually looking at her?

Corr asks him, "Are you Johny?" She sits up some straighter.

Quickly Vogs whispers to her, "I think he said J-o-n-n-y."

58

Corr whispers back to Vogs, without taking her eyes off the man, "You can hear the difference?"

Vogs does not answer her. "Jonny Facemoral, I am Vogs. And this heavenly person beside me is Corr Cor."

The man doesn't answer him. Fastened absolutely on Corr's eyes, Jonny Facemoral says to who knows who, "A dialogue in mono. The eternal night. The moon."

Vogs opens his big mouth. This takes him a while. No one is watching him.

Without looking away from Jonny's face, Vogs again whispers to Corr. "Just before you tried to permanently quiet your earthly brain by ramming it into that post there, I said to you, or, rather, I repeated to you that *dialogue in mono* phrase. Then you said something, and then you said 'the eternal night.' I do not remember, however, either of us mentioning the moon."

"But… Yes!" Or should Corr have said *no*? "That's amazing! I never actually mentioned the moon, Vogs, but I was thinking about the moon and its lucid beauty when I hit the post."

Vogs turns a puzzled face to Corr. He looks quite doubtful. "Really? Are you sure?" He peeks deep into her eyes, sees the bumpy back walls inside her eyeballs.

She winks at him. "Yes, really. Definitely, Dogs!"

Vogs, for no reason that's immediately obvious, drolly distorts his face every which way and presses his hands together side to side like an open book. "Predictably, a relationship that starts off inauspiciously has to mutate into something that changes and enriches both parties."

Cute is Corr's next question. "That's from your chapbook of memorable quotes?"

"'Tis."

The muscles of the left half of Vogs' face return to their customary, undistorted, relaxed settings. "Next, an aside. *Tis*, in this case, with or without the apostrophe, was not the plural of *ti*. Nor was it an abbreviation of *tisane*." The muscles of the other half of Vogs' face follow suit and relax. What is he up to? What is Vogs getting at? He's unmistakably uneasy and wary. Is that why he is taking such a long way around? "I now return to our discussion within a discussion. The words of that 'memorable quote' were the words of a critic. He is not a critic of my work though. He is a critic of the popular arts. I do not offer you his name because chances are that the words were not truly his own words."

"I will assume," says Corr to Vogs, "that what you are doing, my manly monkey, is attempting to adjust the level of predictability of this scene. And I will play along by asking you to tell me, Vogsy, which two of the three of us here comprise the 'both parties' in that quote? Me and you? Me and Jonny? Jonny and you?"

"Don't you recall your already notorious definition of a couple, Corr?"

"I do not know what you are referring to, sir, no."

"The following is a rough condensation of what you said to me earlier this very day, Corr, not so long ago: From the vantage point of any one of the members of a group of three people, there are only two actual people in the group."

"I said that? No!"

Vogs assures her. "You did."

"You did, you did," repeats Jonny.

Slipping into the distant and bemused smile that often shows on her face while she paints, Corr tilts her forehead to press it softly against Vogs' nose. "I don't think Jonny is actually seeing us or even hearing us, love. I think he's all mind."

(8) +

Vogs and Corr do finally make it down to the beach. Jonny Facemoral does not. Discussing this matter as they stroll out onto the sand, Vogs and Corr agree that Jonny is most likely sitting even now where he was seated on the sidewalk when they got up to leave.

"Vogs is standing beside me on the beach."

"Corr Cor is throwing stones at the water."

"The rocks that I select to throw are black and brown and bled and red."

"But did I not see you fling away from us," inquires Vogs in an absurdly normal voice, "several examples of the worldwide gray-speckled species of stone?"

"You are so observant, señor."

Vogs turns to face Corr and sings at very near the utter bottom of his bass voice, "I only have eyes for you, señorita."

And Corr turns to face Vogs. She starts to sing her reply but decides no and just throws it out there. "As long as your lawyer doesn't turn up."

Quick, before Corr's wicked comeback has time to sink in and make a nasty mess in his head, Vogs whirls his head away—"Whop! Whop!"—so that no one will ever be able to say for sure who said those *whops*. His head rolls back but not all the way back to Corr's face. His backbone stiffens, and in a squirrelly voice Vogs says off to that side of Corr, "Did you hear those two identical notes, World? They were, as you certainly already know, Corr Cor and me surging out as if to achieve the far ends of our ropes and suddenly hitting YOUR WALL!" It's not just his backbone; Vogs' whole body has stiffened. The rigidly straight body tips and falls backward like a steel rod onto the gently up-sloping sand.

Corr responds by swinging one good leg over that inflexible, carcass-like body and sitting down on the body's belly facing the body's feet. She plants her heels on the rod-body's knees. Shading her eyes with her hands, looking out just above the surface of the water, she relates how she had once been a fierce, many-colored serpent who roamed the oceans of the world. She was so long and sleek and beautiful that all the fishes in the sea followed her everywhere that she went.

"What happened then?" painfully grunts Vogs.

"What do you mean what happened then?"

"What happened to the glamorous serpent and her countless follower fish?"

"The serpent died on her day to die. And the fish went home."

"May the fully grown person perched as proudly as The Blessed Figurehead on my stomach please realize that she is causing me some discomfort."

"Oh? Why didn't you say so earlier, dear?" Corr rocks back on her ass in order to spring to her feet, causing Vogs pain even more severe.

Corr stands squarely on her feet beside the horizontal-ish, suffering man. She stands as a lone sentinel looking up the beach, looking down the beach. Looking up the beach, looking down the beach. Vogs has raised a trembling hand to her. The quaking hand implores her to, please, help this lug up from the sand. Corr cold-shoulders the hand. Vogs gags and retches as he pathetically struggles to his feet. He's up on his knees, up on his feet—

Tis the female body that wholly stiffens now. "Bang-g-g!" This taut body does not tip over backward like a lifeless rigid rod, however. "Pooch-h-h!" It falls away from its stiffness like a lifeless dropped shirt. Corr's starchless body collapses to the sand.

Afore she passes out of this world, this ever-closing reality, Corr explains to Vogs—in a direfully weak voice, of course—what had just happened to her. "Oh-h-h." Barely is she able to speak; barely is she able to say that she is repeating a message coming to her down a thin, grayish time-tube. And what is that message? "The first sound, that long *bang*, was the never-ending journey of the infamous Last Bullet forcefully entering this part of the world, at last." Corr skillfully melts on the sand like an ice cube on a sunny stone. "Oh-h-h." Another long *oh* surely means there is more message a'coming down the tube. "And closely following that longish blunt report was a second sound, the sound of a deep puncturing, a long *pooch*. That low-pitched sound was the bullet passing right through my chest." Her failing hand covers her torn heart. "Oh-h-h!" End of message.

Vogs stands over her, sneering down at her. He's not kidding now. Strong and cool and disdainful, he starts to walk away. He changes his mind and kneels once more beside Corr. "This is the third time in recent memory that you've fallen to the ground in front of me as if you were dead. The time that you hit the post I can excuse. But the other two times you were clearly trying to frighten me. You succeeded once, but you did not this time. Why do you persist in this spoiled-child behavior?"

Is Vogs truly feeling disdain for Corr? Perhaps not. Perhaps *disdain* is too strong a word. How about *intolerance*? No, too strong again. Let it just be said then that Vogs is sounding a speck unfriendly at the moment.

Corr winks at him. Her wink could have been just a simple wink, or it might have been a subtle reminder to Vogs that—hey!—didn't he just fall down dead as steel himself.

Now Corr addresses Vogs. In a low, even tone. "That was a nice little speech you just made, Vogs. And it was surprisingly articulate for a visual artist." Corr pillows her hands between the back of her head and the sand. "I'll give a speech now, too. I'll make mine even shorter and, I hope, more natural sounding." She vulgarly flips her tongue in and out at Vogs. "I was not *merely* trying to scare you. You are the only audience I have to which I can play my endless grief at the passing of Necky. End of speech."

Inching away from *unfriendly*, or at least trying to, honestly trying to, while sliding a bit toward *curious*, Vogs gives himself a minor head-scratching. "You are falling down before me again and again because you are sad?"

"Sad, yes. And afraid. Afraid of your truelove."

"Laura?"

"That's the one." Corr sits up and knocks the sand from her long, dark and darkening hair. "Your Laura has some kind of weird plan for you, Vogs. Necky was in her way, and I am in her way. I need to be eliminated. And quite possibly, you do, too, eventually."

Vogs shakes his head and hangs his head and gets up from his knees. He is having a hard time with this scene. "Did Laura wave a black flag in your face or something?"

Corr jerks her eyes away.

She's glaring off over the horizon. Her chest tensely rises and tensely it falls, four times, while a shockingly ignoble, *brutish* even, look widens over her face. Her eyes rotate to stare up cruelly at Vogs' ear. "For me, a black flag usually stands for the dubious freedom to do anything one wants."

"Means that to me too, Corr. Did Laura flaunt her black freedom in a way that not even a free radical like you could stand?"

Corr's face is puffing up in anger and confusion.

"You'd better vent, Corr."

"Vogs!"

"Wha-a-at?"

Vogs sounded a bit shrill there. Maybe he had better vent, too.

Corr rails at him. "You're making me sound like some jealous housewife!"

Vogs jerks away and whines miserably.

His impulsive, plaintive cry perks Corr right up. She jumps to her feet to sneer at Vogs' back, to sneer at him the way he had so recently sneered down at her. "Oh, my sad sack, that was such a terrible sound you made. I forgive you everything. I even forgive you for treating me like one of the mob." The sneer she shammed might be cracking into a conditional smile.

Vogs has his back yet turned to Corr. He makes several movements with his hands, then stands silent and unbelievably still. *Positively inhuman those few movements were!* Suddenly, in his most resounding, his most transmundane voice ever, Vogs bellows, "A hush settles over the beach!"

Just as he said and just as he said it, a hush settled over the beach.

He speaks again in that big voice. "Totally quiet is the beach as the darkly-clad wizard lifts his ancient hands to the fuzzy, fussy heavens!" Vogs is acting out what he is relating. "His deeply enigmatic bunch-of-bones slowly...slowly turns around!" Vogs is gradually rotating about to face Corr with his hands and eyes raised high in front of him. "From out of the wizard's cavernous throat booms, 'We will deal again with *Love Of Space*!'"

How is Corr taking all this? How is she relating to Vogs' wizard thing? His farcical maneuver startled her, at first, and not merely because it was loud. Vogs' precipitous change in direction maybe even hurt Corr's feelings. And now? Right at this moment, Corr is looking acutely disappointed. Even so, she jumps onto Vogs' speeding train. "We will! And we will put lots of noise low in the foreground. Noise that is somewhat suggestive of children and oldfolk singing."

Vogs starts staggering about, as if he is under a great weight, as if his uplifted hands are trying to prevent something very heavy from descending to the beach. Aha! The great weight is none other than the sun. Vogs is trying to keep the fading sun up in the sky.

He is not saddened but delighted to lose the battle. "See how Our Sun is setting!" Vogs has not lost the big voice. "Time! Time it is now for us to retreat into the topsoil of our imagination," thunders he who is no longer but was so recently pretending to be a wizard, "which is unbelievably rich and ten feet deep."

Success. With that last *rich and deep* roar, Vogs got Corr's ticklebox going. She laughs and laughs, tries to hang onto Vogs while she's laughing but falls again to the sand. And this time…is she really dead this time? No. Not dead yet. She is still laughing.

Vogs duplicates her fall, dropping to the sand to lie on his side beside her, facing her jovial face. "Sh-h," he says.

As if by magic, Corr stops laughing. She and Vogs lay silent and unmoving while the beach grows darker and darker.

In the dense dark they look like two logs washed up onto the shore. They are not asleep though. A single sharp sound springs Corr&Vogs into action. They push up pronto onto one elbow each to gaze up the beach behind them.

Not far above them is a dim hump on the sand, a seven-point hump that wasn't there before the dark descended. Jonny Facemoral? He kinda sat that way.

Vogs calls out, "Is that Stoick Stone?"

He is answered. "No, it's not. It's Laura Pepin."

"Auughh!" screams Corr. "What is she doing here?"

(9) +

No one of them would take the lead; hence, the unhumble three are forced to walk side by side in the dark. Corr is on the outside, the curb side; Laura is on the inside, next to the buildings and their entrances; and, quite so, Vogs got the dubious honor of being the one in the middle. As he strides along between two very different women, Vogs could be the center of a magnet, with a plus pole to one side of him and a minus pole to the other. Which woman would he see as which pole?

Laura had returned to Vogs' studio, found him not there, and then followed his scent to the beach. Yes, she said that. She said, "Then I followed your scent down here to the beach."

Corr had kicked the sand in scowling contempt before scoffing, "She just plain followed us here. She just stayed out of sight till it got dark."

The three of them are now heading back to Vogs' studio, tramping at a speedy pace indeed up the opposite side of the same street that Corr and Vogs (and perhaps Laura too) had walked down. Corr and Vogs spot Jonny sitting over across the street on the other sidewalk in the pale light from a window. They wave, he doesn't. Laura spends not one second of her precious time looking to see at what or who Corr and Vogs had waved.

She, Laura Pepin, is certainly a potent walker. The uphill grade is evidently not fazing her at all. Is her admitted, "sometimes hourly" single-mindedness an aid in walking fast? Or does she have four little wings up under all that shining gold hair? Vogs and Corr are both in pretty good physical shape, but they are definitely breathing heavier than Laura at keeping this pace.

Corr tries to whisper, tries to whisper softly enough above her heavy breathing that Laura won't hear her. "You are not going to wake up in a brand new life, Vogs."

Vogs snickers and then whispers—not as softly as Corr managed to whisper—a formula return. "Nor in a brand new wife, Corr."

Laura walks on with her eyes straight ahead, unflinchingly pretending she had not even noticed Corr and Vogs were speaking to each other.

Walk. Walk. Walk. Walk. Walk. Walk. Walk. Walk. Walk.

The fleet oscillation of Laura's unstoppable legs slows up not one iota when, less than a minute after Corr and Vogs' *life/wife* exchange, Laura points her index finger at Vogs while pointing the pinkie of the same hand at Corr. Laura's hand is barely discernable in the dim, but it is far easier to make out than the purpose of her question. "What exactly are your relationships to form and color?"

Vogs fires right back, "Let's make this an essay on convergence."

Never to be left behind when Vogs' ripostes get spontaneous, Corr quickly makes an equally unselfconscious, unprompted contribution. "Working with images? Or producing images?"

Laura creases her brow in the darkness. "Do you two always avoid tough questions by responding with essentially unrelated answers?"

That may not have been another tough question, because Vogs answers it directly and without hesitation. "I do!"

Corr chimes in. "I do, too!"

Vogs persists. "Are our *unrelated answers*, as you called them, Laura, all that different from your *problematic question*, your question about Corr's and my relationships to form and color? If we were avoiding that *tough question*—your words again—weren't you just trying to draw our attention to you because you got all upset that Corr and I had a personal conversation, brief as it was?"

Corr is all teeth. This is the very first time Vogs has stuck up for her in the face of Laura. "Yeah! Brief as it was."

The three walk on in silence.

By the sudden grace of a well-lit storefront, both Corr and Vogs catch sight of the smile on Laura's face. *She's not a lawyer at all! Is she even human?*

The threesome trods on, oblivious to its silence, cutting on by two more stores before Laura does the deed.

Hey? Now that Laura has killed the silence, what'd she say?

Laura had turned her head clear away from Vogs and Corr before she spoke, but that in itself is not the reason why what she said will of necessity remain an unknown. Laura could have been talking in a different language, a very different language. Bouncing off the building beside her, her sentence (?) sounded only the faintest bit like she had said: "A father, a mother, one of the children."

Vogs and Corr walk on with their eyes straight ahead, unflinchingly pretending they had not even noticed Laura was talking to the side away from them.

Laura speaks again, directing her words this time at the sidewalk out in front of her feet. While her words are easy enough to understand—no translation needed—she is speaking as if in a loud voice from a great distance. "It is late." She is achieving this loud-but-distant effect with breathy whispering. "I am well away from my abode. You, Corr, said something the day that we met about us all sleeping together."

"You missed your one chance, *sister!*"

Having her idea so roundly dismissed by Corr has little observable effect on Laura. Laura specifically asks Vogs, "What do you think about my spending the night?"

What can Vogs possibly say? Remember: he is in the middle. For a long while he says nothing.

For a long time he says nothing.

He and Corr and Laura have in fact stopped before the main door of his building when next he speaks. "Ok, who all's coming inside?"

Above the door, attached to the building by a thin, down-curving rod, hangs a small lamp. The three players can see each other's faces. Corr, having traveled to the beach and back. Laura, having traveled to the beach and back. Vogs, having traveled to the beach and back.

Corr is not begging. "I can't just leave you to her, Vogs."

"Well, then come on in."

"No."

"Please," begs Laura. Her slick smile. Her hand gently pressed to one ear. Her lowered eyelids.

Corr wants to punch the double-dealing woman.

Vogs sees this *want* and swiftly grabs Corr's wrists.

Corr mutters to herself, "Very vicious vain vixens choke on rotten peach pits."

"Yes or no." Vogs forces Corr to look at him. "Right now, Corr."

"No."

"Then good night." Vogs turns away from Corr, opens his door, and escorts Laura inside.

"Good night!" shrieks Corr as the door closes. As the door clicks closed in her face. She punches the door. She punches the door and kicks the door. Never again does Corr see Vogs. Or hear him or talk to him or anything.

First thing in the morning, the next morning, Corr marches out of her building and over to the meager little table that stands all alone most of the time now on the sidewalk before the big street-window of Vogs' building, once Vogs and Necky's building. Corr sits down at the table, on the single chair that's still at the table, and waits. And she waits and she waits. It's getting dark. She has waited there the whole day! It's dark and no lights have come on in Vogs' building. Nothing. There's no sign of activity inside the building. Finally Corr forces herself to knock. She knocks and then opens the door, because it's not locked. She goes inside and walks through the entire building, searching every nook and cranny. There's nobody there, except her.

Does Corr think that Vogs has been killed by Laura and packed away? Or that Vogs left with Laura willingly? Or that he left without Laura willingly? Vogs never again shows his face in the neighborhood, never comes back. Corr will live half in fear all the while that Laura is the one who will return, that Laura is coming back for her.

Corr turns off the lights she had switched on in Vogs' building and hushedly steps out the door into the night air. Will she stroll bravely back over tomorrow morning to peer in through one of Vogs' studio windows in hopes of seeing him? "There he is, standing in there plain as sunshine, painting. He's waving at me. I wave back. I'll return now to my own studio and go to work." No. Vogs is gone and Corr knows it. She steps carefully into her building and very quietly closes her door behind her.

The next morning, she is painting.

"Launching a search for Vogs would be utterly futile."

While this latest of Corr's "immutable pronouncements" openly invites inquiry, it will be left alone. The sentence will not be disputed, because it was merely a preliminary statement. Corr was just clearing the deck first. She has another, a similar, yet distinctly different hope to express.

"Given that everyone actually constructs everything they encounter, I had to have already known that Vogs would soon be gone. I had to have already determined also how he would disappear. Even if I can't see that *how* right now, I will eventually. And when I do see it, I will try, *in spite of everything*, to go back. I will make a massive attempt to change it all back to just two people alone together on the beach preparing themselves and each other for a period of energetic sexual activity."

Standing with her feet together, facing her easel, Corr closes one eye. Quick, she is dreaming. "I can see Vogs over in our café across the street." Slowly Corr lets her other eyelid drop. "He is sitting in the chair that he likes best with his elbows on our preferred table just inside the window under the sign that he painted, *WELF et al.* I will run outside in this dream. —I rush outside and streak across the street to push my face against the window. It's not Vogs! Someone else is sitting in there."

For weeks after that dream at her easel, Corr is drawn to the window that looks out at the café. Her left eye inevitably closes, and her right eyelid gradually shuts down to mute out the colors and to accentuate the contrast of the blacks and whites. Several times during these little events she has seen Vogs and Laura sitting at the table by the window. But the few times that Corr went across the street to check, it was someone else or no one was there at all.

Six months after Vogs' disappearance, Corr is in her studio working on a painting that will eventually wear the proud old title "A Known And Established Enemy of the People." While painting, she is composing a song, not a song about the recluse poet who wrote "A Known And Established Enemy…" some twenty years before this day, but a little song about not getting to see Milk Mandy posing on the street corner in his most tantalizing outfit. Corr calls the still fragmented song *A Dialogue in Mono*. Someone knocks on her door. It is not Vogs knocking, that much is for sure. As has been stated earlier, Corr never sees, hears, or smells Vogs again.

"I'm screwed up…beyond repair…kaput I am." She is still working on her song when she opens the door. It's not Laura either. And, of course, it's not Necky standing there.

It is not Necky but Necky's brother. "Hello, I'm Jerome, Jerome Watershighagain, Necky's bother. I have not seen Necky since we were children. Yes, I know he is dead. I want to ask you to let me into that building. The fellow in the business across the street said that you probably have a key to it, because he sees you going in and out of there."

"I sneak over there often, yes." Corr is carefully crusty. "I go over there to sleep in either Vogs' bed or Necky's bed."

"Do tell. Who is Vogs?"

"He lived over there, too. Both Vogs and Necky lived and worked in that building. For two or three years."

The man is watching Corr's lips.

Corr softly clears her throat. "If you had been out of contact with Necky for a big part of your lives, how'd you find out where he lived?"

"The police found me to inform me of Necky's death. And the owners of the building—the police must have given them my address—contacted me to ask if I wanted a *last* look around in the building. I think they are about to let someone else have the building. I got the impression there is or was a goodly number of people wanting it." The man is jumpy nervous and as calm as stone at the same time. He does and doesn't look like Necky. "From the way you worded a sentence, I assume this Vogs is not around. Is he dead, too?"

"Don't know. But there's a good chance that he is, yes."

Jerome looks the woman who answered the door straight in her eyes for the longest time.

Laura reaches out her lovely hand to lay it on the shoulder of Jerome Watershighagain. "My name is Corr. Please step inside. I'll get the key."

(10) +

"Dreams do not exist anywhere, I know." Corr's head drops gradually to the side until it lies peacefully on her shoulder. Dragging one foot after the other, she slowly winds about an irregular circle just inside the door of the room that was Necky's bedroom. "Wasn't it just last week that I heard a stranger on the street wanting to impress his confederate by calling dreams merely the battle of entrenched habits trying to keep out newcome habits?" Corr raises her head from her shoulder only enough that she can rotate her head gently on her neck to look over her other shoulder. "I think most everyone nowadays would agree that dreams are only habits made visible. —Yeah, and for all I know, that once esoteric awareness could be taught in today's public schools."

Impatiently, Jerome runs all eight of his fingers back through his hair. "Are we still talking about Necky?" His hair is even darker than Corr's hair. And it's at least as long as hers. His skin is some darker than hers, too. His skin is probably the same color as Necky's but just a little darker.

Corr pops her head up straight and high and then waggles it forward and back as Necky was wont to do in tight times. "Yes, I'm talking about the extended dream that was Necky and Vogs."

Jerome sits down on Necky's bed but springs right back up to his feet. "Well, I don't know about this Vogs guy, but Necky was really here. He wasn't just a dream. He was more than someone's long battle with their habits."

Demonstrating for Jerome probably the stalest of the I'm-skeptical expressions, Cor stares high out the corner of her eyes at nothing. She is nonetheless paying close attention. "Was he? I wonder."

Jerome doesn't take that decrepit bait.

So Corr veers slightly. "The people who lived in this building before Necky and Vogs…they all died, too." She's keeping her eyes fixed up and away from Jerome. "They too are dead and gone by someone else's hand."

"Oh yeah? The cops didn't say anything about that."

"It's true. The whole Thesaurus group." Although Corr's eyes have begun moving about freely, they are still absolutely avoiding looking at Jerome. "Three years before Necky and Vogs moved here."

Jerome scratches the edge of one of his nasal openings. "Were you living/working over there next door at that time too?"

"I had just got set up in the building."

When, again, Jerome does not reply, Corr decides it's time to let her eyes have a look-see.

Her jaw drops in disbelief. She closes her mouth. She frowns deeply. And then…and then she winks at the look in the man's eyes. "No, Jerome. I'm very sorry to have to tell you this, but I am not a revenging roof rat who sneaks down from the rafters at night to kill people. I am the innocent here."

"Do tell." Jerome turns away and wanders about the room looking at this and that again.

Corr's tight eyes follow him closely.

Suddenly her glare jerks left and right and fixes on a window curtain. She mumbles to herself, "That curtain is still drawn. It hasn't been raised since the last night of Necky."

Jerome could not have heard Corr's mumbling, most likely. He stops to pick up something that had apparently fallen between the wall and the nightstand beside the bed. He steps over to Corr and offers it to her. "Are these yours?

Corr does not take the pair of underpants from between Jerome's thumb and forefinger, but she does examine them carefully. Her face is soft and lovely now.

Or at least she pretended to inspect the underpants for what probably seemed like a week-and-two-days to Jerome. "Yes. I almost didn't recognize them. They turned up missing a long time ago."

"Before or after?"

"Pray tell me which before-or-after."

"Before or after Necky was killed."

"Oh, quite a while before, Jerome."

"Then...?"

Corr's eyes get real big and lurch away from the underwear. She squeezes her skull between overwrought hands and cries out in mock horror, "Yes! Yes! You have found us out! Necky and Vogs and I had a completely wide open sex thing going here. You are truly a master detective!"

"Relax." Jerome grins leather-like and pays Corr's fake fit no more mind.

He drops the dusty undies back where he had found them and takes up a book from Necky's desk. "You ever read this one?"

Corr crosses her arms and her legs and flops her head on her shoulder. "Yes."

Tis time now for Jerome to take a turn as the pretender. He cleverly feigns that he is quite unable to keep his eyes on the book and just can't help but gaze longingly at Corr. "I've never before seen anyone stand like you are standing there now and still appear so supremely graceful." Seems Jerome can mock, too.

Did Corr hear his tease?

"Zip!" she barks. "Should I take off my clothes now?"

Throwing back his head as he thrusts his arms high into the air, Jerome shouts victoriously, "Of course!" The book flies high across the room. "Take them off!"

All but concealed in the loudness of his voice was a strange quaking, an unsettling trembling.

Jerome's vivid performance stopped Corr dead. Either that or she suddenly chose to slow herself way-way down. She creeps over to a chair and sits there unnaturally upright, like that stick from that long gone afternoon, the stick with one end pushed into a crack in the sidewalk. Jerome returns to Necky's bed and sits on the edge of it, facing Corr.

They sit dumbly just looking at each other. Erelong Corr's eyes are so damp they could be on the verge of producing tears. Jerome's eyes show a great sadness, too, so much sadness that they will be unable to cry.

Corr slaps her face.

Jerome's eyes blink in disbelief.

"Where do you live?" she demands of him. Corr's eyes are staring wetly at the ceiling now, not at Jerome's heavy face.

Jerome's eyes jump back to life to search the room for Jerome's voice. Jerome's voice is found, and it says, "Way out on the desert."

"Away from people?"

"My nearest neighbor is three miles to the south."

"Oh."

"Do you want to go there with me?"

Corr c-c-can't s-s-say anything back.

"I'll be leaving here tomorrow, if you want to tag along."

Corr waves her head up and down and round and around. Quite slowly she waves her head up and down and round and around and round and around.

Jerome looks frightened. Either he is frightened or he is desperately worried about Corr. He might not even know himself which he is, scared or concerned, if he is not both.

Just to reach the edge of the desert took forever. And that was only the beginning of the journey. Dirt and dust, wind, clouds, sky. Jerome had cautioned Corr to carefully wrap the few things of hers that she brought along. If the sun or wind or dirt didn't get to her stuff, critters big or small would.

Corr lasted a week sleeping in a shack on the desert. The landscapes and skies were beautiful, deeply mysterious, enchanting. But her nose ran and her teeth felt like they were going to crack wide open. So she went home, arriving at her building just as the sun was setting.

She unlocks the door and steps inside. "Wow!" She grins exuberantly. A Known And Established Enemy Of The People is waiting patiently on the easel. Corr had left the painting not quite finished. "First thing tomorrow morning, Akaeeotp."

The next morning. Sure enough, someone is moving in next door.

Corr eventually, after a while, after she has grown, you know, curious enough, goes over there to ask the mover guys, "Hey! Who's moving in?" They tell her, "Some law firm, I think. A woman. I'm not sure of her name right now." Dumbfounded, Corr can't even turn and walk away. Glaring at one man's terribly chapped hands, she grumbles sardonically, "It's a bit hard to believe that two people have been killed in order to make a building available. But times *are* tough in the city." The mover guys have completely stopped doing what they were doing. They are all watching Corr. They are all gaping at the handsome, well bodied, erratically clothed artist. Corr finally comes to her senses, hears her teeth rattling, and notices that the men are observing her. "But that's not *your* problem," she informs them. "Please carry on." And with a gracious wave of her hand, she's strolling away. Actually she's tottering away, tottering back to the safety of her studio, where she will strip off her meager garments, lie down on the floor with her arms and legs spread, and stare at the high ceiling until she can see Heaven.

Heaven? A dirty bird flies into the café. The bird glides over the heads of patrons and across the width of the room to perch on the back of Vogs' favorite chair.

(No one in the café knows this, not even Welf, but under the seat of Vogs' chair-of-choice a fairly long sentence with quotation marks has been compactly written in red paint. Vogs painted the tiny words on the underside of the chair one morning while the café was otherwise empty and Welf was out for his morning walk around the block. "Looked upon by the clearest of eyes, every activity, down to the slightest single action by anyone anywhere at any time, is at best an absurdist parody of the wretchedness of and the very poor quality of *human behavior*." Had Vogs read or heard that knot somewhere, or had he—to quote Laura—created it to look like a memory? Many performances in the past had Vogs avoiding the problem of origin altogether by deftly and simply labeling such a sentence a 'semi-quote.')

Welf sees the bird fly in. He is about to chase the foul fowl outside when Corr, sitting on her chair across the table from Vogs' chair, says, "No. Let him stay, please."

The dust-covered bird turns his head to look at Corr out one eye and turns his head to look at her out his other eye. Then Dirty Bird speaks. In squawks. And not just once. Again and again Dirty Bird delivers the same loud raucous riff as if he is urging Corr to take immediate action.

Corr extends her open palm to the bird.

Dirty Bird guffaws at the empty hand and flies around the room and out the door.

Welf had been raptly watching, wholly witnessing the event. He rubs his upper lip. "What do you make of that, Corr?"

"Don't know, my man. Looks like I just got the word. But in a language I don't understand. Could you make out any of it?" Was Corr serious? She sure sounded as if she were.

Her take on the event so surprised Welf that he laughs out loud. He is laughing recklessly and slapping the wall next to the kitchen doorway. "You are certainly an odd person, my little chickenwicken."

"At least I'm not the mess you are going to look when I get finished with you!" Corr pretends she is *gonna stand up now.*

"No! No! Please don't hurt me!" A broadly grinning Welf waves goodbye-for-now and disappears.

A flash portait of Welf after he waved goodbye and after he slipped around the corner and into his kitchen will suddenly loom up like a white-lit billboard out on the streets one aberrant night in Corr's future.

Long before the morning that the moving crew showed up next door, even way before the day that Jerome Watershighagain knocked on her studio door, Corr had spirited Necky and Vogs' paintings out of their building and into hers. When a representative from Necky's gallery then came moseying around asking questions, Corr lied to him. When a rep from Vogs' gallery came to see why Vogs was ignoring them, Corr told the uptight woman only that no one had seen Vogs for some time. When Jerome inquired why there were no paintings in his brother's studio, Corr merely shrugged her shoulders. So much for heedless moral excellence. With a shrug of her shoulders, Corr gets up from her table and leaves the café.

And none too soon did she leave. Mere moments after Corr had made her exit, Laura sauntered into the café. Corr did not see Laura coming, and Laura caught no sight of Corr going. These two woman have not exchanged glances since they stood with Vogs under his little outside light one night many months ago. All that Corr has seen of her new neighbors is a quick glimpse of a fancy dressed man entering and then leaving *that building.*

Not a half dozen minutes later: "Ugh!" Corr is in her studio experiencing abnormal difficulty getting the cap off a tube of paint. "Double ugh ugh!" She gives up her struggle with the cap and tosses the tube of blue over her shoulder and, yes, onto the paints table.

She begins pacing about the studio, her path unwittingly drawing a series of nearly recognizable shapes on the worn-down, paint-spotted wood floor. "*Subtle* is always related inversely to *normal*." Her steps pick up a bit of speed. "But how is it related to *abnormal*? Everything that is abnormal is then subtle? Me thinks not." Alone she is, trotting all over her studio. Is she talking out loud? She is.

Leaving off discussing the *subtle* question with herself, Corr begins a simple list of lip-curling unpleasantries. "That night…the dark nightmarish walk up from the beach…three ghosts huddling outside the door under a tiny incandescent bulb…" Corr pauses. Her pace slows. Her mouth is open, but the list will grow no longer.

For she falls into a dialogue, a *dialogue* between herself and an idea. This idea is none other than the fancy dressed man from next door, whom she is apparently visualizing as a confidant. She has never actually seen the man's face. Will she make one up for him, or will he remain faceless?

"Why did you use the word *ghost*, Corr?"

"I'm sorry, sir. I use that word too often, I know." The journey of Corr's feet is presently outlining on the floor two broad, squished rectangles that share one short-side. Corr has hid one of her hands inside her smock frock, below her waist. "Most likely I've fixed on the word *ghost* because people are always saying things about me."

"What kind of things?"

"Let me think…. 'Corr moves like a ghost.' Or: 'Even in the daytime Corr Cor can be as quiet and hard to spot as a ghost.' Or: 'She can actually see in the dark, like ghosts do.' But as you can see, Fdm, I'm alive. I'm a hot human being."

"I have noticed no ghostly aspects myself."

"Apparently some people don't ever pick up on *my* aspects."

"Oh, I've noticed your aspects all right, Corr. They're just not ghostly."

Corr extracts her hand from under her smock frock and licks those three fingers as she heads for the door to answer the knock.

Laura prances in as if she will soon own the place. She looks around swiftly, sniffs her nose, steps over to Corr, takes up Corr's hand. Laura draws the moistest three fingers to her face and sniffs at them. She then grins and says to Corr, "Hmm! We're going to have to do something about that, I guess."

Corr Cor jerks her hand free. "You just get out of here!"

Laura Pepin is given no chance whatsoever, no time at all in which to carry out Corr's command. Corr abruptly changes direction and spits out a demand for information. "Tell me what you did with Vogs!"

"That is a personal matter known only to Vogs and his attorney, Laura Pepin. I'm sure he would not want you to know." Laura reaches out her hand to straighten the open neck of Corr's garment. Readily apparent it must be to Laura that the paint-streaked smock frock, made of coarse cotton, is the only clothing Corr has on.

The time is right. Corr punches the haughty woman.

Actually, Corr missed with her blow. Corr's jade fist zoomed past the taller woman's exquisite chin at a million mph. Laura takes a quick step back, formally excuses herself, grins a snake's grin, and promptly leaves the building.

"She took something!"

In a mad rush Corr checks the area, then runs breakneck to the open door. Too late. She sees only Laura's back and yellow hair as Laura passes through *her* doorway into *her* building.

"You have Necky and Vogs' paintings safely stored in a heavily curtained room upstairs."

Ah! The fancy dressed man is still in and about the studio and environs.

"How'd you know that, Fdm?"

"I took myself on a tour of your building, Corr, while you were occupied with my partner, Laura Pepin."

"In that case I should be thankful that I'm merely making you up, Fdm. Of all the people in the world, I would not want Laura Pepin to know about those paintings."

Welf Aceicou never crosses the street. Even when he's out on his morning and afternoon breaks, he limits his energetic walks to the block his café sits on. But tonight he will cross the street. He's locking up his shop to go home—he does have a home—when he hears an awful cry from Corr's building. He runs over there to knock and then to pound on her door. No one answers. No one answers. Lights are burning on both the top and bottom floors. Then Corr opens the door. She's...a mess. She says, "I'm sorry." He says, "Are you all right?" She answers, "Yes." Welf hesitates, then says, "Ok. Good night then. I'll see you tomorrow." Corr says ok and closes her door.

He's locking his door when a horrible cry rings out. Resounds! Resounds from across the street. Her clothes are torn. She has great slashes of paint across her body. She looks terrible.

Her eyes are caves. Black dark caves.

A haunting cry crosses the street like a leaf struggling to stay afloat on a raging, flood-swollen river. Wafting on the whitewater.

He doesn't know what to do. Should he break down her door? Should he run for help? Should he climb up and kick out a window or something? "I don't know!" Welf hesitates, then says, "Ok. Good night then. I'll see you tomorrow." He hurries home.

(12) +

"AND NOW, HERE IS A LIVE BULLETIN FROM YOUR VERY OWN NEIGHBORHOOD: It's a certified fact, folks! Do you get all warm inside when you think of the demented black table standing out in front of Vogs and Necky Watershighagain's building for better than two years? Well, we do! And it's gone! Take a look for yourself, right over there! The precious little table has been underhandedly replaced by FOUR HUGE CONCRETE POTS!" Impersonating a public person, a career news-describer who is supposedly speaking urbanely and confidentially into an audio-video pickup from just outside the scene of an unreasonable crime, a crime in progress, *in your very own neighborhood*, Corr Cor could be heard from a block away if anyone were of a mind to listen. And on she goes. "Hundreds of plants—each and all bearing nondescript, uniformly-sized flowers of primary colors only, thank you—have been trucked in from anonymous plant manufacturing sites far, far away to be methodically crammed into those four monstrous pots to form criminally uncomplicated, *pretty* patterns." Corr abruptly stops her throaty talking to tilt her head to the side and to sneak up an open hand so that she can touch the tip of her index finger to the side of her nose and the tip of her thumb to the corner of her chin. "Please, I am, yes, being just a bit secretive right this minute, yes, because being surreptitious is the generally accepted way-to-act in this type of situation, when one is working for *the greater good*." Her hand falls from her face, and she holds her head high. "AND NOW, BACK TO OUR BULLETIN: Hanging down over this quaint setting is a freshly painted sign. *Pepin et al.*" Smack! Corr had no more than said "*Pepin et al*" when she suddenly slapped her hand hard over her mouth. Was her saying out loud the words on the new sign something she had previously made up her mind to never do? Corr's body stands very still. It could be a dead tree staring down at one of its roots peeking up out of the soil. Or has she found herself on a perilous brink? Has she marched to the unsheltered, windswept rim of her public display? Corr puffs out her cheeks and carefully turns a quarter turn. She is now facing across the street. Loosening up her already unconfined portrait of a public personality, she spitefully snorts a curt, indelicate sign-off. "How totally original!" She could have been referring so viciously there in her sign-off to the lack of originality in the design of the sign or to the whole flowerpots-replacing-table scene.

Where exactly is Corr? She is leaning against the front of her building, standing in the rich sunlight on one foot. She has stood exactly there many times before, always with one or the other of her feet covering the name of the man who laid this sidewalk before she was born.

"I think I'll just slip on down there," she declares, "and pick every last one of those flowers." She has dumped her previous role as a news-describer and is now speaking in thoroughly obnoxious squeaks. She reconsiders her plan. "No. A team of gardeners would be called, immediately." She abandons the squeaks. "And then a big ugly wire fence or something would be erected around the new flowers to keep the likes of me away. Away!" Is Corr speaking conversationally now? Yes, sort of; she appears to be; but, no, so far she has not addressed a person made up for her to gossip with. "And then they'd hire a guard. With a gun. And a uniform. And mean lips. And a long flashlight at night. To shine in my windows. But I'd be ready for this guard guy. I'd secretly tape a broad paintbrush to the bare end of a broomstick, and then I'd run my jerry contraption out the window to paint his face a nice juicy orange."

Grinning wickedly, Corr is making her way back inside her building when she happens to see Welf standing over in the window of his café staring at her. "To Welf or to work?" She rocks her head from side to side in cheery indecision. "Or as Vogs and Necky and I used to ask each other *the question*, 'Are we going to work, lay about, or travel today?' Decisions. All the time these horrendous decisions!" The deer jumps. "Work!" The deer jumps the rest of the way into her building. "Work!" The door slams behind her.

Is Corr needing a new person in her everyday life? Necky is dead, Vogs is gone, Laura's out of the question, Welf is a cafetier. Will Corr suddenly discover someone? If yes, will it be a man or a woman? Or a dog? Corr has tons of friends but not one that she could or would spend hours of time with. And the fancy dressed man looked too stiff in his back. And Jerome positively refused to even try living in the city. A small circular mirror hangs on a string from Corr's easel. On the surface of the mirror are five minuscule words: "No One Cares For Me." Corr painted the words backwards on the mirror so that when she looked at her eyes the words would appear to have been inked permanently on her forehead.

G.J. Horsey Fatts, a curious mix of souls, doesn't bother to knock. He pushes open the door and calls out Corr's name as he steps inside. He is another of the artists from the gallery that showed Vogs' work. The "uptight woman" who came that time to check on Vogs is the housemate of this chap. Vogs used to call the man simply GJ, while Necky had tagged him Horsely. Normally Corr just calls him Hor. (Hor and Corr? Wasn't it Vogs, not Corr, who liked to hear words that almost rhyme with his name?)

Today is not a *Hor* day. When Corr looks up from her work and sees who has entered her studio, she exclaims, "Horsey!" Her bright eyes investigate all over the man. "Haven't seen you in a while."

"Oh-h-h-h!"

Corr looks to be mildly perplexed. "*Oh* what?"

Horsey points his long talented finger. Leaned against the wall, Akaeeotp stands like a fiery demon facing the door. Horsey can't believe his eyes. "Is it finished, Corr?"

"Yes."

"Does it have a name yet?"

Corr is pleased by the attention her painting is getting. "A Known And Established Enemy of the People."

The title impresses Horsey. Has he never heard that string of words before? Yes or no, yes or no, Horsey is certainly dazzled by the painting itself. "It looks like a full-scale phantom image of you moving through the wild night at the very edge/end of the world."

"Actually, Horsey, it's two roses in a vase on a kitchen table."

"Wow! I sometimes forget your genius for sarcasm, woman. Roses indeed! Kitchen table indeed! And I suppose those aren't dogs and cats and rats and mats down along the lower edge."

"Nope. Those are slugs and bugs and rugs."

"What say we jump into bed this very minute, Corr?"

"Oh-h." Corr stalls just long enough to catch her emotional balance. "So that's the reason for your unexpected visit: you heard that Vogs and Necky aren't around any longer, and you came to ravage The Queen with your horseflesh."

"You got me on the first guess."

That said, the big smile evaporates from Horsey's face. He drops his eyes. "When I heard about Necky, I cried all night and the next day I painted a portrait of him from memory."

Horsey wipes his tearless eyes. "And Vogs. Where is he? You still don't know?"

Corr Cor wobbles her head. "I do still not know."

Tis *The Queen* then who points her long talented finger and says, "And I'd rather have rocks in my bed, as one old saying goes."

"This man can make your afternoon pass with a much sweeter song than Rocks In My Bed ever was."

"Oh? Have you found yourself a sweet song now, Horsey? Please, let's hear it. I'd love to listen to this ditty of yours first, before you do me the deed."

Slowly, very slowly Horsey's face turns up in a beautiful smile. "You are not saying no. You are either teasing me or testing me. Or both. Are you testing to see if my mind is sharp enough right now to fill your needs? I will say this, my deed is not dastardly, it is fabulous."

Corr takes her paintbrush from where she had parked it over her ear and lightly touches the wood end of the brush to her cheekbone. "I'm sure it is, son. But first mom must check the medium and the message. Undress yourself and go stand in that window."

Horsey looks at the tall window, looks back at Corr. Corr's eyes are sharp and focused. The Queen is not drooling even the least bit. Horsey then crafts what he thinks is a better idea. "We could undress both of us and go stand in the window together."

They do exactly that.

They spend but a minute standing there, facing out the glass. A minute is long enough: Corr is certain that Welf is not going to return to his café window any time soon, and Horsey is thoroughly erect and whispering in her ear like Necky used to.

"Horseweed. Horse trader. Horsetail. Horseback. Horse-faced. Horseplay. Horsewhip. Horsehead."

That's a shortlist from Horsey At The Window. Those particular eight horse-items were presented here because they are the ones that will stick longest in Corr's head from the hundreds and hundreds that G.J. Horsey Fatts either has hissed to her already or will blip for her in the hours to come.

Not a single rock resides in Corr's studio. So Mr. Fatts gathers up a dozen or so of her old tube caps and spreads them on her bed.

This Horsey person? He's a bit and a dab of everything, which makes it easy for other people to see in him whatever they want. Stop! A point should be made quite clear here: G.J. Horsey Fatts does *not* change, like a chameleon or something. No, people see what *they want* to see in him. Corr might not have made this distinction, and that could be why she used to call him Hor. Now she is calling him Horsey.

Corr has a narrow bed-like thing down in her studio. This is where Horsey laid out his tube-cap trap. But Corr's real bed is upstairs, where Horsey has never been. Unwittingly Corr sidesteps Horsey's paintcap ambush when she calls to him from her big bed. "Up here, Horsey."

Horsey promptly neighs and gallops up the staircase. He turns right, opens the first door in the hallway, and steps into the room where Corr has hidden Vogs and Necky's paintings.

He immediately backs right out of that room and very softly closes the door. Corr is leaning against the jamb of her bedroom door, standing on one foot with her arms crossed. Horsey is really embarrassed. "Sorry, Corr. As far as anyone else in the whole world will ever know, I did not see a thing in there."

"Then come on to bed, my big Horsey. You have your song to sing to me."

Sound dissolves into smell.

(13) +

Corr is sitting quietly, ruminating on her life when Welf approaches her from behind. Sensing his presence drawing near, she whines, "There used to be so many puzzles worth unraveling."

Welf stops dead where he is. He has paused to think.

Having thought, he is nodding his head as he steps around beside Corr to refill her teacup with hot water. He could be weighing something, something other than either Corr's wistful whine or his present trip around the room topping off people's teacups; for, somewhat abruptly, he sets the water pot on the table and plops himself down on Vogs' chair.

Corr's eyes display her amazement at Welf's audacity, but her mouth produces not a sound. Neither does Corr's body change from its ruminating-on-life posture.

"All the puzzles in my life," says Welf with a rising curve in his voice that sounds a lot like surprise, "are turning out to be the *same* puzzle." This might be the very first time this reality has presented itself to this man.

And what does Corr do? She immediately and unceremoniously turns the focus away from Welf and right back on her. "I have one of those universal puzzles, too, Welf. What could be slower than this wristwatch?"

Welf hesitates. No, actually he is *resisting*. It should have been—and most likely was—obvious to Corr that Welf had sat down at her table because he wanted to discuss with her a realization he had made only seconds before. Welf's resistance is short-lived, though. He-who-serves-the-public manages to have only the minutest sharpness to his voice when he says, "Are you talking about that thing there you always have on your arm? It doesn't run, does it?"

"No, it's broke." Corr pushes gently on the handle of her teacup with one finger. The freshly filled cup does not turn on its saucer. "It has never kept time for me. Not for one second. It was given to me as a mean joke. When I was eight."

"You must have liked the joke. Or the joker."

"No. I think I must have liked the puzzle that was introduced into my life that day, Welf. What could be slower than this wristwatch?"

"Oh?" Welf scratches his head.

"Oh!" He quickly grins. "Now I think maybe I see what you are talking about, kiddo. I—"

"It's not a death wish." Corr sighs shallowly. "I'd just like to go to the other side of time, like Vogs probably did sometimes."

Welf had, of course, already worked up and begun a reply to Corr's question ("What could be slower than this wristwatch?") *before* she delivered her next sentence, that five-word declaration ("It's not a death wish.") So what can Welf do now? He re-starts his prepared reply with a different word. "Any—"

Welf stopped his mouth before it could utter a second syllable. Odds are that he realized just in time that he had not understood what Corr was talking about after all.

He shifts his chin and tries again for an appropriate response. "What makes you think Vogs could do such a thing, Corr?" In the months since Vogs disappeared, Welf has been pronouncing his name always in a tone of quiet respect.

Corr answers the question without having to think it over first. "He would shoot the breeze about 'the illusion of time' so much better than I can even now. He had to have had experiences I haven't had yet."

"How about your new male friend?"

Corr's eyes snap to Welf's eyes. Welf stares down at Corr's cup. Corr and Welf hold that pose for a full minute. A minute of interstellar silence is a long time.

A minute of silence is enough: Welf is certain that Corr is not going to answer his question. He asks a different question. Or two. "What about Necky? Did he do that sort of thing, too?"

Corr is still looking beady-eyed at Welf. She crisply cracks, "No!"

Welf blanches but does not up and run away.

Corr jerks up her left hand to rub a finger along the bridge of her nose. This contact with herself enables her to drop her eyes. "Necky was my pureheart. He knew nothing of time. He was more the anti-gravity type, like me—Corr Lighter-Than-Air Cor—even if he was forever denying it."

Corr takes an extravagant deep breath. "Why don't you tell me about *your* puzzle, Welf." She smiles as she softens and relaxes. "—After you tell me why you're sitting down at a table with a customer. I've never seen you do that before."

"Don't tell her, Welf!"

Laura strides up to the table all smiles. "Just joking, Corr. Don't get all upset now. And *do not* try to sock me!"

Is Corr upset? Wow! How could she not be! A lawyer has snuck up on her completely undetected. Has Laura Pepin been practicing Corr Cor's famously unseen ghostwalk? Shoving her dark hair back from her temples, Corr aims to sound stout of heart and spirit and simultaneously bored. "With a stroke of élan, I'll just paint you out, deary. Out-ta!"

Laura looks utterly fabulous. Clothes, body, hair, face, demeanor, hands. Everything is perfect. Welf whistles and covers his eyes.

Corr looks at and sees Welf's hands over his eyes. Then furtively she peeks down into her lap at her own hand, at its broken fingernails and paint-splotched skin.

However imperfect her hand is, Corr does not keep it hidden from sight. (Who would have thought she would!) No, she flips it palm up on the tabletop. From the center of the hand spouts a tall, bright red flame. Corr's hand rises from the table as it turns to aim its flame at Laura's face. Laura raises one of her own hands. She holds her hand up as a shield that she pushes toward Corr's hand. Corr's flame goes out.

Welf uncovers his eyes. "Hello, Laura," he says with simple sincerity. He tips his head at her as he hastily climbs to his feet. "Nice to see you again."

To both of the women he says, "But I have to get back to work."

Laura reaches out to touch Welf's elbow before he turns away. "Just chamomile tea, please, Welf." She sits down so nicely on Necky's chair that she could have been sitting down naked on Necky's lap.

"G.J. Horsey Fatts."

Welf has left them alone. Corr cocks her head in surprise and anger.

Laura repeats herself. "G.J. Horsey Fatts."

Corr springs to her feet.

Calmly but not slowly, Laura stands up, too. She looks quite prepared for whatever Corr might have in mind.

"Here comes your tea!" shouts Welf from the back, as if to forestall a calamity. By the time he actually gets to the table with the tea, Corr is gone.

She's outside, stroking across the street already. "Huffing and puffing I am!" Huffing and puffing she is. "But ya better watch out! For I be just about to burst into a rant to clear my mind of Laura The Perfect Pepin!"

Before that, before Corr erupts into a therapeutic rave, her head clicks hard to the left. To see something? To see what?

"Yiiiip!"

Whatever is Corr looking at high and low in the sky not far from her down the street?

In a crinkling voice she says, "From out of nowhere a startling image has appeared. It does certainly look exactly like a gigantic electric wire hanging down almost to the ground from so high up in the sky that its upper end is totally lost in the blue."

Corr shades her eyes to see better. She has not stopped her walking; yet her pace has slowed to a crawl. So gutsy she is. The apparently uncomplicated yet vigorous image—if Corr is actually seeing a "gigantic electric wire" and not merely describing an improbable vision into existence—holds Corr's attention for as long as it takes her to reach the sidewalk in front of her building. There and then, she eagerly launches into the harangue she had postponed.

"Context? If you look at a different face, you see different things. Context? I have not seen Horsey Fatts for two days now. Context? That does not necessarily mean he is dead. Or even violently missing. Or anything." Corr's every third or fourth or fifth word has a soft yet decidedly rancorous hiss rhythmically hitched to the tail of it. No, these venomous hisses are not intended for the absent Horsey; the cruel sounds are meant to be heard as faint drumbeats helping Corr rid her mind of Laura The Perfect Pepin. "His co-lodger could have put the heavy word on his head, and he doesn't want to offend her. Or he could be painting a huge canvas of me. He could be taking a long walk. He could be petting some dog somewhere." As Corr kicks open her studio door, her monologue shifts temporarily away from Horsey to deal briefly with two other topics. "And in over the threshold the gal throws a petrified foot." Before that stoned foot touches down inside her studio, Corr glances back, behind her. "Bip! The direct wire from heaven is no longer available." All done now with the big wire, her mind swings straightway back to her tirade. "Or he could be right over there in Lawlady's office, lying on her indubitably luxurious couch, sleeping off a long session."

Corr stamps on into her studio, slamming the door behind her. G.J. Horsey Fatts lies on the narrow bed-thing, soundly asleep.

Horsey suddenly wakes up, wakes up suddenly, he's up, he's sitting bolt upright on the bed staring...

He's up. He needs to yawn. He needs to wipe his eyes. He can't. He's sitting bolt upright staring at Corr with a loopy look on his face.

The world is yellow. The world is green. Corr smiles to show herself how pleased she is that she was wrong.

The smile disappears, however, when Corr sees that Horsey was not in bed alone. Right beside where he was stretched out on the bed-thing lies a gun. Is Corr now remembering hearing from several sources that Horsey is known to sometimes pack a de-heater? Is she also remembering that it's easy for others to see in Horsey what they want to see in him? How does this *pale ease* relate to that dark gun? "It does, you know."

"What does what, Corr?" Now Horsey yawns and rubs his eyes. "Tell me. Tell me. Tell me."

Corr is about to speak when Horsey points a finger at the ceiling, pinches his nose closed with the thumb and first finger of his other hand, and falls back on the bed-thing.

Horsey's return to a reclining position has trapped the gun between his back and the raw canvas that Corr has been using as a bedspread down here. Corr automatically raises her hands to block her ears, to protect her hearing from the blast of gunpowder. Nothing happens. She forces her hands down to her sides.

He's snoring already. No, not really snoring. Breathing heavily.

"Did you come here from over there? Over next door?"

Obviously Horsey does not answer Corr.

She steps to the bed and leans over him to whisper, "Or have you been working day and night on that painting of me?"

Corr spins away to jam the butt of her hand against her temple. "He's not painting a painting of you, you *stupitty* woman!"

"Yes, I am."

"If I were to spin back around right now to face Horsey, would he have the gun pointed at me?" Corr is whispering while her back is yet to Horsey. "Has he been hired by Lawlady to get rid of a troublesome neighbor of hers? If that sounds a bit farfetched for me to be thinking right now, consider Necky's fate. And maybe Vogs' too."

"You're going to have to turn around if you want to talk to me that softly, CC."

She does immediately turn around. "You're painting me?"

"I am painting you." Horsey stands up to stretch and yawn again. "Right now your skin is mostly turquoise. Your nails and nipples are snowy white. Your eyes are orange. All the perspectives are focused on you."

"Is there a background?"

"Not really. Not yet. I'm thinking about stripes or tiles. Furiously colored."

"Is that why you haven't been around for a week, Horsey?"

"It has not been even two days yet, lass."

"You didn't answer my question."

"That's part of the reason, Corr."

"And the other part or parts?"

"I've been approached by a lawyer who wants to represent me in a contract deal with a new gallery. It's a biggie, *Deathstacks*. You know, it's the gallery that has the bottom two floors of that new building down in the financial district."

Corr can't breathe. Corr can't breathe. She can't stay standing up. She can't sink to the floor. She can't fly away.

Horsey comes to her and wraps his arms around her. He squeezes her tightly to him.

In a tiny, squeaky voice Corr says, "You've been next door with that woman."

"What next door? You mean Necky and Vogs' building? Not me! I'll never go into that building, not before Vogs is found."

Corr goes limp and lets Horsey catch her up in his arms. (She never shows off her physical strength to him the way she did to Vogs.) Horsey carries her to the bed-thing and lays her gently down. How then did Laura know Horsey's name to spit it in Corr's face?

Gravity rotates to parallel the horizon.

(14) +

"Why did Horsey come to my studio bearing arms when he has never done that, or anything remotely like that, before?"

The above gray and tightly worded question arrived as such a sharp break in Corr's flow that it must have skulked in from somewhere well outside her mood. For Corr is happy. Stark naked and starkly alone, she lies on her back on her bed with her arms and legs spread wide, sighing at her satisfaction. Yes, just one quick breath before that question about Horsey and his gun popped out her mouth, Corr was blithely chinning to her all-remembering bedroom ceiling. She had been cheerfully conversing with the ceiling above her ever since Horsey did his fabulous deed on her downstairs, then did it for her again upstairs here, and then said adiós and went back to his place to work some more on his painting of her.

Corr dry-kisses the ceiling goodbye and rolls over onto her side to lie with one hand between her cheek and the dingy pillow, once Vogs' pillow. "An accurate account of The Final Penalty For Sameness," she says in a quieter voice with her eyes narrowing solely for her own entertainment, "is *not* to be found exclusively in Silly Sammy & Crew's black-hearted reports on their science experiments. No." Her voice springs up out of its softness to say, "It's common know-how too! Yea, even the ordinariest knowledge-bank anywhere has on record that you can just die from having too many of the same things around you. But she's the other extreme. She's not the same kind of thing as anybody." Corr stops short, counts to three, and delivers what could be called an *insert* if she ever finds her way back to that "same kind of thing" string. She softly sings, "Corr has not only turned up on her side and shifted to a totally different topic than Horsey and his gun; her oratory has slipped into a breezy delivery coupled with an offhand content selection and an unbuttoned structure." Corr stops again. This time it is to ask herself, "Could my breezy delivery have *coupled* with a selection *and* a structure? Can one thing couple with two other things?" Her answer comes quickly. "Yes, a delivery can indeed couple with both a selection and a structure." She must have remembered her "notorious definition of a couple," as Vogs once called it. Corr shouts, "For it truly takes three to make a couple!" Corr smiles and pointedly returns to the oratory that she was describing just before that description produced a memory of her venerable discussion with Vogs of the word *couple*. "For example, the very first time that I saw her she was dressed to the nines—but isn't she always? Always, always always! Yet she was standing there stone-still just inches from Vogs, staring at him as if she had no consciousness, none at all, as if she were a straw mannequin, utterly brainless, not aware of anything—except maybe the lack of a healthy aroma from her armpits. How did zee Vogs put it? 'She was gawking at me without intelligent awareness.' Or something like dat dere. And what was the first thing this high-toned woman…this *deluxe* woman said to us? 'You three had your heads down on that table as if you were dead.' As if we were dead? Yeah, sure!" Corr makes a comical face and seals this squishy-wishy paragraph with one last thought, a strangely comforting thought. "And now the table is gone. Our run-down table on the sidewalk is gone, not like Necky is gone, like Vogs is gone."

Slowly Corr slithers her free hand down in between her still damp thighs. She moans softly, like a baby. Then she grunts, not loudly. Then she inhales and exhales rapidly several times. "There's someone downstairs!"

Who will Corr think is downstairs? Someone with a gun looking for Horsey? Or maybe someone with a gun looking for her? It is not Vogs down there. Nor poor Necky. Probably it isn't Horsey returned. And Welf would have at least knocked. "—It's Lawlady!"

Corr leaps from her bed, snatches her robe from its hook, and flies down the hall and stairs. Flashes of luscious skin. Corr looks great in her flying-open robe. The robe is a blue terrycloth with large white spots that each have a darker blue spot at its center. The robe's belt is long lost in the colossal clouds of dust and lint under Corr's bed.

A fully clothed person, tall and erect, stalked straight across Vogs' bedroom to blast Corr and Vogs till they were dead. Dead? Bear in mind a saying that the Corr-Vogs-Necky troupe used to call, at Vogs insistence, The Number One Maxim of the Middle Way: "Real Magic leaves no trace." Real magically, Corr and Vogs were *given* more time to live. Be that as it may, Vogs could be long gone by now. And how about Corr? Has the time of her actual departure finally arrived?

"I admit I was a tad curious about your paintings. Vogs thought I might find them interesting." Standing at the very center of Corr's studio, the stranger rotates her head back and forth to gaze alternately at Akaeeotp and Gcihe (Getting Color In Her Eye). "But I see now that they are mere blobs, rich in color but meaningless."

"Do you mind," Corr immediately flings back, "if I look skeptical?" That was not a polite request. Corr is responding quite hotly to the trespasser. "I have bottomless doubts you are capable of even tiny scabs of curiosity. Incontestable, however, is that you have absolutely no art sense. The meaninglessness you think you see in my paintings has to be deeply rooted in your own sad life. Make that *un-life*." Have Corr's lips ever been this big, red, and flapping like a terry towel in a blustering wind before? "Or better yet, I'll choose a different word, a cutting word that I used to hear sneaking over my shoulder a hundred times a day, *non-life*!"

For some reason Corr does not demand the intruder leave. Noticing that her door to the outside is partly open, Corr tugs her robe more tightly about her and steps over to close the door. "How, where, and why do you know the name *Vogs*?"

The woman had not looked away from the paintings, not once, not even for the quickest glance; so it stands to common reason that she wasn't using Corr's wild lips to gauge the gale blowing out Corr's mouth. If not Corr's lips, what tipped the woman off that the storm has subsided some? Perhaps Corr's last question. The woman turns to face Corr, to look Corr up and down. "I lived with Vogs some ten years ago, before he left the city and took to wandering about the land and eventually met Necky and came back here to live and just happened to land next door to you." The newcomer is as fair of hair as Vogs. Hers is not an oversized head, however. Nor does she suffer any premature thinning of her hair.

Corr strikes a fierce, cutthroat pose and condescendingly wipes her tongue across the outside of her upper teeth. "You must be the Endlessness he talked about." Corr the Pipper cups her hands behind her ears. "Listen! I can hear Vogs wailing to Necky, 'Endlessness haunted me so relentlessly I quit the city and took myself into hiding.'"

The woman sort of snorts, sort of laughs. "Nay, that's not me. *Endlessness* was just one of Vogs' oft used words. No…excuse me please; I spoke incorrectly there. *Endlessness* was *not* just one of his words; it was Vogs' most favorite mood. Me? I was his periodic antidote to endlessness. I say periodic because Vogs enjoyed wallowing in the pain of endlessness. He very much liked it. He was forever constructing excuses for not rising above endlessness."

"How can anyone be an antidote to endlessness? And while you're at it, Gal-in-Green, tell me how you can expect someone to rise above their endlessness."

The woman peers down at her clothes, her own clothing. She appears surprised to see she is dressed all in green. Pants, shirt and shoes. No, she is not surprised; she was merely teasing Corr.

"Wouldn't you really rather know why I'm here, Corr Cor?"

"Your name? As if it matters."

"Char Wrig."

"Char for Charlotte or char for charlatan?"

"Either or neither. Whichever you prefer."

Corr shifts her chin the way Welf does and asks what sounds like a real question. "Did I ever wake up hearing Vogs saying your name in his sleep?"

"Thank you, Corr. You are kind."

"I struck you as kind? Oh! Excuse me then, please. I spoke incorrectly there."

A grin slants across Char's face. "I keep losing track of which of us here is supposed to be the *bicche*."

"*Bicche*? That sounds like a long gone word." Corr pulls on her earlobe. "You're a schoolteacher?"

"Not even close. I caught that old word scribbled on a wall a block from here. Took me the whole time from there to here to figure out what it meant."

Corr squints. "A female dog, right?"

"A makeshift lamp fashioned from a cup of grease and a twisted rag."

"You're pulling my leg, Char Wrig." Corr nearly grinned herself.

"I just might if I get half a chance. I do like Corr's bathrobe."

"It's not for sale, CW."

"Can I just try the yummy thing on?"

"Certainly. And I'll try on your ghoulish green stuff."

Grinning like a ship on the sea as she slips out of her robe, Corr whispers like Necky. "The women exchange clothes. Char takes up residence in the building, and Corr wanders off down the blocks looking for old or new words of her own."

Smiling seductively as she slips out of her greens, Char whispers like Corr. "An address written on a slip of paper is found in the pocket of the green pants. Corr halts her walk-for-words long enough to read once again the faded handwriting. Corr still doesn't recognize the address, yet she is certain she will easily find her way there."

Corr grabs the pants before Char is completely out of them. Char giggles like a girl of five years and does a two-step with her hands atop her head, while Corr searches the pockets of the pants.

Corr looks amazed. "There *is* a piece of paper in here with something written on it!"

Char nods her head. "Sure there is."

Confusion bongs in Corr's voice. "I don't recognize this address."

Char nods again. "But surely you will easily find your way there."

Char retrieves her pants before they drop from Corr's limp hand. She puts them back on. "It was nice meeting you, Corr Cor. I love your body. Goodbye." Char waves as she exits the building, leaving the door standing partway open again.

"So?" Corr climbs the stairs to lie on her bed some more. "So that woman, Char Wrig, used to live with Vogs. So? If I go to that address, who will I find living/working there?" As has been stated again and again, Corr never teas, beers, or bells Vogs again. "Or is the address simply a trap? A trap with Laura Pepin at its base? That doesn't sound particularly logical at the moment." Corr's robe has been left behind, a pile, a relic down on the studio floor.

She tries speading her arms and legs again but finds that position no longer comfortable. She lies on her back straight as a measuring stick. "The beautiful deceiver looked enough like Vogs to be his sister. —Don't start kidding yourself, Corr! Vogs had no sister. She's not a sister! Not a sister! Nonetheless, judging from the things Char said, she must have at least spoken with Vogs since he came back to town. She knew about Necky. She knew about me and my paintings." As Corr is passing from the bed into sleep, she whispers, "Char Wrig, enigma."

Night. Darkness in the room. Horsey has returned and is lying asleep beside Corr when she awakens. He has taken off his clothes. She pets his shoulder, just once. She doesn't want to wake him. He needs his sleep. "What about his housemate? Hasn't she begun to miss Horsey? Obviously she has. Should I worry about the bone-dry woman suddenly showing up for a confrontation?" Corr feels around in the dark to determine if Horsey brought his gun with him again. "His *metal* gun that is." She was not whispering that last time; still, Horsey does not wake up. Corr finds no gun. She kind of whispers, kind of doesn't. "Were you the one who contrived those eerie photo-like pictures that Laura Pepin showed to Vogs and told him they were pictures of his world?" Still Horsey does not wake. "I myself have never heard of you producing anything besides thrilling paintings, G.J. Horsey Fatts."

Horsey is sleeping with just his head lit by faint light coming in through a window. What was that sound? It seems

Horsey is talking softly in his sleep. What is he saying? "You sit where you are told! You do what you are told!"

"Who in the world would even think of telling *you* what to do, my horse? Or are you dreaming that you are the one issuing the orders?"

The sleeper opens one eye to say, "I met with, observed, and studied these people. It was the hottest day in the history of his world."

Corr leans her head really close to Horsey's poorly lit face. "Is this man actually awake and putting me on?" Horsey is plainly not seeing the physical world through that one open eye. "Or is he dreaming an answer to the question that I asked him about the Vogs/Laura pictures? If the latter is the truth, who are 'these people' he mentioned?"

Then Horsey's other eye pops open. He grunts a groggy hi-there.

"Hi there, yourself."

Horsey props himself up on his elbows.

Corr props herself up on one elbow and presses her breast against Horsey's arm. "Have you been working way into the gone light on that painting of me?"

"Actually, I met with the Deathstacks people this evening. I think they are going to want me, Corr. They also asked about Vogs. They were hot about his stuff too."

Corr sniffs her noticeable nose. "What did you tell them about Vogs?"

"The truth. I haven't seen him for months."

"The lawyer went with you?"

"Did."

"A man or a woman?"

"The lawyer? Definitely a man, Corr. No question about it. The robust, athletic type. I'll introduce you, if you would like."

"Nopey nope. No intro needed. Nuff lawyers in my life already."

"He could help you find a new gallery."

"I'm fine where I am."

"You sure, Corr?"

"Am."

Corr nods and abruptly decides to explain why she is sure. "They send someone around, every so often. He or she looks at my new works for a while and then usually says something like: 'Hmm, we'll take all of them. Ok with you?' Next day the carpenters come and box the paintings up and load them on a truck and drive away. A few weeks later, I get a pretty payment slip. That's the way I like it."

"You never have to show your lovely face to your public?"

"Never, Horsey."

"Actually," Horsey raises his eyebrows, "to tell the whole truth now, I've heard that about you, Corr. I've heard it a good number of times, but I thought it was just another of the tall stories running unchecked through the arts. I didn't know any gallery would actually allow its artists to not appear upon demand."

Horsey drops back flat on the bed. "But if that's the life you prefer…" He winks at Corr. "Me, I like the being-there part, particularly the flashy openings."

"Deathstacks! What a name for an art house! But if you get into this new gallery, Mr. Fatts, I'll make an exception and attend your opening. If you want me to. I can see how you might want me not to go."

"Oh, I'd love for you to go *with me*, Corr. We could dress up outrageously alike and take turns saying stu-u-u-pid stuff at the tops of our voices."

"Well, that quick you talked me right out of going." Corr flops back flat on the bed, too. "I'll just draw a line around my life before this moment and paint everything outside the line black."

Turning up on his side to face Corr in the dim, Horsey blows softly in her ear. "Or we could go separately and pretend we are meeting for the first time at the opening. People there who know we already knew each other would just join us in the joke. And then! And then one very perceptive attendee would recognize you as the subject of that great painting over there. You would suddenly be the center of attention. Everyone would marvel at your refined beauty. And they would all agree that you are the most perfect subject for a painting who ever lived."

"Whew!" Corr sits up. "What a rick-rocking crock that was. I'm getting up. You go back to sleep if you want."

"If the light got switched on right now, would I find that you are blushing, Corr?"

"Not on your life, lov-aah boy."

(15) +

"What about that address? Maybe I should ask Horsey to go with me to check it out."

Horsey is sound asleep when Corr returns to bed. And Corr is sound asleep when Horsey wakes up in the early morning. He kicks around down in the studio for a while, hoping Corr will wake up. She doesn't, he leaves.

Fear not, Corr Cor *will* eventually awaken; she has not up and left life eternally behind. See that, right there! Corr's hand moved. And there again! Her eyebrow twitched. No great expanse of time has passed since Horsey left the building, and Corr is already showing signs of returning from her typically touchless world. What will be her first thought put to words in this, her typically touchable world?

Her eyes are still closed when she says, "Where's that flesh gun of yours, Horsey?"

Corr gets no answer. She opens her eyes and turns her head to look beside her on the bed. "No Horsey there, no sirree."

Corr can see into the bathroom from her bed, and Horsey is not in there either. She calls out again, a bit louder. "Hey, Horse!"

She gets no answer. "Nopey nope."

Corr sits up in bed and stretches. "Guess it's back to basics then. A cup of tea at *WELF et al.* But put on some clothes first, Nectar Crotch. Brush those teeth. Smile like you mean it while crossing the road. With any luck, you'll fall into a hole and never be seen of again." Who is Corr imitating? Probably some actress of yore once made an impression on Corr Cor.

All dressed for tea and down in her studio, Corr picks a piece of chalk from the easel tray and scratches it against the note-area on the wall. "Social Couples Kissing." She smirks needlessly at her robe still lying like a pyre-for-love on the floor and makes her escape into the sunlight.

"Zow! The sun! It's so bright!" Corr staggers with joy.

She composes herself. In fact she overly composes herself. Perhaps she is still seeing herself as that actress. "Smile. Cross the street, my little chicken. Like you mean it. My little chickenwicken."

None of the holes in the street are so deep today as to swallow Corr. And Welf is actually waiting for her at the door.

Surely Corr sees Welf standing there half in and half out of his cafe, waiting expectantly for her. Yet she neither stops nor even slows as she approaches the door.

"Good morning, Corr. There—"

Welf was cut off by a snap of Corr's fingers as she raised her wrist as if to check her watch smartly on the fly. "Yes, it is still morning," Corr reports. Slick and quick, she clips on by the café's proprietor. "And a good morning back to you, Welf." She strides straight over to her table, where she nearly sits down on someone's lap.

"Y-y-y-y-y!" Corr vaults away from the person on her chair.

"Have no fear. I do not bite," the man assures her. "Not normally," he adds facetiously. He is saying all the letters in all of his words. "To prove my goodwill, I will move over to this other chair so that you can have this one."

The occupant of Corr's usual chair is the overdressed man, the very man Corr was fantasying about when Laura danced into her studio that time. Corr had gotten herself all juicy thinking about him then, but later she decided that Fdm, the fancy dressed man, looked too stiff in his back to be of interest to a rambunctious woman like herself.

The man stands up. He is a noticeably tall and erect person. Corr takes note of this.

The man waits serenely for Corr to make up her mind. When her face cracks into a nervous half smile, he makes the moves to help her take a seat on the chair he had offered her. He sits himself down on another chair, once Necky's chair.

"Do I know you?" Corr is examining the man's face.

Suddenly Welf is standing beside her. "Tea, Corr?"

Startled, Corr babbles like a flock of birds outside the window.

Welf nods his head as if he had understood her and leaves the table.

"Not to my knowledge. Although we are neighbors in a way." The man smiles decorously. "I work in the building next door to your building. I work with and for Laura Pepin."

Corr fixes her icy gaze on the man's nice clothing. She whispers real low, "Is this Necky's killer?" She looks up again at the man's face. He smiles again at hers. Although his eyes are blue, as blue as Laura Pepin's, his skin is darker than Corr's.

Whispering not so quietly this time, Corr asks, "Is your name to be the tardy arrival?"

"Gett Resu," returns the man, with not a shadow of hesitation. His darkly pigmented hair is not straight like Corr's.

"Corr Cor."

"Yes, I know. Laura has spoken of you."

"Has she also spoken of the two men who lived in the building that you and she are now making use of?"

"Yes. She has spoken of the two artists. No. I cannot tell you what she said about them."

Welf is back already with Corr's tea. He places the cup and saucer carefully before her.

Welf glances at Gett Resu. Then Welf's eyes return to Corr, to her nose in particular. "There you go." Welf pats the back of Corr's hand.

"There I go. Thank you, Welf." Corr reaches out to touch Welf's elbow before he turns away, the way she once saw Laura do.

Gett Resu was watching Corr. He reaches over in front of her and draws his cup and saucer to his new place. He had had something to eat too. He pulls that empty plate well out of Corr's way.

All this considerate treatment by Welf and Gett Resu goes right to Corr's head. "Am I looking giddy to you?" Corr at least appeared as if she were asking Gett Resu. She does indeed look giddy.

Gett remains alertly silent.

"Before I start reeling about and perhaps fall from my chair, I'll raise my right hand and lay it flat to cover the exact top of my head." Corr raises her hand to the top of her head and sternly commands herself to slam closed the door to the part of her mind that allows her to feel lighthearted and harebrained.

Corr's *manual* turnabout tickles Gett. He asks her, "Are you now going to get all rough and tough with me?" He raises a hand to protect his face.

"Yes. Did you kill my friend?"

Gett Resu does not look especially knocked back by Corr's shameless question. Perhaps he has been forewarned by Laura about Corr's unpredictability. He lowers his hand lightly to his lap. "I might have," he says slyly. "What was his or her name?"

"His name was Necky Watershighagain."

"Isn't that one of the two men you just asked me about?"

"Yes." Corr is glaring unsparingly into Gett Resu's eyes.

"And my response to your first question about this man was...?"

"That you won't tell me what Laura said about Necky or Vogs."

"Your second question about this man will get much the same answer. I cannot tell you anything about him."

The consummate calm of the man is upsetting Corr and shaking her confidence. "You don't deny killing Necky Watershighagain?"

"I don't have anything to say about him or the other man. Nothing."

"You—"

Just as Corr had cut off Welf at the door, Gett Resu cuts off her here at the table. He does this by pointing his index finger at the ceiling and rotating its tip in a small, slick and quick circle. Didn't Laura Pepin do that with her finger, too? But she used her little finger, didn't she. Horsey also did something like that once, but without the turning of the finger. "I must go now," says Gett. "We will dine together again. Please."

He's up and away before Corr can think of what to say. Here comes Welf.

"I wanted to warn you, Corr."

"That's all right, Welf. No harm was done. And I do appreciate your thoughtfulness. Does he come in here very often?"

"You know that I can't talk about my customers, Corr. They need their privacy."

"Ok, Welf. I read you loud and clear. He and Laura Pepin have recently started coming in here frequently, and they always sit at this table. Gett Resu generally sits at my place here, and she flops her tainted thing on Vogs' chair. I thank you."

Welf nearly nods his head.

"What are you planning to do?" he diffidently queries Corr.

Corr mimics someone, not some hoary actress this time, someone "rough and tough." Someone rough and tough and cool-to-cold. "Nothing for the moment. I've got the table to myself, haven't I?" Corr scoots her butt back and forth on the seat of her chair. "I'm parked on the bark!"

She squints tightly down at her lap and says with a faint whistle in her voice, "Maybe not in front of me, but they will in time have to eat their insult, this insult to Vogs and Necky and me."

(16) +

Horsey looks grand and probably feels that way too. "Would you read the painting for us?" He was addressing Corr.

Corr hesitates. She checks Horsey's eyes again and again. "I'll start with the eyes. Ok?"

Tis an hour into Horsey's opening at Deathstacks. People are gathered around him. These people all know by now that Corr is the principal figure in the painting they are facing.

"Good choice, Corr."

"My eyes—that you once said were orange, Horsey, but are now yellow-orange azo with tiny streaks or flicks of emerald green—are gazing directly out of the painting. Am I making eye contact with the painter? Or later with the viewer? My skin is rose and turquoise and dusk. My nails, nipples, lips vary from parchment to white. An easel looms up behind me. A partial roll of canvas stands beside me. My hands are on my knees, my feet are apart, the toes are spread. Walls. Partitions. Something that works like a ceiling. Everything is violently colored. Stripes and triangles and lines. Dashes. Sea creatures. Caricatures? Yes, little cartoon beings. And a flaming halo floats nearby. Blues, purples, reds, greens. Everything is centered on me. And…" Corr falters. "And a colorless necklace hangs from my neck."

Horsey eggs her on. "What does the painting seem to you to mean?"

"It means that you think I am beautiful beyond belief but definitely not placid."

Apparently the women of the group bunched around Horsey all enjoyed Corr's answer, for they demonstrate a variety of laughs, from nervous and twitty to thrilling and grossly overconfident. The men in the group don't seem to know what the women are laughing at.

Horsey is careful of what he says next because he does not want Corr to end her description there. "That's good, so far."

"I'm intense. I'm perceptive. I am mostly looking at myself."

"Good! Good!"

"The world conforms to my vision."

"Ahh!"

"I am a vessel, a deep ship filled to the brim with lust and art."

Horsey more than agrees. "You are certainly that!"

"That…that gray necklace is a substitute for my wristwatch. And for my life. It's dead. It's not here. Just like my watch and my life were dead before they were given to me."

Horsey's head tilts and falls to the side. "Wo-o-o!"

Two of his artist friends (both males) start cheering.

Horsey hugs Corr tight to him. He's laughing. There's no end. Or the end comes too suddenly to be noticed.

And now. It's much later. The last looker has left; the opening at Deathstacks is officially over; the gallery is closed. Horsey and Corr are walking the streets to Corr's building, not a short distance away.

"I see the painting of you as a… What's that word? I see the painting as a *generalized* statement, Corr," confides Horsey, using more than a few hand gestures, "not as something personal to you." Horsey did not sound as if he were telling the flat truth there; he sounded as if he were trying to comfort Corr.

"It was a great opening, Horsey. Everything went swell. Your paintings were all well received." It's not cold out tonight, but Corr has her arms across her chest with her hands gripping her upper arms. "I'm not the world's expert on the matter, obviously; but the fact that I heard not one snide comment about your work tonight has got to be some kind of a record for an opening in a name gallery."

"What did you really think about the painting of you?"

"I won't say."

"Why not? Don't be afraid to hurt my feelings."

"That's not what I'm afraid of."

Corr can see that Horsey is indeed starting to hurt inside. He's hurting because she won't tell him what she thinks. Corr seems to be fighting with herself. "I can't afford to buy the painting, and I don't want you to think I'm asking for it."

Horsey explodes. "It's yours, Corr! How could I sell it to someone? I told the gallery right up front that it's not for sale. I want nothing more than to give it to you."

Corr collapses to the sidewalk. (Good thing Vogs didn't see her do that.)

Horsey collapses to the sidewalk, too. Two painters-without-pillows lie gazing up at the night's sky.

Horsey has never once asked Corr to accompany him to either his living place or his working place. And Corr—for one reason or another or for no reason—has never once mentioned this omission to him. But has she ever entertained the thought of taking herself to either or both of Horsey's spaces in absence of an invitation? The idea of her walking into Horsey's world uninvited could be rolling around in there in her brain, or it could be still so low in her consciousness that it hasn't yet turned into rollable words.

The show "Paintings by G.J. Horsey Fatts" was up for two weeks. Next day, the day after the show closed, a van from the gallery pulls up in front of Corr's building. The big van is stark white except for one huge blue/black word on either side of the tall box, *Deathstacks*. The deliverymen treat Corr as if she were actually rich enough to have purchased the painting from the gallery. At least that's what Corr will tell Horsey later. The two men carry the painting in and lean it against the wall of her studio. One of them asks, "Where would you like us to hang it, ma'am?" Corr thinks for one second before replying, "Upstairs, in my bedroom."

She chitchats with the men. When they tell her that only one of Horsey's paintings did not sell and that the unsold painting is out in the truck, Corr grins with delight. She talks the men into wrapping up Akaeeotp (also known as "A Known And Established Enemy of the People") and delivering it to Horsey when they return his unsold painting to him. In other words, Corr and Horsey exchange paintings, a centuries-old tradition in the fine arts. Horsey gets EOTP, and Corr hangs herself upstairs.

"Didn't even have to slow down for that one."

(17) +

"I always thought it perfectly reasonable to believe that everyone everywhere now and then finds themselves in a drab frame of mind." Judy rocks her head in artful amazement. She cautiously maintains her reserve, however, and does not smile one bitsy bit. "But you! You're so vibrant I can't even visualize you in such a state. Do you ever find yourself in a neutral mood?"

Corr feigns a clumsy hem-and-haw before she answers, "Often when blue turns to purple, I feel all my desires diminishing." Corr draws the points of her shoulders as close together in front of her as they will come, as though to illustrate with her physical dimensions the diminution of her desires. "Desire can fade in me until I'm a thoughtless blob."

"You? A blob?" Judy is looking down the bridge of her nose at Corr.

Corr's shoulders roll out and proudly back to expose her ample bosom. "If desire is removed from the equation before a certain discipline is achieved, it stands to reason then that awareness will certainly and immediately follow suit. Zip, awareness is gone. Hence, the blob."

"That isn't quite what I was asking you—"

Corr hears where Horsey's housemate is going and breaks in on the woman before she can finish her sentence. "Wait a short shake! You used the word *mood*, didn't you? A mood is a more or less conscious state of mind. The blob is hardly conscious at all. So I guess my answer should have been *no*. No, I never find myself in a conscious state of mind that is neutral, that is without color, that is without fire and zeal and stupidity."

Judy heard *that* word. She squinches her face. "Stupidity?"

Corr responds promptly and directly to the question that was asked. "Right. Stupidity. Flat-out ignorance. Hence, the confusion. Hence, the rash profusion."

Judy Blue—the uptight woman/the bone-dry woman/the rep from Vogs and Horsey's ex-gallery—coughs lightly in her hand. She had sat in the café for over an hour waiting for Corr Cor to make one of her periodic appearances. Judy Blue might have had to wait another couple of hours if Corr hadn't looked out the window of her building and seen the woman looking out the café window at her. Corr remembered the woman's face from when the gallery had sent someone around to check on Vogs. When Corr then strolled into the café and walked across the room and sat down to stare over the unfamiliar table at Judy, Judy said in a cracked voice that she would like to talk about Corr's "missing neighbor" again. Judy Blue has not yet said so, but, of course, she wants to talk to Corr about Horsey too.

Up to the present moment, the name of neither man has actually been said by either woman. So far, Judy has allowed the conversation to be dominated by Corr talking about herself.

Here! Here is the change. Corr has suddenly turned silent, seemingly granting Judy the freedom to speak her mind.

Judy is not ready to do so, however. She sticks to the old formula for maintaining a safe position in a conversation: make a complimentary observation, ask an easy question, provide any needed small bit of clarification. "*Rash profusion.* Those two words of yours produced in me an interesting image, Corr. Are they completely yours? The words, that is."

"Who knows who owns words?" Corr leans hands-under-elbows on the tabletop. "That's why I paint. But I'll sell those two to you if you really want to buy some words."

"This is not a shopping trip for me."

There is a beat in the air from somewhere. Corr secretly whispers, "Attitude is still all there is."

Then crisply aloud she says to Judy, "What kind of trip is it for you then, Judy Blue?"

Almost continuously since Corr sat down opposite her, Judy has been watching Corr's eyes. Finally she asks Corr, "Have you even noticed the other people in this café?" Sweeping her hand in a broad gesture, Judy may be nearly ready now to speak her mind.

Pointedly not turning her head to look around the room, Corr gazes at Judy from beneath half-closed eyelids. "Not really. I pay them little mind." She coldly, tauntingly winks one eye. "Is there someone in here you want me to take particular note of?"

"As I said before, you are a vibrant person, Corr Cor. Apparently some people enjoy your art, while others don't see that it has any value at all."

"Are you going to get to some point soon, madam?"

"Where are Vogs' paintings?"

Corr's eyes pop wide open, and she gives Judy a big false soundless shrug.

"Necky Watershighagain wasn't one of our artist's, but we are curious about the disappearance of his paintings, too."

"Are you indeed?"

"We can get a search warrant."

"Can you indeed?"

Judy wants to grin perceptively. "Is your blue suddenly turning to purple, Corr? You are very much more subdued now. Will I actually get to witness you becoming a thoughtless blob?"

"Don't kid yourself for one minute, Judy Blue." Corr pops the edge of the table quite hard with the four fingers of one hand held tightly together, and everything on the table rattles. "I've got more energy in my left nipple right now than you've ever had in your entire skinny, dried-up body."

Corr is not finished. She brushes her hair back with both of her whizzo hands. "I heard you threaten me with a search warrant. I doubt you could get one. Besides, where would you search? Vogs is long gone. His building is still here, but it has been thoroughly re-occupied. And by a lawyer et al. Our Lawlady just might have something to say about your nonexistent search warrant."

"The warrant would be for your building."

"My building?" Corr's lips flutter. "Boy, you are really reaching now!" She laughs loudly with her eyes running all over the ceiling. "What's the matter, sweet-so? Horsey won't do his fabulous deed on your carcass anymore?"

No. No. No. Judy Blue did not yell, "I'll kill you for that remark, you filthy cur!" What Judy Blue did do was squinch up her face and gauntly smile and squint out the side of her eyes and faintly say, "Good day. It has been interesting meeting you."

Corr ignores the woman and glances at her usual table. It's empty now. Corr stands up just as Judy is standing up. Corr gives Judy the finger she had inherited from a boy on the street the afternoon of her last walk with Vogs. She haughtily takes possession of her real table.

Judy is out the door now. Welf shuffles up beside Corr. Corr titters at Welf's humble approach. Humble, too, is his utterance. "What?"

Corr is still trying to arrange "the leafy brown maze that is myself" comfortably on her chair. (That short quote was set and allowed to remain in the middle of the previous sentence because Corr, when she gets as all-ruffled-up as she is now, often refers to *herself* as "the leafy brown maze that is myself." She once meticulously explained to Necky and Vogs, who both just happened to be quite asleep at the time, that she repeats that "leafy brown maze" thing in honor of a huge autumnal painting from early in the previous century, a painting Corr had seen in her early teens hanging the slightest bit crooked in a museum. According to Corr's memory, centered on the bottom member of the vast painting's intricately carved frame was a broad brass plate that bore this inscription: "Only Gradually Does One Discover the Reality of the Place." What Corr did not explain to Necky and Vogs, or to anyone else for that matter, was that the painter of this infinitely detailed recountal of a state-of-nature that had dematerialized before Corr rose up from the clay in this world had the same last name as the last name Corr Cor had only recently made up for herself.) Upwardly addressing the side of Welf's neck, Corr remarks, "She lives—or is it *lived?*—with that male friend of mine who you once asked me about."

"Oh. I guess that explains something."

"It does, Welf. My usual tea, please-o-please."

Something else that Corr never explained to Necky and Vogs—and no, Corr has never mentioned this second incident to anyone else either, except maybe in her dreams—is the haunting circumstance that immediately followed her stirring discovery of "the leafy brown maze that is myself." She had turned that day from studying the *mature* painting titled "Only Gradually Does One Discover the Reality of the Place" to read the curator's description of an equally aged painting on the opposite wall. Included in this description was a quote, "Four parameters are necessary to determine an event, namely the three which determine its position and the one which determines its time. — PheW Bee." Corr Cor had stared steadily at that quote till she understood its words and had invented a dark enough category for them. "One of the oldest of art's enemies."

Corr has not checked out the address she found tucked in Char's pants.

(18) +

"Char's pants. Char's green pants." Corr sings an airy tune as she flits high and lightly down the sidewalk on butterfly wings. "The address is in the pocket. Was in a pocket."

But the world can change without notice. Suddenly those broad, garish wings hesitate. They falter. Corr's feet touch the ground. "Horsey?" She cries, "Horsey has not come to see Corr for some time now." She staggers. "Not since the day of Corr Cor's irksome verbal bout with irksome Judy Blue." The big butterfly wings collapse to Corr's sides and cease their pumping altogether. "Is Horsey *not* wanting to do his magic trick on my lurid body?"

The wings are kaput, but Camp Corr is not that easily defeated. Not only does she declare in a touchy, touching voice that she will burst again into song; she describes the means by which the song will be rhythmically embellished. "De-winged, I will do my dim-damnedest to combine into one harmonious happening the pulse of my now outstretching strides and the singing of the words and a two-handed rubbing of my scalp."

Damnedest is what is normally considered *a word*, clumsy and antiquated though it is. *Dim-damnedest* was presumably constructed either offhand or from *d* scraps in Corr's memory.

She begins her attempt at a "harmonious happening" by warbling in a plaintive yet sexy voice, "Is he *not* wanting to do his magic trick on my lurid body?"

Corr stops her song and starts over, without breaking either her stride or her stride's symmetric cousin, the two-handed head-rubbing. "Is he wanting to *not* do his magic trick on my lurid body?"

She again stops singing. "Nope, that one's a no-go, too."

Once more, Corr starts the song. "Is he wanting to do his magic trick *not* on my lurid body?"

No matter where Corr inserted the *not*, the question had not worked as an opening line for her song. She quits her singing and stops rubbing her head. "But she keeps on keeping on down the avenue." True, as Corr just said of herself in old-talk as if someone else had said it, she keeps on striding speedily down the street.

She's fussing yet about the absence of Horsey. "More likely Horsey has found someone new, perhaps someone at Deathstacks." The words are falling behind; clearly Corr's speech is no longer even trying to keep up with her strides. What might this slowing of her words mean? It could mean that she is tiring of the on-and-on about her dreary dearth of Horsey. It could also mean that this same cheerless topic will haunt today's hike downhill for only a few more sentences. "Hmm. New gallery, new woman. Why not? Maybe I was just a transitional thing for him. But to just write off Judy Blue that quickly may not be the wisest thing for me to doeth." Corr harrumphs pedantically. "Or would that be *doest*?"

The disagreement between the two archaic words dissolves as Corr's progress downgrade is brought to an unscheduled halt. She stopped to examine a post. She circles the tall post, smiling. "This is the one all right, the very one I ran into." She whistles shrilly and bestows a name on her rediscovery of the pole, as if she expects that her second meeting with the pole will eventually be seen as a major event in the long history of art. "Tis a disarmingly plain and unaggressive title that expresses quiet respect for this one-legger's stiff upness: A Solitary Pole Rises From The Sidewalk."

Dumping the smile to put on a pucker, Corr's head impersonates that big bulb or whatever it is that revolves in the lighthouse on the point way down the beach. "But I don't see any Jonny Facemoral parked on the sidewalk anywhere around here. Maybe someone-with-a-truck pulled over, threw Jonny up in the back, and hauled him on down to the beach."

Now it is the pucker that Corr's head dumps, along with a mild frown of concentration. The happy, whistling smile is back. This *fun* smile will not last long, however; for Corr's lips have already started twisting into a *shrewd* smile. "I will no doubt never know if that be the case, since I'll be making a right turn several blocks before a person in my shoes would otherwise reach the beach. Hah! Reach the beach!" She gives the post a shrewd (to match her smile) pat, then slips-and-slides on down the sidewalk. "And after I make that turn, how far do I still have to go? That, folks, is today's unknown."

Corr is making good time down the slope.

Corr was making good time down the slope until all at once her head and neck jerked rigidly into their most upright positions as her pace slowed drastically. And her pace is slowing again. She does not come completely to a halt this time, but her whole show slows way down before she starts chanting.

Chanting. Her head and neck shed their rigidity, yet both hold on dearly to their elevated postures. For thirty-five paces Corr chants out loud once per step in a rooted, applied voice, "Doesn't make any difference."

A second set of thirty-five paces—Corr doesn't waste one step while switching that first word-string for another—is accompanied by "Make a difference!"

In a third suite of paces of equal number, she chants, "Doesn't amount to much."

From between her moist, faded-ruby lips thirty-five times comes "Rich in color but meaningless."

And finally, as Corr reaches and makes her right turn, she finishes her five-set session with "Don't see that it has any value at all."

This is more or less a new street for Corr. She has crossed the street called FOX many times before but has never walked along its length. She knew even before she left her building that she would have to turn right at this intersection, because FOX ends here.

She comes upon two rundown buildings, twin businesses, squatting side by side. One storefront is signed "All The Red Cards." The other is signed "All The Black Cards." What do these places sell? Corr peers into the small buildings. Both are completely empty, gutted. "I surmise that at one time these two enterprises supplied *High-level Serious Discussion*. Yes, I can see depressed folk carting themselves into the Black Cards business for some curative talk with others who are in similar desperate plights. Over-stimulated humans in need of a bit of corrective powwowing would have rushed into Red Cards. Or is it vice versa with the red and black? No matter. One way or the other, anyone who felt the need and had the money and wasn't particularly physically or verbally violent was welcome." As Corr moves on past the two buildings, she glances back at them. High on the sidewall of the last building, painted by hand in luminous white paint using a six inch brush, are these words, including the quote marks: "Mutual Defense Against Aggression Either By Law or Arms." The message has been up there for all to see long enough that the paint is now flaking and fading, rendering the text more ethereal than physical. Corr slams the butt of her hand against her forehead and makes her next stride extra long. "Someone should cuff the daylights out of this here moron. Those were not huts of help! They were but bastions of defense."

Someone is walking toward her on the sidewalk. Not someone she knows. The person stops when Corr stops. They are directly facing each other. Both are smiling. Slowly Corr raises her straight arms from her sides till they're parallel and level out in front of her. The other person does the same. Their finger tips almost touch.

Corr says, "I was saying to meself that I could say 'Hey!' to this person. *Hey* can express interrogation or surprise or exultation or be of indefinite meaning."

Without hesitation the other person says back to Corr, "I was saying to meself that I could shout 'Outgrow your ego!' at this new person and see what she says back to me."

"What would I say in return?" Corr lifts her eyebrows. "I would say, 'A fine introduction to twelve-tone music you are.'"

"Hah! Very good. And a good day to you."

Not waiting to watch the other person continue on down the sidewalk, Corr happily continues on up the sidewalk. Her one hundred and seventy-five steps of chanting are paying off.

"Can't see or hear the ocean from here…but sure can smell it. What was that number? Yes, 832 FOX. That's 743 over there. So the address that I'm looking for must be in the middle of the next block on this downhill side of the street. It could be that tall red building up there."

Like the majority of structures on this part of FOX, the three-story red building looks to have been built as a single unit for dwelling, meaning it's a home, not a converted commercial structure. Corr knocks on the front door. No one answers. Corr rings the bell. No answer. Corr waits. No answer. Frilly curtains block any seeing into the house's ground floor windows.

From where she is standing at the front door, Corr can see that shorter, two-story homes hug up tightly against either side of the house. So Cor cannot walk around back of 832 FOX to see if anyone is back there.

"Try the doorhandle, kid." When Corr turns the handle and pushes, the door swings open. "Simple, huh."

Corr prances into the house the way Laura gamboled into Corr's studio one dark and difficult day: as if she will soon own the place. "Nice house." Corr strolls from room to room saying hellos but mostly gawking at all the homey furniture, rugs, knickknacks etc.

When Corr enters the dining room and stops to admire the formal layout, she notices that on the corner of the shining table—a splendid oak dining table—lies a lone piece of paper. Corr tramps straightway to the marvelous table to take up the paper in both her hands. It's a note. "Welcome, Corr. Sit down, relax, make yourself at home. There is nothing in this house that is off limits to you."

Corr gulps in surprise. She throws the note back down on the table and yells blisteringly, "Laura Pepin!"

Not one sound comes to Corr from within the house. Does she realize that she is gripping the edge of the table? Timidly she calls, "Vogs?" She does not call out Char Wrig's name. Corr must believe that Char was indeed only a messenger.

Upstairs, Corr finds a sitting room, three good-sized bedrooms, an office, two more baths, and a great porch on the top floor rear that looks out over the houses to the ocean. Unlike the view from Corr and Vogs' buildings, the view from the topmost floor of this building includes not only the waves "way out on the ocean" but the waves that break against the beach as well. Actually, Corr can see quite a bit of the beach itself.

In a big closet on a wall of the largest bedroom, Corr finds clothes that would fit her nicely. "If I wore this sort of thing, that is!" In a not-quite-so-big closet on the opposite wall are clothes for a man. "These would fit Vogs, I think. But he would most certainly never allow himself to be seen in such extravagant garb. *Garb* as in *garbage*." Corr starts to close the second closet door but then jerks it back open. "Horsey, would you wear this stuff?" She shakes her head and closes the door. "Do Laura and I wear close enough to the same sizes? And Gett Resu, as far as I can know, always wears posh clothes like those in the second closet." No, no. Gett Resu is way too tall for the man's clothes. And Laura Pepin is too tall, too. The clothes in the first closet wouldn't fit Laura at all; she is as tall as Vogs was, and her thin body is not entirely in use, as is Corr's body. Does this bring Corr's listing of possibilities back to Char Wrig? "No, this place has very much the wrong ambience for Char in Green."

Corr steps over to a dressing table, sits down on its petite chair, and gazes at herself in the mirror. "I am embarrassed to say that I have never ascertained whether or not Laura Pepin and/or Gett Resu *live* in the building next to mine." She pushes a finger up under her lower lip. "Laura and Gett. Gett and Laura. Minor indispositions will take the two. And nasty sores will unexplainably appear on their skin." Corr does seem to be enjoying herself. She does not open the drawers beside her nor any of the little boxes sitting on the polished, dustless surface before her.

Waxing melodramatic, she says for herself to watch in the mirror, "Yet something is amiss in this setup. Or should I have said that something is missing here? Yes. There isn't anything *wrong* as far as I can tell; there's just something *not here*."

Corr stands up, takes off her few clothes, and goes over to lie down on the bed. "How long will I have to wait for this missing something to appear?" She falls instantly into sleep and dreams out loud.

"I'm dreaming of a word. I'm in a library. The word is shimmering above the head of a person in a faded blue shirt. This person is sitting with his back to me at the next table ahead of mine. The word is *Tommy*. I rotate my head to the left and see another word. This word is printed in hard black ink on the bright red spine of a book on the row of shelves next to me. *Pigdoctors*."

Corr turns up on her side. "I'm sleeping. Yes, I do know that I am asleep. I know also that I can dream. So I dream for a while—of painting and sex and companionship—then I stop dreaming. I pass the flimsy barrier of death and enter death. I die and die. I look for Necky. He's not anywhere to be seen. I do not only not see Necky, I don't see anyone." Corr rolls back onto her back. "There is a perception reminiscent of light and a percept of perfect moisture, but there is no solidity or volume or personality. And there's no time! Vogs told me that would be the case: no time. 'Time is but a pieced-together illusion that you are better off without.' My eyes are only partly closed, as if I were squinting at something on the ceiling, a drawing of a young tom turkey perhaps. Yet my eyes are not seeing anything in the room. Room? I am *not* flattened on a bed, I'm lying comfortably on my back on a raft at the junction of many rivers. Although the gently swirling waters slowly turn the raft, the sun is always smiling at my face, at my partly-opened eyes. *To be free of anything that restrains or fastens."* Now Corr is whispering. *"I am but one of the parts into which something naturally separates.* If I were to wake up right now, I wouldn't know where I am. I might not even know who I am. *The artist's individuality is minimized."*

The light level in the room is sinking. The sun has dropped below the ocean. Corr is not waking up. Soon this world will be dark, and the three honey bears will be returning home from their walk in the woods.

(19) +

Dreaming out loud. Will Corr title her next painting *Dreaming Out Loud On An Unknown Bed?* Vogs used to tease Corr about her having long conversations with "the real one" while she was asleep. Beyond the teasing, Vogs was convinced that even though Corr professed to want to get to "the other side of time," she will never get there if she keeps on talking to herself, talking to herself while she is awake as well as while she is asleep. And what was Corr's incisive reply to Vogs' advice? "Rats and pearls and little red girls."

That rhyming titbit, "rats and pearls and little red girls," does sounds now as if it could have been a spin-off of a funny jingle that Horsey once presented to Corr. —No! Not true! Definitely not. It can't be true, because Horsey gave his slightly longer verse (four items instead of three) to Corr *after* Vogs had disappeared. So maybe just the opposite is true. Had there been a closed circuit of communication: Corr to Vogs, Vogs to Horsey, Horsey to Corr? Why not?

"That's how saying are made. And they always eventually come back home to roost." Saying that, Corr wakes up.

Her head heaves up from the bed like a shot. Her eyes are big. Sitting up fast as she can, she opens her yap but discovers she can't even squeek. Straining her eyes, she searches the dark that has filled the room. The room is so strangely distorted by the feeble light that Corr could have leaked into another world. (No incidental music is playing. Not even the melodious babel of a city faintly in the distance.) Corr's hands are spread on the bed to brace her, yet her whole body quakes. Suddenly she is capable of speech. "Who-o-o is that standing there at the foot of the bed?"

The big window that looks out toward the ocean is a little lighter than the rest of the room, the doorway to the hall is darker than the room, and the other window cannot be made out at all. There is no one standing at the foot of the bed. No one.

Cautiously Corr climbs off the bed and stumbles over to where she had taken off her clothes. There are no clothes, no shoes there. Even her underwear is gone. Corr is standing with her arms hanging wet-rag at her sides. She shivers. It is not at all cold in the room. Corr doesn't move. She can in fact feel warm air being pumped into the room.

"Heat? What does that mean? That there is someone here somewhere in this house? No, not necessarily so. The house is certainly respectable enough that it could be sailing along on an auto-maintenance setting. —Stop! Think, imbecile! How do I explain my missing clothes if I'm on an automatic ship and there isn't anyone here with me? Tiny robots? Carpet that eats clothes? Pack rats with a hang-up for women's personal things? Strong, silent vacuum cleaners built into the walls? At least I didn't dream

I was frenetically running in the dark. You know, running in the dark in the freezing rain with someone—yaahh!—in pursuit. Yaahh, what I need right now is that little piece of something I once overheard Vogs saying to Necky. What is it? How does it go? Repeating it always calms me right down." Corr crosses her forearms over her eyes. "'…the timeless ultra-reality that deep-sleep so poorly imitates…' Yes, that's it."

Remembering that sequence of words must have had a strong effect on Corr, for she confidently stretches and yawns and struts over to closet number one.

She turns on the light; but before she steps inside the closet, she has something important to say. It's a warning, a caution for a vaguely identified set or class of persons to not misjudge her. "Hear me out there in Blear Eyed Land. I have no choice whatsoever. I have to pick out something to wear from this swanky trash."

She does that picking-out slowly and carefully. Corr tries on many things. And she sits down on the finely crafted chair in the closet and tries on pair after pair of shoes. Everything fits. This fact is not lost on her. She quotes some long-forgotten somebody: "But only the intellectually wasted will argue with perfection like this."

Yet when she emerges from the closet, she is still naked. She takes herself over to closet number two and turns on its light.

Her second try-on session takes not nearly so long. When she emerges from the closet, she is still naked.

She visits the other two bedrooms. In the only closet in the last bedroom, she finds her clothes. They have been folded and laid symmetrically on a shelf. "I think I see a message here. Either I wear those overdone clothes and sleep in that big bedroom, or I wear my kind of clothes and flop here in the smallest bedroom. Obviously the next thing to do—after I get dressed—is to ascertain whether I can exit the building."

The street door opens just as easily as it did when she entered the house. Corr steps out into the night and carefully and quietly closes the door behind her.

(20) +

"Apprehensive of danger," recites Corr from memory. "Apprehensive for one's life." Anxiously she swings her left hand a little higher this time and twists its wrist to peer at her timeless watch. Naturally the watch tells her nothing, other than that it still doesn't work, if the watch can be seen in the dark at all. The city's time is half past midnight. In the dead of night a truck is motoring very slowly along FOX, lingering behind Corr. Corr strides a little faster down the sidewalk in the weest hour of morning, but the truck stays the same distance in back of her. Corr may soon be running in the dark after all.

The truck speeds up and pulls alongside of Corr. A gold oval painted on the door of the truck catches a little light from a distant streetlamp. In the oval are the names Oltan Blagg & Alaber Krisco. Corr stops. The truck stops.

The driver leans over to crank down the window.

Before the driver can say the first word, Corr demands to know, "Are you Oltan or Alaber?"

The driver grins. Teeth shine in the night. "I think both Oltan and Alaber have been dead for years. Look at how old this vehicle is."

Corr pushes her head closer to the window opening. "Hey! It's Horsey!"

"Yes. It is genuinely me, Corr."

Corr grabs the loose handle, yanks open the worn door, and literally jumps inside the truck.

"Why were you trolling along back there behind me, Horsey?" Pressing the palm of her left hand down flat against the blanket stretched loosely over the creaky frame of the original seat, Corr softly tells Horsey, "I fear the answer."

"Nay, I'm a good boy. I just couldn't make up my mind whether it was you out there on the sidewalk in the middle of the night."

Corr cocks her head and sounds almost proud to tell him, "I've been on an adventure. Maybe it was a solitary adventure, maybe not. I may never know."

"Let me give you a ride home, Corr." Horsey corrects his posture on the seat and does little things to the truck to prepare it for departure. He looks happy to see Corr. He is still grinning toothily. "And I will definitely allow you time on the way to tell me about your adventure."

"Right. Fine idea, sir."

Horsey starts the truck to moving. From the inside it really sounds like an old vehicle.

Wasn't it just yesterday, on her way down here from her building, that Corr was imagining that someone in a truck pulled alongside of Jonny Facemoral and threw him up in the back and drove away? Where to? Oh yes, Jonny was taken down to the beach. If that mental construction is yet visible in Corr's head, she might be decidedly curious which way Horsey will turn this truck off FOX tonight. To the left, in the direction of her building, or to the right, down toward the beach.

Surprise. Horsey asks Corr which way he should turn. He asks her if she needs to go straight home or if she would like to sit on the sand and listen to the waves for awhile.

Going to the beach might be interesting, especially if it turns out that Jonny is actually there. But maybe Corr has had enough of the unknown for the time being. Maybe she would like to just go home and crawl into bed with a warm Horsey. Corr does not answer Horsey's question until the very last second before they need to turn one way or the other. Afore that, though—it's a ways yet before they reach the critical intersection—she asks him, "New truck for you?" Corr caresses an area of smooth metal on the door-panel beside her where the paint and primer have been worn completely away.

"No. It's Judy's. The woman I share with. She loaned it to me so that I could haul some stuff today. Her dad keeps it running for her."

Corr turned deathly silent. Her hand jerks away from the door-panel. She crams that hand in her lap. Horsey had never before said the word *Judy* in Corr's presence.

Horsey has not been around to see Corr even once since Corr commented on Judy's "dried-up carcass" to Judy's face. And now Corr Cor must accept that G.J. Horsey Fatts and Judy Blue are still *sharing*.

On the dashboard, in the low-powered glow from the instrument panel, is a greenish, fossilized sticker that still reads, "Be Free From All Mental Activities And Fabrications." Corr reads this old word-to-the-wise out loud.

She turns her head to look out the window and says in a sweet yet stainless voice as if she were watching a beautiful scene passing by outside as the truck is just about to enter the *T* intersection, "I should be going home then. And I'll be saying a good-night to you there as I climb out the door of Judy's truck."

Given Corr's highly agitated state and Horsey's tendency to never argue with anyone about anything, it is not a stunner that the dark truck-trip up the grade from FOX is unpunctuated by human voices. When C&H arrive at C's building, Corr gingerly opens the truck's door, starts to get out, but looks back at Horsey.

Horsey only shakes his head.

The first thing that Corr said to Horsey tonight was a demand, a demand to know if he were Oltan or Alaber. And the next to the last thing she says to him tonight is also delivered in a demanding voice. "What are you pursing your lips at me for?"

Horsey's return is barely audible. "If your works are generally concerned with analysis of perception, Corr, why are you so blind?"

Corr is shocked. *Horsey never accuses anyone of anything.*

Corr tumbles out of the truck and musters her courage to stand tall and calmly reply and not slam the old door in Horsey's face. "I heard your accusation—that slur—as a direct insult to me, to my work, to my life."

Now she slams the door.

Corr marches from the curb to her building. She does not look behind her. She abruptly stops just one hand's width from the building and presses her nose to the rough outside of her door. Her eyes are closed. Corr whispers to her door. "My awareness is not totally dependent on my surroundings." She is crying.

"I assume that it is so," the door whispers back to her.

(21) +

She's inside.

Now she slams the door.

Now she slams the door.

Now she slams the door.

Corr takes the pitch-black stairs three at a time. She sprints through the always open doorway to her bedroom and leaps like a flying squirrel onto the bed.

Some years later…

Not years. No! Not even one. Tis but *seconds* later.

Seconds later, staring soberly upward from her sturdy bed, lying as flat in the velvet darkness as she can possibly make herself, with her fists tightly clenched and her toes curled up in her shoes, Corr makes another list. "Who could possibly be the mastermind of my *adventure?* We can assume now that Horsey was not hiding behind the red house; Hor Fats can be infuriatingly close-lipped about some things, but he doesn't lie. *Oh, by the way, drat and phew on G.J. Horsey Fatts!* We can make no such assumption, however, about Lawlady and/or her blue-eyed, dark-skinned man. Char can be safely eliminated from consideration, although she obviously knows at least something. Judy Blue is out, too. She doesn't have the necessary imagination. Mr. Incurably Ironic Vogs is still a remote possibility. Welf? Maybe Welf Aceicou has used up all of his savings to buy me a proper house. Oh! I won't hold my breath over that one." Poing! Corr is asleep.

A long black snake of silky peace slithers by.

The deep silence. Is broken by a sudden, piercing thermal POP. From the roof? From a wall? One of the floors? From where in the building did that sharp sound come? As if the sound's lingering image were a cue, Corr's lips part to let out, "Is the world opening up for me or closing down on me?"

This would have been her second session of sleep-talk tonight—little is left of the night—but, lo, Corr voices nothing more after that one lonely question. She lies so still she all but disappears. Till noon.

Corr is up. She has undressed, she has redressed. She is downstairs and headed for *Welf et al.* Except she stops. Corr was reaching for the handle of her studio's most used door-to-the-outside when she paused.

(While the outer surface of this same door was described last night as being rough against Corr's nose, the door's interior surface is glass smooth, in large part because Corr has recently repainted the inside of the door. What color? Cobalt blue with just a tad of cadmium yellow mixed in.)

She locates a piece of chalk and records a reminder in the note-area nearby on the studio wall. "Thermal Death Point." Under that, she scribbles a second reminder that is a very long note for her. "The raucous honking of a gaggle of geese flying so low overhead they nearly slam into this building."

Corr stands very still for a moment, staring at what she has written. As she turns to leave for the café, she crisply informs the words on the wall. "You seem meaningful to me right now, but you are only a key, a key that will disappear before the first poop of paint hits the canvas." Just the writing down of those two evanescent memos may have been the initial tangible step toward Corr's next painting, whether or not that painting is eventually titled *Dreaming Out Loud On An Unknown Bed.*

Shouting loud three sudden sounds—"Bang! Slap! Crackle!"—Corr swiftly looks this way and that as she jauntily steps out of her building. But she immediately does a double take. A triple take. "Wha-a-a?" Corr comes to a total stop and crosses her eyes to clear her brain. "Whew! I thought I just saw Jerome Watershighagain sitting down there on one of Lawlady's monstrous flowerpots, looking much like a flower himself." Or did Corr cross her brain to clear her eyes?

She tries again looking this way and thataway. "It's a no on the Jerome and a yes on the flowers, trillions of uniformly colored blossoms all jammed together suffocatingly tight into four grotesque, potty pots. Tis a crime, truly a crime of enormous scope."

"Are you a person believed to be possessed of clairvoyance?"

Corr jumps straight up in wild alarm.

She drops into a low, defensive crouch and looks every which way. "Who-o-o or what was that?"

No answer.

"As they settle down in my memory, the words sound just like Jonny Facemoral's not quite perfect voice!" Speaking of not quite perfect voices, Corr's last sentence was nearly mush. "But no Jonny is to be seen."

Slowly she stands back up. Corr's caution is dead serious.

Nothing untoward happens. She dances a solemn little jig. Still, nothing bad happens to her. So she starts out stiff-legging't across the street, keeping herself ever ready to come at once to an standstill. "Did I nearly see Jerome? Did I almost hear Jonny? When I woke up in that red house, I thought maybe I had slid into another world. But what is this that's going on now?

132

This is where I live; it's not some strange house on an unfamiliar street. And it's broad daylight."

Corr all but trips and falls as she enters the café.

"Watch it, kid," toots Welf from the back.

"Yah yah!" answers Corr. She makes it to her table and drops her wondrously firm bottom on her chair.

Suddenly, flabbergasted, Corr gapes down at her clothes. What does she have on that dismays her so? Pants, shirt and, yes, shoes: she is dressed all in green.

"This is not a dream or a fantasy or a vision; it is actually happening in time and space. But I don't own a single piece of green clothes!" Be that as it may.

Corr deliriously presses the palm of her hand to the middle of her forehead while she tries to remember. "I got up from the bed, took off yesterday's clothes, stepped over to the chair, took up some clothes and put them on. This pair of pants? Those shoes down there? This shirt? How would they have gotten there on the chair? I should have looked in a mirror: maybe I've turned into Char Wrig." Fretting over that possibility, Corr has a bright idea. It is also a comforting idea. "Welf would not have called me kid if I were Char Wrig coming in the door."

Here's Welf now.

"You're either a bit early or a bit late today, Corr. Nice outfit, though. Something new for you, huh?"

"Don't ask me. I have no idea where it came from."

"Oh." Welf doesn't know if Corr is joking or in earnest. He tries to sound amused and amusing. "Did these items of attire just suddenly appear on your body from out of the *green*?"

"That's as good an explanation as any I've come up with so far, Welf."

"Do tell?" Is Welf beginning to believe Corr? He remembers the pot of tea he has packed out for her. He places the pot and cup and saucer and a spoon wrapped in a paper napkin in front of her on the table. "You aren't shucking me now, are you?"

"Nary a bit, sir."

"Are you feeling all right, Corr?"

"As far as I can tell, I am."

"Wait! Wait just a minute!" Does Welf have a bright, comforting idea, too? "A woman came in earlier, a couple of hours ago, and sat down on this chair that you always sit on. And! I would have sworn she was wearing clothes I have seen you wearing." Welf watches for Corr's reaction, then says, "Do you think that woman could have anything to do with these mysterious clothes you have on?"

"She didn't up and tell you her name?"

"No. I didn't speak with her, except to take her order. She was about your size, but with blondish hair."

"Sounds more and more like Char Wrig." Corr nods her head more than once. "So Char just might be involved with the red house after all."

"I'd never seen the woman before, and I don't recognize that name. Nor do I know anything about a red house."

"Good, Welf. Then I can cross your name off the list."

"What list?"

"That was just another aren't-we-precious saying. It didn't mean anything in real time."

"Oh. OK."

Welf has left the tableside. He does have other customers to attend. Corr is pensive. No visible part of her body has moved since Welf turned away. Who is the last person Corr would want to walk into the café and come over to sit down with her right now? Correct. Laura Pepin. So it is not Laura Pepin who enters the café. It is her man, Laura's man, the man that Corr asked pointblank if he killed Necky.

Gett Resu looks different. He looks tired, a tad tattered, even the tiniest bit scruffy. And this time, instead of Corr, it is he who is not paying sufficient attention to his surroundings. He walks over to the table and nearly reenacts Corr's nearly sitting down on his lap. He doesn't "Y-y-y-y-y!" like Corr did, but he gasps quite audibly.

"This is my chair, sir." Corr is glaring up at Gett through half closed eyes. "But have no fear," she enlightens him, returning to him the very words he once bestowed on her, "I do not bite." Sarcastically she adds, "Not normally anyway."

"Please, madam, excuse my clumsiness, if that is at all possible." Gett Resu lowers his watery blue eyes and bows his head. "I often sit on that chair. It is apparent now, though, that I only sit there when you are not in the café, too."

"What did you say? 'It is apparent *now*? Hah! Likely story. I recall my making the fact that this is my chair completely apparent to you *some time ago*." Corr is coming on strong. "Are you running short on memory cells? You don't look that old and/or wise."

"You have no idea how old I am."

"So now you're a bloodsucking shade forty centuries old? Sure! Right! You can sit down over there," Corr points across the table, "where, I assume, your sweetie normally sits."

"You are very kind."

Gett Resu not only looks different; he is talking differently, acting differently. Most noticeable is that his pronunciation of words is not so deadly precise. His words are still understandable enough, yet they are fuzzy today and just slightly blurred. And his manner is diffident. In fact, he sounds downright timid. He looks and sounds as if he has lost his confidence. Has he learned to distrust his once mighty powers? Awkwardly he sits down on the chair allotted to him.

Corr grins insufferably. Obviously she is not remembering that she herself was even more mush-mouth just a short while ago.

She goes directly to the real point. "Did you kill Necky?"

Gett may be presently lacking in confidence, but he's not yet a blockhead. He provides Corr with nothing that she could construe as an answer. From an inside pocket of a severely rumpled suit coat, he takes out a wad of papers and begins to peruse the papers carefully, only occasionally glancing up at Corr. Once, he seemed to stare for three long seconds at Corr's green clothes.

Welf delivers to the table a tall glass of something dark and ugly. To drink? He is also toting a miniature sandwich on a saucer, which he places beside the glass in front of Gett.

Again Gett Resu sounds conspicuously fainthearted. "I thank you, Welf."

Welf grunts and immediately disappears. Whether he looked at Corr while he was at the table is not known.

Now in walks Laura. Tall, slender, beautiful, Laura touches one hand to her golden hair when she notices that Corr the Puncher is in the room. What will Laura do? Corr is already eyeing her harshly, and Gett is plunked down on her accustomed chair. Gett has his back to the door; so he hasn't picked up yet on Laura's presence.

Laura takes herself to a table clear over on the far side of the room. She sits down there and smiles radiantly across the room at an area behind Corr, where Welf is working.

Laura's eyes may have shifted. Yes, she seems now to be staring at someone other than Welf. Corr generally pays little or no attention to the other patrons in the café, but today she looks where Laura is looking. "It's Vogs!"

That's impossible. It is not Vogs but someone who looks like him.

Corr shudders. Her hands are shaking. She must think the man *is* Vogs. She gets up from her chair and flounders over to that other table. She stops a *reasonable* distance from the man but then pushes her head closer and closer to him.

The man looks up at her. He smiles, tips his head at her, then returns to what he was doing. He does look very much like Vogs.

Corr jerks her head away from looking at the man to look at Laura. Laura is smiling at her either shrewdly or complacently.

Corr hesitantly returns to her chair. She raps on the center of the table to get Gett's attention. She has to knock again before he looks up at her. She points a finger at the Vogs look-alike. "Who is that?"

Gett does not want to participate. But he yields and turns on his chair to have a better view of the man.

Corr can't wait for his answer. "Is that Vogs?"

"Of course not."

Those were the first three words Gett has said to Corr today with certainty in his voice. Corr notes that fact.

Her eyes stay tight on Gett's face. "If you don't personally know that man over there, as I assume you do not, how would you know that he is not Vogs? You have never before seen Vogs."

Gett's watery eyes return to his papers. He pays no more attention to Corr.

With a frustrated shrug, Corr gives up questioning Gett. She whispers knowingly to herself, "Gett Resu will not ever sink so low as to speak to me again."

She leans forward and off to one side in order to look up through the window at the sign hanging outside, the sign that Vogs painted for the café. "No change with the sign."

What did she expect?

Her eyes come back inside. Addressing no one in particular this time, Corr asks another question that will never be answered. "Why did this man who looks so much like Vogs just happen to show up in the café today when Lawlady and I are both here to see him?"

Corr is maybe staring at Gett again, if a look so blank can be successfully named a stare. "*And* the last time that Laura Pepin and I were in this café at the same time," she says, drawling out her next insoluble riddle, "she surprised me by knowing Horsey's name. What does Lawlady want from me?"

Gett gives absolutely no indication he heard anything that Corr said.

Corr's attention rolls slowly back to the look-alike. From her chair Corr studies that Vogsish man in his chair, until he gets nervous and ineptly leaves the café. "Like a pack of dogs in flight," says Corr of the fleeing not-Vogs.

Corr stares once more at Gett Resu, staring at him not blankly but actively this time. She might just as well have been sitting all alone on the beach.

Corr tries staring at Laura Pepin. Laura is chatting and laughing with Welf. And when Welf eventually leaves Laura's table, Laura Pepin pays not the slimmest heed to Corr Cor.

(22) +

"A fellow I once knew named Vogs, as in *bogs*, used to throw water at the sky while going on and on about an idea that he called Endlessness. I don't think his Endlessness meant the same thing that I am meaning here, though. Hiding behind his usage there always seemed to be something sweet and eternally beautiful, even though he denied that vehemently every time I brought it up. 'No! No!' he would insist. But I kept hearing 'the faultless white glaze on a perfect handmade vase that rests on an invisible pedestal at the very center of the universe.' I once talked with a woman who had lived with this Vogs. She called herself *his periodic antidote to endlessness* and told me that Vogs enjoyed the pain he found in endlessness. Of course that's all beside the point. Anyway, that's where the word came from. Or, more correctly speaking, that's where it came from *for me*. Me? I'm using it here in the title of this painting because… I'm using it to mean something vaguely like *onerously severe perpetuity*. So,

ENDLESSNESS AGAIN is sort of like saying ONEROUSLY SEVERE PERPETUITY ON A CLOSED LOOP. Right? Which might make a good title itself—OSPOACL. In the end, though, I thought it sounded a bit much. So we have ENDLESSNESS AGAIN."

"Is this unpleasant never-ending-ness, to coin a word here, the reality of your life, Corr?"

"Don't know. It might be. I just don't know."

Nalaen is looking yet at the painting. He says something, speaking very softly.

Corr sees his lips moving but can't quite hear the words. So she says something that he will not quite hear. "Persistent rhythmic ground bass and florid figurations of a simple melody." Is that what Nalaen's soft-talk had sounded like to Corr, a mothballed definition of *boogey-woogie*?

Nalaen Figg takes several steps to the left of EA to stand in front of the next painting leaning against the wall. "And this one, DREAMING OUT LOUD ON AN UNKNOWN BED— it was painted before or after ENDLESSNESS AGAIN?"

"DREAMING OUT… is my latest painting. It's barely dry."

"It's so pale and strangely distorted!" Nalaen moves up closer to the painting. "Just looking at it is like waking up on another planet."

Corr has been slowly turning a tube of paint in one hand. "My intention exactly."

Nalaen is truly surprised. "No kidding?" He steps back a bit from the painting. "I thought I was probably way off track."

"No, you got it right on." Corr lays the tube down lightly on her easel's tray. She doesn't say anything further, not immediately. But surely she will want to explain to Nalaen both the why and the where-from of the pale distortion that he noticed right off in her most recent painting.

She is not dreaming. She is *here*. Corr looks more comfortable with herself, less scattered, very mellow. Her words are just as purposeful as ever, yet they are lacking their usual aggressiveness. No openly hostile attitudes are being flaunted here by Corr, and her sentences are unburdened by hidden or doubtful meanings. No, she has not turned out to be a "quietly compatible person" after all. Not by a long shot. So? Whence came this calm aplomb? All evidence points to Corr having produced it herself, as a naked response to the engaging manner of the man, Nalaen Figg. Corr is enjoying herself. She is having a great time chewing the rag with the rep sent by her gallery to find out if she would agree to participate in a group show. She would also be expected to attend the opening, Nalaen said, something that Corr has never had to do before.

She finds it necessary to bring up Vogs again. "That same guy, Vogs, during our last afternoon before he unexplainably disappeared from my life, was telling me about some extraordinary pictures he had been shown. As he talked to me about the pictures, bizarre images started forming in my head. Then, months later, I got tricked into going to an unknown address. I fell asleep there in that unfamiliar house and dreamed a thrilling dream. It was dark when I awoke on a clean bed in a strange house. In the pale light I felt I had left the earth behind." Corr walks a circle around Nalaen. "I looked around me, and in the dark in that house I was certain that I was almost but not quite seeing what Vogs had seen in those pictures." Corr stops and stands close beside Nalaen. "From that night came this painting."

Several seconds hang softly quiet.

"Your story explains the ON AN UNKNOWN BED part, Corr. But what about the DREAMING OUT LOUD half of the title?"

"I dream out loud."

"Oh. Really." Nalaen wiggles his head in confusion and delight. "Always?"

"Probably so."

They exchange meaningful glances.

Corr has sealed off the room in which Vogs and Necky's paintings are hidden.

"Well, are you going to do it, Corr?"

"The show?"

"Yes. The show."

"I am."

"Very good! I'll get out a formal invitation to you right away, tonight. And the truck will be stopping by here in a couple of days to pick up the paintings. I'll instruct the men to be extra careful with this, your latest painting. Is that all perfectly all right with you?"

"Quite."

They shake hands. Nalaen lets himself out. He looks back, grins and waves to Corr as he closes the door behind him.

"He *closed* the door."

Corr slides over to a street window to watch the man walk away. "How'd you like your sex last night, Vogs? How'd you like your sex last night, Necky?" She tries to wiggle her head the way Nalaen wiggled his head.

(23) +

"I wiggle my eyes. Wiggle wiggle wiggle. And after my eyes have been thoroughly squirmed and have then settled down nicely, what strikes me first? I clear the mighty husk in my throat and answer that the tall glass doors have been swung open and locked to stay that way."

As Corr passes in through the doorway, a card is pushed into her hand. The dispenser of cards—smallish, frizzy-headed, at least momentarily unclassifiable as to gender—flashes twenty too many titanium dioxide teeth at Corr before turning sharply away to shove a card at the next person coming in. The graphite-on-pink handwritten card reads: "Three paintings (approx. 4'x5' each) audaciously confront the arriving guests."

Presumably the card directs attention to the unflinching trio of 4'x5's cleverly mounted on the freestanding partition that separates the entry area from the main gallery space. Corr quickly checks 'em out. "Can't say why at this moment; nonetheless, it seems certain to me that the person who gave me this card is not the painter of these three paintings." Obviously a series—probably by a woman but that is far from incontestable—the paintings are striking compositions indeed. From left to right, they are titled: "Why Do I See Them And You Don't You Ask," "Well I Know They Are There," "You Can't See Anything You Don't Know Is There." Many greens, thin yellows, luscious reds and browns applied to heavy, blue-black foundations.

In the formal invitation-to-show promptly sent to her by Nalaen Figg, Corr was asked if she would like to hang her paintings herself or if she would prefer that he do it. Corr did not reply in any way to the invitation. Even so, the men showed up in their truck and took her paintings. "Away."

Only once before tonight has Corr's physical body actually been inside this gallery. That one time was way back when Corr was soliciting a gallery to represent her. The place has changed considerably since then. It's bigger now, much more spacious.

Spotting her paintings all alone and *glowing* on the huge rear wall, Corr loses her breath for a moment. "Oh my!" It is beyond any question that she was given the top display surface for paintings.

And there is Nalaen Figg, smiling wider-than-widely at her from across the room.

"And who is standing right beside My Sir Nalaen Figg, having just been talking to him? Am I seeing Char Wrig Or Laura Pepin or Horsey or Judy Blue or Jon Doc Luis?"

The truth is that Nalaen is standing purposely alone, looking real spiffy in an outfit of many tones of blue, totally waiting for Corr to come over to him or for her to wave for him to come to her.

Corr doesn't move, doesn't even twitch.

Very next moment, she's glancing nervously around her. "People swarming!" She rubs the back of her thumb with her other thumb. "Two dozen trifling, coy, hand-shaking scenarios come instantly to mind." Corr, of course, is decked out in her new outfit, the all green one. The all-the-same-tone-of-green one. "And I'm not going to take part in any such collusion! I'm leaving."

Nalaen sees Corr turn to leave, and he sprints after her. He begs her to stop.

She does. Corr turns, approaches Nalaen, and stands beside him as if she had not been leaving the place at all. She passes her eyes over the crowd. "What is that word that is like *arrogant* or *complacent* or *smug*—that's it! *Smug* is the word. I've got to remember to use the word *smug*. It's a good word."

Nalaen grins so big he's nearly laughing. "Seems to me that *artfully playful* would be the more appropriate word to remember at this gathering, even if it is two words."

He lays his ear on his shoulder and whispers to Corr. "A goodly number of these people here tonight have been waiting a very long while to meet the creator of the paintings that are hanging in their homes and/or businesses."

Corr stands with her hands decorously clasped behind her. "After many long years of arduous struggle, years that necessarily began in my early childhood, I have learned to see selflessness not as some humbling moral state but as simply being without a self. And, hence, being without the hideous clumsiness inherent in selfhood, also known as *ipseity*." Now gently clasping her hands in front of her, Corr peacefully continues. "I now understand why so many people consider selflessness a concept vital to all humans. Profound ideas should be protected from cultural conditioning and experienced for what they actually are."

Nalaen pretends to mop his brow. He has not lost the big grin. "Have you memorized all this? Or are you that quick?"

Corr grins, too, but marks her return with mock disdain. "I am quick. I never say anything that I have already thought."

"You don't say! —No play on words intended. That's very interesting. I will reexamine your paintings through that filter." Nalaen's amazement is not entirely pretended.

"It's not as uncommon as you might think."

"And where did you conduct your survey, Corr Cor? And who were the subjects of the survey? Maybe *totally unpremeditated speech* is not unusual in some very select group of our accomplices in art, but I doubt that too."

Corr spreads her arms and opens her hands to the big room. "This doesn't even exist in the world, unless I'm having a nightmare."

Nalaen spreads his arms, too. "All of this? Wooo!"

Then he wraps himself tightly in his arms. "What does that make me, Corr? A blue ogre?" He grins like a blue orge.

"Never! You are with me. People like me only marginally exist. People like you keep people like me close enough to the ground that we don't become birds in the outer space."

Nalaen's lips twist tightly, as if he has been knocked off balance by what Corr just said to him. Has Nalaen grown hopelessly accustomed to being that person in a conversation who is seen by everyone else as a "bird in outer space"? Is he quite used to being *the strange one* himself? Is *the keeper* a newish role for him? "So who is having this nightmare, Corr?"

Though it at first seemed confused, Nalaen's question was actually very much to the point. And Corr's rhetorical smokescreen is thinning fast. Is she yet unable to fess up, to reveal how she actually feels about being here tonight? "OK. I am sufficiently mixed up now, Mr. Figg. We can change the subject."

Nalaen laughs loudly, and people turn to see what is so funny.

"Changing the subject…would be just fine…with me,…Corr." Nalaen is having some difficulty speaking and has to cover his mouth until his laughter subsides.

He then thoughtfully asks, "Do you approve of my hanging of your paintings, Corr? Or should we go over there for a closer look before you dare answer?"

"I can see them from here. You did a marvelous job."

Nalaen tries to sound tongue-in-cheek but betrays his utter delight at Corr's praise by picking a teenage voice in which to say, "Fireflies flashing in the meadow. Thank you for the compliment. I am pleased that you like what I did." He is probably not aware that his head is bobbing.

"Now it is you who is glowing, Nalaen."

Nalaen could be thinking right now that Corr had just compared the present look on his face to his adorable "fireflies flashing in the meadow" floater. But more likely Corr had compared the glow still on Nalaen's face to the glow on the wall at the end of the room when she first spotted her paintings.

"I am just a small boy lost some somewhere in the universe," says Nalaen in an even younger voice. Is he trying to impress Corr with the number of well-defined voices he stocks in his quiver?

Corr looks long at his mouth. She grins, just barely exposing her teeth. "Sure. Sure," she says to him. "A likely story. I believe that." Corr curls up both corners of her mouth. "But how's 'bout I check with your shadow to be certain?"

"My shadow?"

"She is coming. I can smell the blood of a jealous woman."

Nalaen turns around in a circle. "I see neither a shadow nor a jealous woman."

"Let us calmly count to thirty."

Nalaen shrugs his shoulders. "Why not?"

They have counted off twenty-eight seconds when a woman strolls up behind Nalaen and lays her hand intimately on his back. This person is not Char Wrig or Laura Pepin or Judy Blue or Jon Doc Luis—if this last name is or could ever be a woman's name. The woman gazes at Corr's eyes. "Are you going to introduce us, Nale?"

Completely taken aback, Nalaen bypasses the woman's question to ask Corr, "*This* is my shadow?"

Corr indicates the woman's hand on Nalaen's back. "Isn't she hooked to you like a shadow."

Nalaen might have answered that non-question had he been permitted to try.

"Tee-hee." Corr's utterly false titter nimbly blocked all possibility of Nalaen responding to her. And Corr stays on top by following the disgusting titter with a lurid promise: "I will boldly pinch her cheeks and then further reward her with a cheesy *Hello there.*"

The woman instantly steps back, necessarily dropping her hand from Nalaen's back.

Nalaen is not laughing or even grinning at Corr's antics. He reaches out and lays his hand gently on the woman's shoulder. "This is the new owner of the gallery, Corr. This show was entirely her idea. She expressly requested that I try to talk Corr Cor into taking part in the show."

Plainly, Nalaen and the woman are now waiting for Corr. Corr the Cor wipes the smut off her face. She flicks a couple of fingers through her hair. She makes several other as-if-habitual gestures, then announces, "I shall forthwith pass into a stupa." She drops to her knees and raises her hands pressed together palm to palm above her head.

The waiting woman—whose name has not been said—silently drops to her knees, too, and puts her hands together above her head.

Nalaen does the same.

One by one, everyone in the gallery assumes Corr's posture.

Filtering through the chichi pastels of the lamp's curvy-wurvy shade, the light from five tiny uncoated bulbs lends a gay, carefree glow to the pair of gleefully laughing naked folks. The folks, the lovers, have settled down somewhat to lie side by side on their backs on the artistically disheveled bedding. The laughing man flops his head to the side to run his merry eyes down the laughing woman's lithe arm. Sneaking two fingers under her arm, he lifts her wrist an inch. "Is this here the famous unworking watch?" The laughing woman tries to pooh-pooh the laughing man's question, but the strength of her laughter prevents the escape from her mouth of even the first pooh. The extravagantly shaped and glazed and shaded lamp is new. Twas an after-the-show surprise present for Corr. Nalaen had not fashioned it himself; a friend had made the over-the-top artsy lamp at Nalaen's request.

True, the laughing woman could not produce a pooh when a pooh was rightly called for; however, contradictorily, almost immediately thereafter she can and does take back her wrist and reply, "Was that a roomful of stupas, Nalaen?"

Nalaen's laughter burgeons now totally without constraint. Corr's "roomful of stupas" must have really struck his fancy.

But now...? What is this? Is Nalaen choking himself? Is he cutting off his air to rein in his laughter? Why would he want to stop laughing? Does he have a bright, comforting idea? "Roll over on your stomach," he, quite short of breath, suggests, "and I'll polish your butt a bit."

Corr sniggers up and over her untamed laughter. And what be her verbal response to Nalaen's proposal?

"Sam! Sam! Sam!"

Three *sams* said that fast evidently means she thoroughly approves of Nalaen's idea. Her lush merriness cuts loose a rainbowed stream of bubbling giggles. "With your hands or your face or with your curved-to-the-left friend again?" She does not wait for Nalaen's answer. Corr springs flatly upward to revolve in the air and land on her stomach with a soft thud, wowing Nalaen.

"Now *that* was impressive! You do continue to amaze me, enchanting woman."

In place of a thank-you, Corr says, "It is Corr Cor's job in life to astound people into reassessing their lives. If someone absolutely refuses to be astounded, I then flat-out bewilder that person."

Nalaen whews and then winks. "That being the case, Corr, I am so pleased that I am repeatedly astounded by you. Bewilderment can be decidedly unpleasant."

Knock! Knock!

Immediately Corr and Nalaen cut their talking. That pair of jarring, nearly identical sounds had to have crossed the studio from the main door and climbed the stairs and advanced down the hall and into Corr's bedroom without losing its demand. The two folks on the bed look at each other.

Corr asks, "What time is it, Nale?" If the owner of the gallery—still unnamed in Corr's presence—can call Nalaen Figg *Nale*, then so can Corr.

"It must be around 1:30 am."

"Do you know who is at the door?"

"It's your door, Corr."

"It's your shadow, sir."

"What? Do you mean…?"

"That is precisely what I mean."

"How can you possibly know that?"

"I can smell the blood of a jealous woman through a two foot thick stone wall. And each and every woman trapped in a jealous condition smells just the teensiest bit different."

"You *are* trying to bewilder me!"

"Am I succeeding?"

"Should I go down and let her in, Corr?"

"No need for that. The door is not locked. We will sedately wait and see if she can find her way up here."

Three oceanic minutes dissolve into the never-ending imagining of the world. Toot, toot, toot.

"Was that a soft footstep?" It is Corr's turn to narrate. "And then another? Yes, this is again the physical world, and there is indeed someone ascending the stairs." Corr rolls back over onto her back.

Corr and Nalaen prop themselves up on their elbows to peer intently out over their toes, out over the end of the bed, through the doorway and out into the dark hall.

They hear the sound of a doorknob being tried. But the mechanism will not turn. That would be the door to the very locked room of Vogs and Necky's paintings.

Nalaen takes a quick turn at narrating. "Footsteps in the murky hall."

Corr takes her next turn in a low whisper. "Ahh, there she is, peeking around the edge of the doorway."

"Hi," says Nalaen.

"Hi," repeats the woman.

"Come on in out of the dim," says Corr.

The woman steps through the doorway and into the pretty light of the lamp. A handsome woman. Dark brown hair. Tanned skin. Penetrating green eyes. And below the comely lips stands a shapely body skillfully attired.

"Lise Tenwotom, you met Corr this evening, but the two of you were never actually introduced. This is Corr Cor. And, Corr, this is Lise Tenwotom."

The woman approaches, leans over the bed, and gently tugs on Corr's big toe. "Good to meet you, Corr." She has a noticeable, unusual accent.

Corr sits up and leans way forward to take the woman's head softly, gently between her hands. "Thank you, Lise. Thank you for the invitation to show. Thank you for sending Nalaen to convince me to attend." Corr is caressing Lise's ears. "And thank you for coming to visit my home tonight."

(25) +

"Did Lise creep into my building in the middle of the night last night to see me or to see Nalaen?" Unaware that Welf has come up beside her, Corr continues speculating. "Probably both of us. Yes...I think so. It would be both of us."

"Your regular tea, madam?"

Startled by the unexpected nearby words, Corr cries out—"Oh!"—as she blinks her eyes and urgently touches her hand to her cheek. When she then turns her head and suddenly sees Welf standing so close, she cries out again—"Oh!"—at the same time that she again blinks both her eyes. Corr tries to smile for Welf but can't. She takes in a breath. She is still touching her cheek. "You got me, you did. Twice!" She ambiguously waves her uncheeked hand. And when a curious Welf looks her directly in the eye, she squeaks like a talking mouse, "Good morning, Welf. Right. Nothing unusual today. Same ol' tame ol'."

Welf nods and waits and has all but started to turn away when Corr twangs into song.

"Just me and my sha-a-a-do-o-ow...all alone and fe-e-eling...like a multi-tone blue ou-ou-outfit."

"Rough night, huh?" Welf is sympathetic.

"Not at all, my dearest man! Wonderful, wonderful night!" Corr dons a funny face. "It may, however, have been just a bit long on this end."

"Gotcha. Long night." Welf pats Corr's shoulder. "I'll be right back with your medicine."

"He didn't understand." Over her patted shoulder, Corr watches Welf leaving her area. "And why did he not understand?

150

Because I was wearing a frown! That's why. Before I forced it away with a false face, my face bore the frown of an ugly. I was scowling even though I am feeling just great. I must-must-must do something about my habitual facial expressions!" Corr draws her lips back from her teeth as she twiddles her thumbs under her chin. She looks (unwittingly?) like an early adolescent weighing unspeakable pros and cons. "But I don't want to get so smiley nicey-poo that I turn into a waxwork."

"Little chance of that."

This time Corr was not frowning like an ugly. She blinks again, quickly touches her cheek again. "Oh!" she exclaims once more as she coquettishly glances up over her shoulder, her other shoulder, not the one she had looked up and seen Welf over. Her curvaceous body shimmies from the base of its neck to the thoroughly warmed seat of its chair. "Who said that?"

The obvious truth, that there is not a soul standing beside or behind Corr, doesn't appear to bother her. (Was that a confusing sentence? Its sole purpose was to convey that learning the truth of the situation apparently did not bother Corr; it did *not* mean that the truth did not make an appearance before Corr in order to bother her.) "And the man who approaches me to inquire if he could join me at my table...what would he have looked like *this* morning? Right! Spot on! He would again have looked very much unlike anyone ever seen on this planet. Even so, today, he would have subtly resembled both Nalaen and Lise."

Welf is back with Corr's tea and paraphernalia, which he arranges for her on the table. He stands tall and rubs his hands together and smiles confidently. "This ought to fix you right up, Corr." Necky used to call that unwavering smile "Welf's witchdoctor face."

Our professional worker of familiar magic—to use one of Vogs' descriptive phrases for Welf when he is in this mode—suddenly swing his eyes to the door. Normally Welf would have conversed some more with Corr, but he shakes his head and returns straightway to his kitchen.

Vaguely inquisitive, Corr looks where Welf had looked. "The sun?"

Indeed, the warming light from the sun is shining in the open doorway. Yet beholding the miraculous white light flowing into his café is not what caused Welf to abandon Corr's table. Someone had stepped into the building before Corr looked over at the door. Who has strolled in out of the sun looking immaculately clear and bright herself?

Not appearing in the least surprised to see Corr in the café, Laura Pepin does her long-legged walk straight across the room to the table. (A *no* and then a *yes*. No way is LP as full of herself as she wants to appear. *Yes*, she is one good example of a *slippery customer*.) She pulls back her chair, sits herself right down. "How'd your show opening go, Corr honey? Sorry, but I couldn't make it myself."

Corr does not say one word. Not one sound does she make. She stares without blinking at the eyes-and-nose area of Laura Pepin's face. Corr's mouth slowly opens to show that veteran tongue of hers sliding potently over the backsides of her upper and lower front teeth.

"You're running with a pretty fancy group of artists there, gal."

Still Corr doesn't speak. Between the middle two fingers of her right hand, she picks up the spoon Welf had left for her. Corr holds the spoon up level with her chin. Her tongue has not stopped doing that thing behind her teeth. Corr's eyes jump from Laura's face to the spoon, from the spoon to Laura's face.

"You are fun to watch," grants Laura, "a real pleasure. Provided one does not take this incredibly threatening performance of yours too seriously, you look positively scrumptious enough to eat."

Suddenly the slippery silvery spoon slides from between Corr's fingers to crash-land on the tabletop.

Corr hastily retrieves the spoon and lays it on her saucer. She gathers up tightly *the leafy brown maze that is myself*. "Where is Vogs?" She was trying for the leathery face and voice that Jerome used on her just that once.

"What makes you think I know?"

"Why did your Gett Resu kill Necky?"

"I was not aware that he did."

"What do you want from me?"

"The sex you promised me, Corr."

Corr ducks.

Was her duck instantaneous? Yes, twas, indeed. In one split second, Corr's head had dropped, her back had bowed, and her fingers had spread strangely askew on the tabletop. Why? Why had Corr dipped down so incredibly fast? Had Laura's unexpected, sexy reply kicked Corr undone? Had Corr been thrown without warning into a panic and rendered far too vulnerable?

Eyes zero in on each other across the table. Hard eyes from Corr, fraught with danger. Soft eyes from Laura, entreating but dishonest.

Corr's lips curl. She sits up straight. She snarls, "Vogs maybe had sex with you, and he has never been seen again."

"I'm sure he is being seen again *somewhere*."

Major surprise! Corr neither jumped right up to punch Laura's snotty face nor gazed up ever so innocently at some spot on the ceiling while she was tipping the whole table over into Laura's genteel lap.

Where has Corr Cor gone? Why has she suddenly stopped smelling like a boiling bomb? Why are her eyes no longer struggling with all their might to burn deep holes into Laura's vexing face? It would appear that Corr has been distracted, deeply distracted, perhaps by the thought of Vogs being seen *somewhere*.

Corr is looking thoroughly lost. Have Laura's confident words carried Corr to that same "somewhere" where Vogs is being seen, and Corr does not recognize the place and has no idea—relative to her own world and its extensions—where she is?

Corr Cor has to open her mouth thrice before her first word drops out. (What a beautiful, quick sight: Corr's mouth is open, the word is falling out.) Her voice falters. "Could…I see the pictures that you showed to Vogs?"

"No."

"Why not?"

"I can offer you two reasons, Corr. First: I don't have them, and I can't get them again. They are not mine. Two: You would not be able to see the pictures even if you were holding them in your hands. They would look like blank sheets."

"Who has them, and who made them?"

"I don't know who made them. And I can't talk about who might have them."

If Corr was lost just a while ago, she is back now. "Could *you* see the pictures?"

Laura's eyes lock on Corr's eyes. "No, Corr. They were blank sheets for me too."

"Vogs told me that he kept repeating a phrase to himself. 'A dialogue in mono.' What does it mean?"

Laura cocks her eyes away and nicely shrugs her shoulders. "You got me. I never heard him say that."

"What happened that night after you went into his building with him and left me outside?"

"You were invited in, too, Corr," purrs Laura.

"I've not forgotten that fact!" snaps Corr. "What happened?"

Laura scratches her head as if she is trying hard to remember. Is she merely hassling Corr, or is she actually endeavoring to recall something?

Laura could well have been searching her database for two sentences she had said to Corr one day in Corr's studio, for Laura repeats those sentences here in the café. "That is a personal matter known only to Vogs and his attorney, Laura Pepin. I'm sure he would not want you to know."

Chances are very good that Laura would have been much happier for at least the next few minutes of her life if she had been unable to remember those two sentences and had said something else, something like "What would you like to know, Corr?" For Corr throws her hot tea at Laura's classy blouse. And Corr Cor does not miss this time.

Corr ignores Laura's scream. Corr looks completely immersed in thought as she stands up and pushes her chair to the table. On her way to the door now, she is mumbling something. "Not photographs...not real ones...constructed on a machine...no doubt about it...very clever though...insidiously realistic."

(26) +

Now she slams the door.

Now she stomps across countless colored stars on an old wooden upside-down sky to her paint-crusted easel. Now she spins about and stomps right back across that impossible sky to stand not altogether facing her memo-space on the wall. She reaches out her hand; and in that disheveled, two-dimensioned space she writes with slashing letters, "Don't EVER talk to that woman again!"

Assuming "that woman" is Laura Pepin, chances are not very good that Corr will obey for long the command she wrote on her wall. But who knows?

Corr tears off all her clothes and then...changes her mood. She calmed down. And how was this tricky transformation accomplished so fast and easily? Corr pacified her choppy waters by doing up her hair, handily binding her hair into a fountain, a dark spout of hair that shoots straight up from the top of her head six inches before it crests and the hairs drop back down to lay their free ends peacefully on Corr's head. She kneels on her prayer rug. Down she goes, down into the hole in her self.

"I will now launch a narrative that will center my vision on my hole."

Her eyes are open and clear but unfocused.

"It was Vogs who told me that everyone has a hole in their self and that art is one of the primary tools used to locate this hole and then to put the hole to use. For what seemed like forever after Vogs informed me of the existence of my hole, I was unable to spot it. But one day, there it was, right where it must have always been. I was so excited I ran over to Vogs' studio to tell him. He laughed and waved his hands in the air but went right back to work. It was two weeks before I found my hole again. At first, looking through the hole was like peering through an opening in the clouds at the clear sky above. Eventually I learned how to turn the hole to point at the world. Viewed through an opening in my self, the world appeared so strange it could have been an entirely separate place.

"To the preceding short history of my discovery of the aperture in my self, I will now add a touch of today's attitude: The great majority of the many things I learned—and am still learning—from this new skill of mine are thrillingly positive, growth oriented. One thing was not so pleasant, though. One thing was a problem for me. This new way of seeing split humanity into two distinct camps: those who can view the world that's outside of their selves and those who cannot. Vogs said that in time I would get over this troublesome incongruity, but I am not so sure he was right. I'm not sure he would know, for he never actually had this problem, at least not to the extent that I did/do. My guess is that his self was/is far more transparent to him than mine is to me and, therefore, there was not such a major difference for him between his self's world and the outer world."

Twenty-five minutes later, where is Corr? She has not moved; she is kneeling yet on her fading rug in her studio. Her back is straight, her head is high, her eyes are still perfectly clear. Her lips begin to quiver. Corr might be returning now from the world outside her self. Her head tilts a couple of degrees. "Gett Resu!"

That sudden, painful cry sounded like fear. What could have provoked Corr to cry out Gett's name in fear? While chances are low that Corr is afraid *for* Gett, is she afraid *of* him? Oop, the obvious *next* question just popped up. What in the world would Corr have to fear from Gett if the truth is indeed as Corr herself so knowingly said it is: Gett Resu will not ever say another word to Corr Cor? The simplest straightforward answer to that question seems to be that Gett Resu could explode into Corr's studio bent on revenging the burning of Laura's breasts *and* say absolutely nothing to Corr. Was the murderer, whoever that may be, required to speak to Necky before killing him? The startling emergence of a thought-image of Gett Resu racing to the studio right this minute with his mouth taped shut just might explain why Corr all of a sudden yelped out his name.

Her head tilts the other way. Again Corr cries out in agony. This time she cries the name of the person she instructed herself to never speak to again. "Laura Pepin!"

Corr's second painful cry had exactly the same horrible, panicky ring to it as her first. Two impulsive screeches—could they both have been reactions to internal images? Is it thinkable that Corr is now braving an unexpected image of a crazed Laura Pepin on the loose?

"If Gett Resu, why not Laur-like-far herself?"

Ha! That arched question from Corr's lips instantly tipped the scales of probability the other way. Rather than Corr being assaulted by an unexpected image of Laura Pepin, Corr could well have *constructed* an image of LP. In fact, both of Corr's screams could have been imitations of Laura's scream when she realized Corr's hot tea had been flung against her chest.

"Lawlady could come crashing through the door any second with her tomahawk raised." Corr rotates her eyes to fix her keen gaze on the doorknob. "Will Lawlady be coldly intent or wild in her eyes? Will her bosom be all whitely bandaged under her tea-stained blouse, or will her breasts be completely exposed and flame red?"

Corr pops straight up from her knees to stand with her feet well apart. Rub! Rub! She rubs hard everywhere on her bare body reachable with her hands. Rub!

Having sufficiently shined her flesh, she steps over to position herself just four feet from the smooth blue door to the outside. She's standing with her feet spread again. If someone comes along and opens that door, Corr will be directly facing the street in all her impudent glory.

She remains right there, standing superbly erect without moving, for hours. The sun goes down, again. The studio darkens. A gang of boohoos slips in under the door and attacks her spunk. Corr fights back gallantly in the face of defeat. She crumples to the floor, weeping, weeping silently for she is not known to be a bawler.

In the dark, on the floor, Corr, the painter, rolls onto her back and presses the butts of her hands against her temples. "Hark! Is that Vogs' Endlessness knocking now on this lonely woman's door? No, methinks it be only a wind outside, no doubt a death wind come to sweep the quaint cobbled streets in the failing light."

(27) +

(Day one.) Jerome Watershighagain turns up in town again. Corr barely managed to stay a week in his shack on the desert. He has traveled all the way back up here from that wilderness solely to see her.

(Day four.) Woe, Jerome lasted but three days in Corr's city. He really liked Corr's ocean, saw it as profound and beautiful, much like his desert. But the constant noise of the city hurt his ears, the constant bustle squeezed his brain, the constant greed insulted his view of humanity. So yesterday he went home.

Even though the sun has been up for a couple of hours now, the light in the room is still a mix. That is to say today's sun has not totally overpowered the weirdness of last night's full moon. Some minds hold that the poles of strongest turning are not midnight and noon but three in the morning and three in the afternoon—and the moon's face had become entirely visible at precisely three a.m.

And those smoky smears on THE BED? That is not *smears*; that is not any several things. It is one thing, the body of a female. Laid out on its back with its limbs all knotted up in the graying bedclothes and with its head turned way to one side, sandwiching one ear between its head and a pillow, the body is alive but breathing quite shallowly. The eyes are open and staring blankly at yon wall. Yon wall stares blankly back at the two eyes. The window behind the head has splashed a streak of sunlight across the upper, not-sandwiched ear; and the room's open doorway softly woos the dormant but definitely not sleeping painter with the hum from the coldbox downstairs.

The eyes blink. Just once. Her mouth opens and Corr is ON. "What is my mummied mind seeing right now? Ah, I see what it is seeing. It is gaping with utter loathing at the principal problem of my life. It is grudgingly yet dutifully reexamining my everlasting *either-or/neither-nor* habit. Either up or down, neither you nor me, this-that, if not assertion, then repression." The lid of Corr's lower eye flutters and closes. And reopens. "But this handicap of mine is one filthy addiction that even Jerome would acknowledge as being nearly universal with humanity. It's a suffocating dependence that even being totally alone out on the desert won't necessarily rid him of. Just as my being alone and all but anonymous in the city hasn't stripped the scurvy stinker from me. Me, the full-tilt, full-service artist whom Jerome left behind here!"

Does Corr Cor spring unbelievably upward from lying flat on her back to land lightly on her feet? Nay, not today. *Slow* and *sluggish* are the descriptive words as she DOES NOT GET UP AFTER ALL. All she does is roll her draggy head from lying on one ear to lying on its other ear. By that minimal means she hauled her eyes away from the staring-right-back-atcha wall and over to the open, sunlit window on the opposing wall. For a pigeon has landed on the window's sill.

When the bird sees Corr looking at him, he starts cooing at her. He stops the cooing the instant Corr's lips part. He listens attentively to her.

She says to him, "The weight is the world. Take the world away and there is no weight."

The pigeon bob-i-bobs his head as if to say thank you. And in return for Corr's nice gift to him, the bird gives her one eye and then his other eye, the way friendly birds do. (Friendly birds and birds delivering indecipherable warning messages. Dirty Bird in the café, for example.)

Corr speaks again. "What did I think, you ask, after I had gone to the gallery and seen my paintings there? I thought— No, I *knew* that there is someone, probably a man, who has stood looking at every one of my finished paintings, from the very first one that I showed publicly to the last painting I did for that last show. He has never seen me, as I have never seen him. But he is watching my shadow. Over the years he has watched my shadow move from painting to painting."

The bird shakes his head in utter disgust and flies away.

The lack of understanding/compassion of the pigeon has no obvious perturbing effect on Corr. The Indomitable One sits up to untangle her arms and legs and to throw off the covers. She pivots on her butt and stiffly lowers her feet to the floor. Her ascent from the bed? How does she fare there? Her standing up, her rising from the very cloth she has warmed with her own body, is, in a quiet way, magnificent. She does wobble a bit before she finds her land legs.

"Stretching. I am stretching, stretching."

Rubbing her eyes with her fists, Corr shambles over to a chair to get the clothes she laid out last night to put on this morning, the green clothes.

"What's this?" She is astonished. "They're not here! Clothes are here on the chair all right; and, yes, they are my clothes; but it has been a good while since I have even seen *these* clothes!" She is visibly upset. Her hands are actually shaking.

Corr shakes her head too. And nods her head, too. "Char Wrig again?" Corr is seriously hugging herself. "Or a clandestine clothes maven?" Corr starts to shiver. She had best get at least her upper body into clothes of some sort. "The third choice here would be a trickster left behind by the desert man. Must I watch out for all three candidates at the same time? Musteye? Life keeps playing curious switcheroos with my art-bred expectations. Therefore. Maybe I should return immediately to bed."

If Corr does not go back to bed but, instead, looks about her bedroom more closely, she might spot the green clothes. The greens are laid over another chair on the other side of the room. Why is Corr not seeing the green clothes? Perhaps the answer is simply that she never hangs clothes on that chair over there. Or is the answer not quite that plain? Will the clothes not being where Corr thought she had left them add meaningful mystery to what promises to be a drab day?

"Drab day alone!" Corr wheels on her heels and hikes to the open window.

"Sure, I saw the greens on the other chair on my way over to this bright window." She checks for bird crap on the window sill, then sticks her head and shoulders outside. "But, no, I'm not going to wear them there clothes now. Not today!"

There is a first time for everything. Corr sees Laura looking out a small window of Laura's building. Laura is staring directly at Corr Cor in Corr's window on Corr's building. How could Corr have forgotten this window-to-window possibility? She and Vogs and Necky used to send and receive carnal messages by this means. "Frequently. All the time."

Laura opens wide her blouse. It's a fresh blouse, of course.

"I can't see well enough to tell if I'm being shown Lawlady's permanently scarred breasts or if I am expected to be totally in awe of those darlings over there or if I am supposed to be getting all steamed up over the two."

Laura yanks a shade down over her window.

There is no shade on Corr's window.

"That silver shade over there certainly wasn't on the window when the building was Vogs and Necky's."

Corr pulls her body parts back into her bedroom and closes the window. As she passes by the green bearing chair, she kicks the chair, knocking it over and dumping the greens on the floor.

"If I wandered over to Lawlady's right now, would I be looking for a fight or looking to get licked?" Corr takes up her *old* clothes from the number one chair and packs them into the bathroom. "Doesn't matter at all, I guess. Because I'm not in the slightest interested in either."

Corr stops. She looks quickly behind her. She looks down at her feet on the bathroom tiles. "What *am* I interested in?"

She turns on the water in the tub. Ho, she's going to bathe today instead of taking a shower.

"Art comes to mind."

She climbs in while the tub is still filling. "Patterns On Silk Seen Through Patterns On Silk: a title, an aggressively nasty title."

She thumbs her nose. "Vogs is not lying waterlogged in some bog. I ask him to wash my back. He gladly does so."

Who in the world now would feel free enough to just walk into Corr's bathroom and jump into the tub with her? There have been quite a number of such people in Corr's life, yet there does not seem to be a one right now, except perhaps Nalaen and/or Lise. But Corr appears to not be counting on those two darling tits.

"Then there is the lady with golden hair."

Aren't good artists endlessly resourceful?

Corr lies back in the old cast-iron tub with her arms extended along the curved-over top of the sides. "Lawlady had no trouble brazenly trotting into my studio downstairs uninvited. If she took a mind to waltz on up the stairs and in here, there is nothing in all creation that could stop her."

Corr clucks her tongue. "Half smiling, LP would urbanely lower her expensively clothed rear end to that toilet seat cover over there. She would suavely cross her long, thin, creamy-white legs and rest at least one elbow on her upper knee before offhandedly mentioning something unbearably cruel to me. I would have to spit back at her in my most ugly voice, like I did that day downstairs, which was also, I'm remembering now, the day that my fist narrowly missed connecting with Lawlady's chin, 'You just get out of here!' But this time she would not leave…"

(28) +

"What's to do? Paint, of course. Or not paint, of course. Walk to the beach, of course. Or walk *toward* the beach but turn right on FOX and at least pause at 832…of course."

Corr smiles a big toothless *U*. She yanks up on the chain for the drainpipe's plug, climbs out of the gurgling tub, throws her body into the not-green clothes, and heads on down the grade. "Maybe old Horsey will just happen by in Judy Blue's truck with Judy Blue's dad riding shotgun and Jonny Facemoral sitting out in back behind the cab giving voice to Vogs' *dialogue in mono*. My oh my, four elusive gents."

The tall red house.

"It's gone!"

The red house could have been moved from the site where Corr is looking for it; that is entirely possible. Or the house could have been standing over across the street ever since it was built.

"Oh! There it is, across the street." Corr gives a little jump of joy. "Bingo." Her arms shoot up straight above her head. She wiggles her fingers. "Whoosh!" She sportively wiggles her elevated fingers. Maybe half a minute goes by like this.

Corr ceases wiggling her high fingers but doesn't lower them. Maybe another half of a minute goes by.

Corr's eyes have glazed over. She is standing on one heel now, still facing the red house on the other side of the street. Suddenly her head drops way back, and she whispers up into the air between her yet vertical arms. "If it were not for my initial explosive reaction—'It's gone!'—I would probably have dismissed my not spotting the red house right off as merely an innocent oversight. My little spit of verbal violence informs me, however, that I mislocated the house because I still suspect the green clothes were moved to another chair by someone other than myself. While I was asleep."

Corr crosses the street to replay the scene cold. Cool as a ruby red popsicle, she knocks on the front door. No answer. She rings the bell. No answer. She waits. No answer. So far, everything has been a loud echo of the first time she stood waiting on this doorstep. The next move will be Corr boldly turning the door's handle as she enters the building.

"Oh! —Ow!"

Corr bumped her forehead hard against the door. The door did not swing wide open this time, did not budge one bit. The door could not cooperate with Corr's replay because it is securely locked.

What will Corr do? She still can't see in the windows. She still can't walk around to the back of the building. She knocks on the door of the house to the left of Tall Red. She knocks on the door to the right of Tall Red. No answer and no answer.

"There's no one at home anywhere. The nests are empty. Vacant. Uninhabited. Deserted."

Corr spins around and parades briskly out into the street, where she whispers to her hand, "Or the occupants are day-sleepers." Corr has halted on the road's unpainted centerline. She pivots about to stand facing Tall Red with her feet close together and her arms extended straight out to the side from her shoulders. Loudly she divulges, "Or they are furtively peeking out their curtains at me right now."

Not wiggling so much as one single finger, Corr stands as a crisp epigram. "Between the pavement under my feet and the grown-over soft spot at the very top of my head, no exterior part of me moves or moves or even moves, except for my eyes. And of course my mouth. My eyes search the curtains of the windows on all three floors of Tall Red. My diligent eyes also check the windows of both of Red's shorter neighbors."

Corr sighs. Her tee collapses, and her hands slap-slap against the side of her thighs. "'Tis actual. The nests are empty."

What will she do now?

"Sit down right here on this spot and wait for the Blue's truck to run me over." Corr sits herself down crosslegs on the blacktop.

"The Blue's truck? Naw, the *blues* truck! The blues truck! Run over by a blazing blues truck!"

She flops back on her back to stare up into the majestic heavens. Her legs are still crossed. "In a state of *extreme prostration and depression*, I'll lie here flattened and stuck to this hard, rough surface till time's end, when Vogs will reappear riding on a silver cloud over the city, picking up all his lost children to take them home."

A dog wanders by, notices the unusual heap lying in the middle of the road, and steps smartly over to check it out.

His pointed head is right above Corr's head. Now he's gazing down into her eyes. She smiles up at him. Apparently not noticing Corr's infamous ghostly aspects, the dog licks her nose. Corr laughs and sits up to pet him. She has been saved in the nick of time again, by a dog this time. She uncrosses her legs and climbs to her feet. The dog nods good day and trots away.

"Not green clothes. Not the blues truck. Not Tall Red. Not glistening gold hair. Not red-into-blue-into-brown eyes. Or even orange eyes. Not a gray necklace hanging from my neck. Not a purple thoughtless blob. Not skin that's mostly turquoise. Nor a big black bird disappearing into the thick white fog. Neither nails nor nipples of rose or dusk. No yummy colors whatsoever! —No yucky colors either. Just clear paint on clear glass applied with a banshee's brush."

Is Corr merely using up time now, either not wanting to leave the scene or not having anywhere to go?

Honk!

A vehicle is approaching, and the road is not wide enough for the mottled maroon machine to go either left or right around Corr.

Honk! Honk!

Corr doesn't budge. It's a standoff.

Honk! Honk! Honk! Honk!

(29) +

A woman and man sit touchingly close to each other at one end of a bench. They are both very still: every so often a head or hand of theirs will move inconsequentially, but the two people have not spoken to each other for ten minutes or more.

The silence that the two are sharing is broken by the woman. "It's a grayish folder."

166

The man promptly replies in a voice broken by lack of use. "No, it's not."

She spoke, he spoke, and the pair returned forthwith to their quiet, their mutual mum being marked this time by a series of tiny tips of the man's head.

The man stops tipping his head. Sounding quite certain of himself, he tells the woman in a now smooth voice, "It's a newspaper." With a fresh wet grin on his face, he leans a tad closer to her to humorously confide, "They still *print* them, you know."

The woman neither looks at the man nor comments on his inside dope.

Still grinning, the man returns to his opinion, to expand upon it. He nods his head affirmatively. "It's a standard newspaper that is folded...let me picture the count in my head...yes, folded in half *three* times." He smiles wide at his wisdom.

The woman smiles some, too, but still does not yield. "Looks like a big folder filled with loose papers to me."

Neither does the man yield. "It's a newspaper. Take my fuzzy herd for it. Look at him. That guy would have no use in the world for a folder full of papers, particularly down there on the beach. But he *can* read."

The woman shakes her head no and turns to Corr. "What do you think it is?"

Corr? Sitting all alone on the other end of that same bench, the weatherworn bench that looks out over the beach at the ocean from along the edge of the last road, Corr is surprised the woman even spoke to her. The five feet of unoccupied wood that separates Corr from the woman is normally enough of a buffer in the city to prevent strangers from starting up a conversation.

The woman is about Corr's age. And a quick glance at the man as he leans his head to look around the woman at Corr reveals that he is close to the same age.

Uncertain as to how she should proceed, Corr answers, "I couldn't help but hear you two. Even so, I don't know what is at the center of your amiable dispute."

"The man lying down there on the beach…on that striped towel." The woman leans toward Corr and spreads her hand on the bench seat to prop her torso on one arm. She has large teeth. "What is that lying on the towel beside him?"

"It's a newspaper," chimes the man. He has quick eyes.

Corr looks long at the object of concern. "I really can't say." She sounded a bit surprised at herself there. "It could be either a newspaper or a folder." Would Corr have been able to make out the object just fine if it had been lying not in wavy beach light but in the dark?

Corr is staring yet at that thing down on the towel when her head suddenly rebounds as if her blues truck had just run into and over an unseen speed bump. She whispers, "Good thing I wasn't Jonny up in the back of the Blue's truck. That unforeseen force would surely have thrown him out."

The woman seems to understand she wasn't supposed to hear what Corr just said.

"Ok," barks Corr. Freshly filled to the top with self-assurance, she proclaims to the couple, "I'll stroll down by that towel and then come back up here to tell you the answer."

"Hey!" The woman gives Corr a great grinning view of her teeth. "Would you?"

The man says, "Great idea." He thoroughly approves of Corr's decision.

Corr bounces to her feet. "Sure thing," she chirps back over her shoulder as she strides away from the bench.

The man and woman watch Corr. They don't take their eyes off her.

Corr struts on down toward the ocean some distance past the towel. Pretending she has forgotten something, she stops and turns around and starts back up as if to return to the bench. She drops to her knees on the striped towel and picks up the object. It is a folder. She opens it up and thumbs through its contents. The man lying beside her is asleep.

Corr returns to her spot on the bench. "*Folder* is the correct answer. *Newspaper* is the not-correct answer. Judging from the folder's insides, I would quess the sound sleeper down there is a real estate agent." Corr jabs an index finger twice at the sky. "Mission accomplished."

"Wowee!" The woman scoots over half the distance to tap Corr on the shoulder. "Good work, fearless warrior."

Corr sets the woman straight. "I'm part lion, actually. So it was not at all biggish for me."

The woman lowers her chin and smiles without showing her teeth. "I can see the lion in you, yes."

"What are the other parts of you?" The man wants to know. He scoots over to be sitting right next to the woman again, next to the woman and therefore closer to Corr.

"Calo." The woman lays her hand on her own chest. "Calo Colm."

"Hey, I'm a *C. C.*, too. I'm Corr Cor."

"Hello, Corr," says Calo Colm.

"Hello, Corr Cor," says the man.

The woman, Calo, then points her head at the man. "This is Stiff Wind."

"No kidding?" Corr looks the man up and down. "*Stiff* as in S-t-i-f-f?"

"Right," the man answers. "You got it. And W-i-n-d."

Corr is grinning. "Do you use both of the names as one unit? Or as two units?"

"Friends usually call me *Stiff*. Or *Stiffer*. Or *Stump*."

Corr's grin widens. "As in *Stiff Stump*?"

The man looks a bit embarrassed by this latest turn in the conversation, but he is not blushing or retreating in the slightest. "Right. You got it, I think." Stiff reaches around in front of Calo to offer Corr his hand. Here and now, there is little room for doubt as to which way Stiff Wind's wind is blowing.

Corr lightly takes his hand and gives it a tiny shake.

When Corr releases his hand, Stiff says, "We live together…in the same house anyway. That one there." He points his hand-shaking hand behind them at the ancient house directly across the road. He then purposely drops that same hand to Calo's knee.

Stiff is at most two years Corr's senior, and Calo would be within a year either way of Corr. Corr wonders out loud. "You could be brother and sister if it weren't for your last names being different. No, even with different last names you could be brother and sister."

Calo giggles jauntily. "We are not related in any way. We have just spent more than enough time together to look alike." She edges closer to Corr.

Stiff quickly closes the gap. "Do you live around here, Corr? Or are you just passing through? I hope you don't mind me asking."

"Don't mind." Corr runs her fingers through her hair. "I live up that way, a good walk from here."

Pretending to pull wryly on her chin, Calo asks, "Have we seen you before, Corr?"

"Maybe. I come down to the beach often enough—"

Corr stopped herself. For a long, slow moment her countenance darkens. "Come to think of it, though, it has been quite a while now since I've been here."

She does a passable imitation of Calo's sprightly giggle. "But I've never ever *sot* on this bench before."

Stiff makes a two-handed regal gesture at the sea. "Calo and I were getting about ready to take a break from our ocean beholding. Would you like to join us for a late lunch?"

Corr's mouth drops open. In amazement? Or is she kidding de folks? "Come to think of it, I've not had one bite of food to eat so far today."

Calo bounds to her feet to tug on Corr's sleeve. "Then let us go get some grub. You and me and him."

Corr doesn't do any of her superphysical, shooting-straight-up-in-the-air stuff. No tricks. None. "Sure. Why not?" She rises demurely to her feet.

That is Stiff giggling at Corr's coy gravity.

Stiff's giggle was not at all like either Calo or Corr's. His was bumpy, like fast-flowing shallow water, with an imperfectly concealed smell of danger.

He's up from the bench. Everyone is up now. They are walking. They are crossing the road. That is not Vogs in the middle. It is Corr. Calo and Corr and Stiff are all smiles. No, they are not holding hands.

Stiff is taller than he appeared to be while sitting on the bench. His back is straight, his head is high. He unlocks the door, pushes it open, and bows to allow the women to enter first. He sniffs twice, once for each woman swishing by him.

"The house is old, for sure, but quite nice. Would I call it refined? Well…it's scrubbed, for sure." Corr is whispering to herself as she tours the house while the others are fixing lunch. "The trappings of educated folk. The smell of wood and imported carpets." She does not go into the bedroom. Nor the baths. Nor out onto the back porch. She sums up her tour with one more whisper before she wanders into the kitchen. "No perceivable primary focal point."

"It's about ready." Calo is setting a dish of cold vegetables on the table.

Stiff is proudly drying his hands. "Pick a chair, Corr. Any chair is fine."

"Ahh, the food smells great." Corr gambols over to a chair.

All three sit down at the table. The food dishes are passed around.

Friskily Corr slides behind her sly mask. "What did I miss in my survey of your house?"

Stiff peers out the top of his eyes at Corr. "Your good friend Necky."

"What?" Corr shudders. Suddenly Corr shudders in cold fear.

Calo calmly confides, "He laughed from a sick heart."

Corr springs to her feet, knocking her chair over backward. She spins about and runs at breakneck speed, somehow not colliding with a single thing on her way out of the house. The front door had been left standing open.

(30) +

The city's police department was not interested in either Calo Colm or Stiff Wind. Both Colm and Wind had already been closely investigated, long ago. They had been friends and occasional playmates with Necky Watershighagain.

Corr had run the whole way home without stopping. Even so, even after she had raced breathlessly uphill all the way from the beach road to her building, she had had a hugely hard time talking herself into contacting the police and telling them about the two people who live in a house down across the street from the beach. "And now I realize that my first instinct was right. *Keep your mouth shut!* Nothing is ever gained by bringing policía into *any* predicament."

So why did she do it? Why did she yell for help? Corr explained it to herself this way: "If Calo Colm and Stiff Wind knew Necky and also knew or somehow figured out that I was Necky's good friend, then they know where I live. Stiff Wind could have just casually rambled up to my building and killed me, like I thought he had killed Necky and was flaunting it in my face at their kitchen table."

No one is going to just casually meander into Corr's studio right now: the front door is doubly locked.

It's evening, and she's shivering while trying to paint.

It's nighttime, and she's shivering under a sheet.

172

It's morning, and she's shivering in a hot shower.

Corr puts on the greens.

She goes downstairs, unlocks the door, peeks outside.

"The coast *looks* clear."

Corr steps outside and locks up the door behind her.

It's time for her tea, and she's shivering while crossing the street. A loud bang somewhere behind her nearly knocks her knees out from under her. She panics, covers her ears with her wrists, and runs the rest of the way across the street. She is shivering violently and gasping for air when she bashes through the door and staggers into the café.

Welf stops to stare at her. "What a sight you are!"

Corr struggles to come back razor sharp. "That was not said disparagingly, I hope. Nor was it a compliment, I assume."

Corr's puny, shapeless attempt at cleverness didn't even register on Welf's face. No less anxious about Corr's condition, he starts toward her. "What is it, Corr? Are you sick?"

"The world is fast becoming otherworldly, Mister Manager."

Corr may or may not have been joking. Welf stops just far enough from her to not crowd her. Apparently he took her statement seriously.

"It's curious you said that, Corr. Several of my customers have confided to me lately that for them this past couple of months has been like being on a different planet."

Now that was an uncharacteristic thing for a supposedly worried Welf to say. Whatever was his intent? He provides not a clue.

Did Welf's curiously deliberate recollection turn Corr's mind to remembering? Is she recalling Vogs' description of the effect that Laura's pictures had on him? "It's as if a series of doors has been permanently opened to a new world." Or is Corr reliving her own waking up in the dark in the big bedroom at 832 FOX, where the faint light was distorting everything so strangely she could have been transmitted bodily to another world while she was asleep? Or is she remembering now that she had mentioned this eerie experience in the house on FOX to Nalaen *after* he had said of one of her paintings, "Just looking at it is like waking up on another planet." Which, any, or all of these possibilities? Corr provides not a clue.

Instead she quips, "It's curious you said that, Welf. Several of my nerve endings lately have confided to me that for them this past couple of *years* has been like being on a different planet."

"That was weak, Corr. And you don't need to be mean to me."

"Sorry, Welf. Truly."

"Apology accepted."

Welf takes Corr by the elbow and guides her to her table. The table is indeed unoccupied. He has her sit down. "How's your wristwatch? Still not working?" Welf does not glance at Corr's wrist to see for himself.

"Right. You got it, I think."

Corr blanches with horror. She mouths the words *Stiff* and *Wind*. Her answer to Welf's wristwatch question just now was exactly, word for word, Stiff Wind's answer to her *Stiff Stump* question. When Welf has left her side to get her tea, Corr says softly, "I must rid myself of those two before their words and everything else about them turn into foul habits for me. First I will throw out their foul names. Done. Then their foul images. Done. Then their foul presences. Done. Then the negative spaces left behind in my foul brain. Done. Done."

Corr glances over her shoulder to see if Welf is returning with her tea yet. No, he is standing in the kitchen doorway staring at her.

It takes Welf a moment to realize that Corr is looking back at him. He snaps a hand-wave at her and retreats into his kitchen.

Corr slumps in her chair. Waiting for her tea, she is reminded of why she pays little or no attention to the other patrons of the café. Two men at the next table are talking louder than they need to, in whiney voices.

First voice: "Look at what I found at a little sale yesterday, an antique book of matches. See the bold red letters outlined in white on a patriotic blue background. '*Subauling is the name. Fame is my game.*' I can't guess what that means. But this matchbook is so old the font employed hasn't been used for many a year, to my knowledge. It has that quaint old-fashioned elegance."

Second voice: "Elegance? How could you chose that word? I would describe our cast of major and minor characters here as having more like an outmoded, naïve, trashy sense of symmetry. And two parallel lines of four words each? Ha! And eight words that just spell gobbledygook? Ha!"

"You don't like what I bought?"

"Do the matches still work?"

"I didn't want to spoil the book by trying one."

(31) +

"What does that word *gobbledygook* mean?"

Corr frowns tightly and produces for herself what she thinks might be an example of gobbledygook. "Once it could be said that some went down to the sea, while some just went down to the cellar to check the furnace. Some still go down to town. And some still go down in flames, while some just sink below the horizon." One of Corr's countless talents—yes, this would be the same talent that Nalaen-in-blue labeled "totally unpremeditated speech" just a short moment before Corr told him that he was the good-party preventing her from becoming a bird in the outer space—had enabled her to erect and deliver her example of gobbledygook so quickly that the construction sounded as if it had been previously prepared and memorized. The downturn of

Corr's mouth dissolves. Her eyes start to sparkle. Up! She smiles crookedly, tickled hot-pink with herself. For a painter who is not also a writer, just listening to herself saying all that totally unpremeditated gobbledygook could have been quite a visual experience.

Corr has returned to her studio from the café. Smiling sweetly now, she flicks her middle finger against the taut surface of a newly stretched and gessoed canvas. Pho-o-o-onk!

"Pell-mell to the sea, to the cellar, to town in flames below the horizon."

That must have been the condensed version of her nonsense construction.

Usually Corr doesn't draw anything on the canvas before she starts applying paint. Today she tries a sketch. Over and over again she attempts a sketch. Every time, it comes out a naked man.

"No, these men are not people I recognize. Not by any stretch of any imagination." Corr rubs out her latest man. "Maybe they're dead relatives. Or famous men from the past. Or men I will someday meet."

Knock. Knock.

Corr wrinkles up her nose. "Did not those two knocks on my door sound oh so very much like another two knocks on my door?"

Relaxing her nose and wrinkling up her lips, Corr calls, as if she does not already know, "Who is there?"

"It's Lise."

Corr grins wide and lays her soft pencil down on the easel tray. "Then get on in here."

Lise Tenwotom parades her tan good-looks in through the door. Her sharp green eyes dance about the room. "Hiya, Corr." She closes the door behind her. From where is that accent of hers? And why was the door not locked and doubly locked?

"Hello, Lise. Either a good morning or a good noon to you. And what brings you out this way?"

"A social call on one of the gallery's more talented artists."

"And you stopped by here on your way to see this talented artist?"

Lise pushes at her rich brown hair as she gazes off over her other shoulder. "I'm not going to answer that *innocent* question. I've praised you quite enough for now."

Corr takes a couple of moments to admire Lise's strikingly well-proportioned body. If Corr were to take up her pencil right now, she might draw a woman instead of a man. "Nice clothes, Lise."

It's Lise's turn to check out Corr. "Do you dress all in that one color as a matter of style?"

"What?" Corr is confused. She looks down and remembers she's in the greens. "No, definitely not. This is a clear-cut aberration of my normal dressing habits." Corr may be too agitated right now to catch Lise's reference to Corr's having also worn today's outfit to the opening at Lise's gallery. "In fact, I'll go up and take them off right now, Lise. Be back in a second. Wander around. Look."

Corr has all but removed the greens from her body when Lise ambles into her bedroom.

"You are certainly luscious to look at, Corr. And I must say that you are as talented at sex as you are at painting."

"You liked the three-way romp that night, I take it."

"I did! I did!"

"But that is not why you have come here, Lise?"

"Right." Lise dons a more serious expression as she somewhat stiffly walks over to look out a window. "Do you know a woman named Judy Blue?" Lise closes the window glass. Her words bounce off the glass. "She thinks you are illegally in possession of the paintings of the known artist Vogs, who her gallery represented before he up and disappeared. She also thinks you have the last paintings of Necky Watershighagain, who was from a different gallery. She also thinks that another popular local artist, named G.J. Horsey Fatts—who also was once with the gallery that Judy Blue works for—knows that you have these paintings but he just won't say so."

"Ahh." Corr stacks her fists one on top of the other on top of her head. "Thank you for bringing me up to date on the fantasies of Judy Blue, a sour woman."

"Sour? Yes, I agree. She is an acid fruit." As Lise turns around to face Corr, she steps to one side of the window, where she leans back against the wall. "But Judy Blue is not as stupid as she might seem to you, Corr. I have come here to warn you to be careful."

"What can she do if it's not true?"

"Whether what she claims is true or not, Corr, Judy Blue can make your life mucho messy for an extended period of time."

"How did you learn all this?"

Lise smiles mischievously up at the dusty old overhead light fixture. "One professional took another into her confidence."

Lise is now piling her fists on top of her head in imitation of Corr, who has by this time more or less lowered her hands. "I think Judy Blue is wanting to come work for me, Corr."

Corr sputters. "Gad! What a thought!" She has to bite her forearm to prevent an outbreak of lunatic laughter.

Lise's eyes light right up as she, unlike Corr, does not hold back even for one second after she has screeched her two exclamations, "Gadzooks! My sentiments exactly!" She bursts into laughter, laughing openly, gaily, immodestly.

Corr's mouth spits out Corr's arm. Corr's mouth opens way wider; and out of this mammoth slick-walled cave explodes a mighty, ecstatic, hot-orange *yah*. "YAH!" The big orange word splats joyfully against Lise's gorgeous forehead.

Fast, quick as she possibly can, Lise, her eyes flish-flashing crazily, returns Corr's good deed with a vigorous *yah* of her own. "Ya-a-h-h-h-h-h-h!"

(Please, Lise's *joyful word* was, no, not a copy of Corr's monochromatic big jazzy flattened note. Lise's long yah was a scintillating, prismatic portamento. And please, a *portamento* is a continuous glide effected by the voice in passing from one tone to another.)

Does Corr laugh and laugh uproariously? And does she hug her stomach while deliriously running in place? And does Corr deCor try the very best she ever has to speak understandably as she sends up a long, colorful word-banner twisting and curling like a snake overhead?

"Of course the resident artist is stark naked all the while that the visiting gallery owner is beautifully dressed," the shrieked banner reads, "an unmistakably observable fact that adds a certain historical dynamic to today's little conclave in the artist's bedroom."

"Historical?" Lise is the one sputtering now. "Don't you mean *hysterical?*"

(32) +

"I wasn't actually picking up word-by-word what he was saying. So I thought that he said, 'I am vaguely remembering being in this space before.' In retrospect I can hear that truly he said, 'I am vaguely not remembering being in this space before.' That one word, *not*, makes a great difference. He was viewing the world from the other side."

Corr fakes a guffaw. "Is it possible to 'vaguely not remember'?"

From a safe distance Welf watches the two women for a while before returning to his simple work.

"Yes, I'm beginning to think that it is." Nodding her head honestly, Lise stares thoughtfully down into her tea. She and Corr are discussing Nalaen Figg. "I think Nalaen was standing on the bright side of the world, where it's normal to expect that everything is apparent, nothing is hidden, nothing is lost in time. But when he said that sentence to me, he was looking over toward the darker side, where I live, where things are forgotten over time, where most things are hidden from sight."

"You've thought about this a lot." Corr squints one eye like a would-be marksman. "Haven't you?"

"Yes, it took me some time to even begin to understand the man."

Corr draws in a deep breath, crosses her sinewy arms below her breasts, leans back in her chair. "You didn't exactly say so, Lise; but you implied, I think, that on Nalaen's 'side of the world' normally nothing is forgotten. Are you seriously proposing that the man has total recall?"

"Wouldn't total recall fix the difference entirely inside the person, Corr? No, I get the impression that the whole world is different when seen from where Nalaen is."

Corr uncrosses her arms, screws up her mouth, and lays the backs of her fingers on the tabletop. In a tone that's a touch tough she asks, "Other than that one *not* word, what makes you think this guy is *from the bright side?*"

A rush of nervous laughter cascades from Lise. She presses a fingertip to the point of her nose while eyeing Corr's famously noticeable nose. "The way he bats his baby blues?"

Corr looks a little put off by Lise's tease, if Lise was teasing. In fact Corr is acting now as if she is tiring of Lise's company. Lise Tenwotom may have gone on too long about Nalaen Figg without once acknowledging straight out that he has infatuated her. Corr asks from a safe distance, "What does he do, besides work in the gallery?"

"Nalaen was once a painter." Gazing up at the café's ceiling with her head tilted a tad back, Lise makes her list. "He was once a playwright. He was once an office worker. He was most recently a novelist hiding out as a street person—no, no, make that 'a park person.' What is he doing now, besides working in my gallery? He is busy writing the novel that he slept in the park for months to prepare himself for."

Corr's eyes narrow.

Looking yet up at the ceiling, Lise grins eagerly. She licks her lips. Has something with a delicious aftertaste just occurred inside her? Lise's soft and sensual gaze dives from the ceiling into Corr's eyes. "Speaking of sleep! He was disappointed that you didn't dream out loud for him."

"Hoy!" Corr jumps back into the conversation with renewed interest shining in her eyes. "I don't think I ever got all the way to sleep while he was in my bed. Maybe we can try again. I'd definitely like another opinion on the matter."

(33) +

"So what if his eyes were baby blue! *Now* they're baby green, and he's no longer safe to have around!"

What could that possibly mean? No, it was not the long roar of a dragon, a roar that only sounds like words. It was Corr Cor dreaming out loud in a strong voice. Listen, she has more to say in that same voice.

"Rudely ripped out of her context, she no longer fits into the class of common humans contemporarily and indiscriminately captioned *Safely Underpowered*!"

Huh, again. Corr's lead-in protest—in which "baby blue" eyes became, by some as yet unexplained turn of events, unsafe "baby green" eyes—has now been joined by an equally muddy "rudely ripped" exclamation. Were these two forceful utterances meaningful to Corr or mere rhetoric? Or are they further examples of gobbledygook?

Tis possible the sleeper was quite pleased with her "rudely ripped" sentence; for she says in a much milder voice, quoting herself from the very last time she and Vogs conversed with each other on the beach, "That was a nice little speech you just made. It was. And it was surprisingly articulate for a visual artist."

Onto that last run of words—her "much milder" string—Corr hangs an even quieter tag: "And particularly for a visual artist who's quite asleep."

Ah, it does seem Corr was at least momentarily aware she is asleep.

Her next bunch-of-words will end even more abruptly than it begins.

"Exhibitionism, public. The door not only quits its closing when it is closed, it quits its opening when it is open. If *trepidatious* is not a word, use *trepidation*. A hemispherical speed bump on the road to Neckyland—"

Even while Corr is fast asleep, her forehead can draw down into an intimidating scowl. "Why does this dream of mine keep jerking so catawampusly?"

Corr cuts the irregular, *catawampus* flow of spoken words, cuts it altogether and lies so still on her bed she could be dead. Seconds go creeping by. Is she still breathing? –Lo! Is that a low, heavy, rumbling sound? Yes. But where is it coming from? No, there is still not a fleet of fiery dragons flying this way. There! The rumbling stopped. The sound had come from deep in Corr's throat. It sounded much like the grumble that Welf sometimes makes when he is displeased and frustrated. Corr's mouth opens. Sturdy, sensible words walk out. "Dreams follow various systems of connectedness that oftener than not swerve drastically away from the deliberate coherence of awake time." Corr sounded like someone reading from a reference book. Is she searching her memory, trying to come up with an explanation for the zigzag trace of her dream?

Her dreaming out loud is not for Nalaen. Nor for Lise. Alas, Corr is fully dressed and quite alone on her bed. Lise had to go somewhere else after their—as Lise called it—chummy confab in the café. It is roughly the middle of that same afternoon. So why is Corr lying on the bed? Why is she asleep? "I have definitely acclimatized to the world's getting colder." She doesn't sound as if she is especially enjoying herself. "Yes, I am definitely pointed towards the world getting colder."

Corr crows about her hoax. Hoax? Yes, maybe a minute after her terse clarification of how she feels about the world cooling off, if it is, Corr opened her eyes and sat up on her bed and boasted that she had not been asleep at all. And she is saying that again, right now, for the third time. "I was not asleep at all." How could she have been not asleep? If her dreaming out loud was truly a hoax, for who's deception was she make-believing sleep?

"A long painting sterilizes the highway."

Has Corr changed the subject, or is this some more of her gloating?

She's up. She's up from the bed. She doesn't have to get dressed. She bounds down the stairs to the studio, to the easel, to quickly dust the loose graphite from the gesso of the otherwise naked canvas.

Busily mixing three colors of paint on a glass dish, Corr sings in her next-to-highest voice, "Walking a path along the edge of a park, a dirt path, I hear from one of the deluxe houses off to my right, through open deck-doors, a man saying, 'I don't know how to explain it to you, dear; but I know what it is.' That, yes, is what the man said to his dear. So say some. So say some. So say some. —Yo! Stop me! What a fool I am! Oh why did I judge that man sight unseen? Only sublime beings can pick out of the crowd those who truly know *what it is*. What it is. What it is. The things of the world are empty."

The song is over and the new color is ready. Corr applies the paint to the canvas with an inch-wide flat, one of her "powerful yet precise" brushes. "Slap dash rack pack slim do red."

She has painted a line from the top edge of the canvas to the bottom edge. Corr steps back to eyeball her work. The line, starting out bravely on its journey from the leftmost quarter of the top edge, descends nearly half of the canvas in a gentle curve to the right. It switches to a straight down heading for a short while, then starts wiggling frantically as it approaches the rightmost quarter of the bottom edge of the rectangle. The painted inch-line reaches the bottom and appears to drop into invisibility below the canvas. "Presto! A Long Painting Sterilizes The Highway."

From out of Corr's most recent dreaming-out-loud session—declared afterward to have been not sleep at all—has come the first stroke of a new painting. What it is.

(34) +

"Can I believe it? I passed not a single soul on my trip, the entire trip, all the way down to the beach and then all the way back up to here. How very, very strange. Even for this late at night."

What it is.

(In less than a minute, this last *What it is*, the effortless three-worder sitting directly above this paragraph and hanging right below Corr's comments on her strange voyage down to and up from the beach, will lose all of what little fitness it has there. In fact, in a sense, that once nonchalant, soon inane saying will ring this time as regrettably inappropriate. Appalling news awaits Corr, news that will permanently mark her life with a distinct and previously unknown flavor. Therefore, immediately following this paragraph a replacement line will be inserted.)

Oh, yoo-hoo! This here night is not over!

Upon returning to her building from her midnight walk, Corr immediately discovers things are not right. First, her street door is not locked. "I can clearly remember locking it." Warily she opens the door and slinks into her studio. The lights she had left on are on, and only the lights she had left on are on. "Nope, nothing seems out of sorts here." But suddenly she understands. "I hear what the ding-ding bell in my head is saying!" She races up the stairs. "Drat!" The locks are unlocked, and the door stands open a crack.

Corr does not enter the room. She doesn't even push open the door a little more to look in. She pivots away and stumbles blindly back downstairs, where she bumbles through the making of a cup of tea—the café won't open for hours—and then immediately curls up in a ball in her dilapidated overstuffed chair. "What it is...is a waste." She is soon fast asleep. She has forgotten to lock the street door after she skulked in through it.

This time she is unquestionably asleep. And this time her dreaming out loud consists of only one sentence, one peanut wish. "I would sit before a glowing potbelly in a tiny shack in a graveyard in a heavy rain, forever cooking the skin of my face."

When Corr awakens in her chair, the light of morning is wandering in the windows like the proverbial gray-white flock of tourists. The first solid thing that Corr sees is a plain man in a dark suit. He is standing, looking fixedly at her new canvas. Her tea is stone cold, but she won't notice that for some time.

The man turns his head to look at her, sees that she is awake now, says, "I'm wearing a gun." He opens one side of his coat to prove that he is indeed packing a death device. "I wanted you to know that up front, so you wouldn't up and panic if you happened to notice it."

Corr's eyes are the eyes of a big fish staring out through the curved glass of an undersized aquarium. Her mouth doesn't move.

The man takes one small step toward her. "I am presently employed by *Pepin et al.*"

Corr does not so much as blink.

The man cocks his head. "From next door, you know." He starts to take another step toward Corr, but then, suddenly, his eyes drop to her hands.

Corr's hands, having lain all knotted up together in her lap all the while that she slept, have let go of each other and are now slowly rising from her lap in a series of pale, truly shocking afterimages of themselves.

They, the amazing pair of hands, cease their ghostly ascent and hover out in front of Corr just barely below the level of her shoulders. Three…four…five empty seconds pass like long, chilly northern nights. Corr's entire body starts to rise the same slow, chimeric way her hands had risen. Her body rises from the beat-up chair in one unbroken movement to stand its tallest, facing the man.

The man crimps his lips and exhales audibly. "I've never before seen anyone…so clearly defy gravity!"

Corr remains. She is an incredible timeless immovable standing stone, until, all at once, she cocks her head and smiles sweetly. "Congratulations. Most people can't see it."

"Whew!" The man relaxes his shoulders by pumping his arms. "What say you warn me first next time."

When he then notices that Corr's sugar smile is fastly fading, the man snappily inquires, "Does the color of that line have a name?" He rotates his upper body around to point a finger at the canvas on the easel.

"It's a mix. No name. Why the gun?"

"That's who I am. A gunman."

"Why are you standing in my studio, gunman?"

"Laura Pepin of *Pepin et al* has instructed me to inform you that someone surreptitiously entered your building last night and removed a number of objects. She would be honored to represent you in the matter."

"Represent me in *what* matter?"

"Laura Pepin is of the opinion that the objects that were removed from your building were not yours to have in the first place."

"Is Pepin of *Pepin et al* going to show me some mysterious pictures, too?"

"I'm sorry, but I have not an inkling of what you were asking there. Do you prefer to be addressed as Correggio Corato or as Corr Cor?"

Corr glares at the man so intensely her eyes draw together till they merge. For the length of her next question Corr is a cyclops. "How is it you know that I am also Correggio Corato?"

"Being able to find out who people really are—or once were—is a major requirement of my business."

"As major as the gun?"

"Truly."

"Does Lawlady know where the removed objects are?"

"We did not discuss that point."

"Then does she know who took them?"

The man shakes his head. He has donned a thin, colorless smile. "That's another point we did not discuss."

"How did Lawlady learn so quickly that this removal occurred? Was she watching from her window? Or did she partake of the pleasures of burglary herself?"

The man is buttoning the coat of his custom suit. "You'll have to discuss all that with her in person." He is now straightening the tails of the coat.

"If you don't know anything, why are you here, Mr. Gunman? Or would you rather be addressed as Sly Redder?"

Blonk! Knocked back on his heels, the man emits a long, ragged whistle of surprise. He is the one with the big fish eyes now. "Pow! That was as impressive as your anti-gravity trick. How did you do it?"

Corr barely grins. "How did I do which?"

"Know my name."

Corr presses the palms of her almost back-to-normal hands very softly to her cheeks. "My getting up from the chair was not a trick. My knowing your name was."

The man begs. "Tell me how it's done."

"No. You should leave here now."

Clinching his teeth and squinting his eyes, the man elbows the gun under his coat. But Corr does not bend the slightest. She points a high, stern finger at the door. The man leaves.

"Of course he left. He had no choice." Corr crudely spits at the door. "One more minute of that scene and I would have had to kick the pissy mode load code out'a him."

The spray of tiny, hardly noticeable particles from Corr's mouth (check the previous paragraph) had a maximum trajectory (before total evaporation) of eleven to twelve inches. Corr has insisted a number of times to a number of different people that her inability to spit accurately and voluminously is one of the whacking drawbacks of her being a woman.

"And no," she sharply appends to her threat as she shoves her fist at the door, "I don't know what a pissy mode load code *is*."

(35) +

"Amass King."

"You're asking what?"

"Ha-ha. Ho-ho. Ho-hum. I have suffered that response five thousand and twenty-two times before. I am not asking anything! Amass King is my name."

Welf raises both of his eyebrows. "A-m-a-s?"

"No. Put two *s*'s at the end."

"Well, then what can I do for you, Amass King?"

"I want to work here."

"Really? That's amazing. Please tell me why."

"Not only am I an excellent worker; my family had a business much like this one in our hometown; therefore, I would already know what to do and how to do it. But far more important is that I wish to spend as much time as possible as close as possible to the artist who lives across the street from *WELF et al.*"

"Corr?"

"Yes, Corr Cor the painter."

"What is your interest in Corr?"

"She is a beautiful woman whose paintings make me weep in deep distress and laugh with ecstatic joy. She is said to come in here frequently. I want to be the one who serves her her tea."

When Welf then proceeds to give the arrogant young man a goodly list of reasons why he works alone in the café, Amass King turns surly. AK's hair is dark, straight, and longish like Corr's; his skin is copper brown in color; and his eyes are the same surprising blue as paleskinned Laura Pepin's and darkskinned Gett Resu's. Amass King's slender body is probably not as fragile as it looks. Welf brusquely escorts Amass King's body out of the café. Again, the proprietor of *WELF et al* is not a small man.

Minutes later, Corr Cor the painter just happens to glance out her studio window and catch Welf Aceicou staring out his café window at her. She returns to her work, but before long she returns to her window. "Welf is over there again—or is it *still*—looking straight at my window." Sure, Corr gets curious. She cleans her brushes and strolls across the avenue.

"What's the story, Welf? Have I not been coming in here often enough for you?"

Welf leads Corr to her table, sits her down, tells her he will be right back with her tea and that he needs to talk with her. When he returns, he actually sits down at the table. Fairly unusual it is for Welf to sit down with a customer, any customer. (Correct, this wise custom of Welf's was mentioned earlier.) He sits down with Corr and relates how a man named Amass King had come into the café just a while ago wanting a job so that he could be near to her.

"So?" Corr shrugs like a true celebrity, which she is not, as far as she knows.

"I got a bad take on him, Corr. I think he's trouble for you."

"Hmm." Corr reaches out her hand and lays her fingers on Welf's hairy forearm. "I appreciate your concern, Welf. We'll just have to wait and see, I guess. Point him out to me, please, if he shows up while I'm around."

Welf points.

Corr turns her head to see what Welf is pointing his finger at. A slightly built, well dressed man, a year or two younger than Corr, has entered the café and is coming directly toward Corr's table.

Welf jumps to his feet to confront Amass King.

Corr says calmingly to Welf, "Give us five minutes, please."

Welf doesn't budge.

Amass King stops a mere two feet in front of Welf.

Welf and Amass glare at each other.

Welf growls over his shoulder to Corr, "Just whistle." He pivots on his heels and exits left.

Corr notices her tea. It might be close enough to her preferred drinking temperature by now. Taking a trial sip, Corr gazes into Amass's blue eyes. "Hello," she purrs. "Won't you sit down? Be you Amass King?"

"Hello. Yes, I will. Yes, I am." The man gladly takes the chair that was once Vogs'. Although Amass is plainly excited, he controls himself quite well.

"You would take a job here and serve me my tea?"

As a lark salutes the dawn, the man salutes Corr Cor: "I am Amass King, and I worship your paintings."

"Worship?"

"I would accept a job here, yes, to serve you."

"Whew! I am a big bit astonished and a little bit discomforted, Amass. I don't get all that many direct compliments."

"You don't?" Amass is a bit astonished now himself. He shakes his head thoroughly. "If you say so, it must be true. Yet I cannot see how it could be so, Corr Cor."

"Just Corr is good enough."

"Thank you, Corr."

Corr leans back in her chair and stares frankly at the man's face.

She takes another sip of her tea. "Do you paint, Amass?"

"Not exactly."

"How did you come upon this café?"

The man talks. "I had been trying for a very long time to get your address. No one would give it to me, your gallery included. So I went to the opening of the last group show there—the first showing of your work that you have ever attended in person. I know that to be a fact because I have been to every one of your hangings." Amass is speaking a touch too fast. "And it was certainly well worth my time to go to that last show, for I did and do love each and all of the paintings you hung in it…particularly *A Known And Established Enemy of the People*. Anyway! After the show, I followed you and that gallery guy to your studio over there. Then all I had to do was come back the next day and ask around the neighborhood. 'Yes, Corr Cor lives right there.' 'Yes, Corr Cor frequents that café over there.' Everyone has been very helpful. —Except the guy who runs this place."

Actually, Corr gave *A Known And Established Enemy of the People* to G.J. Horsey Fatts shortly after his first showing at Deathstacks, which was quite some time before the opening of the group show at Corr's gallery that Amass is referring to.

"You followed me home."

Amass replies to Corr's statement as if it had been a question. "That I did. I am resourceful."

"What did you mean when you said you don't exactly paint?"

"I don't paint, but I do make pictures."

"You *make* pictures? How do you make pictures?"

"I have a machine that makes pictures from the thoughts in my mind."

Corr leans *way* back in her chair this time. And this time she isn't examining the man's face. She's staring at the mirror inside herself.

Amass waits patiently. Minutes pass. Welf is over there waiting, too, waiting to show the insufferable Amass King the door again.

At last Corr leans forward and plants her elbows on the table. "Let me do some guessing here, please."

Amass eagerly nods his head.

"This machine of yours turns out realistic yet unrecognizable outdoorsy scenes, in gray-scale, on page-sized sheets of some kind of unknown high-quality paper or paper replacement, in a secret medium."

Amass is stunned. He has arched his eyebrows the same way Welf raised his brows while trying to guess the spelling of *Amass*. Weakly he asks, "How'd you know?"

"One of my secret tricks. Where's Vogs?"

Amass King leans back in his chair. He locks his hands behind his head and cleans the inside of his mouth with his tongue.

Corr does not take this fine opportunity to ask Amass why she didn't notice him at the opening. Or why he didn't come up and talk to her then and there. She yawns and says, "Tell me the name of another painting of mine you liked in the group show, Amass." Corr flicks the tip of her finger against the edge of her teacup.

She waits.

But Amass King never does jump zestfully to his feet to shout, "DREAMING OUT LOUD ON AN UNKNOWN

BED." Nor does Amass deliver from the seat of Vogs' chair, "ENDLESSNESS AGAIN." Nor does he so much as whisper a list from behind his hand: "QUITE VERTICAL...DEATH AND DISAPPEARANCE...WE HAVE HEARD FROM THE CLOCKS AND THEY ARE IN AGREEMENT...BUT IT LEAVES ME AS I WOULD BE IF I WERE THERE..." Or any of Corr's other suggestive/murmurous titles.

As she has a tendency to do in such circumstances, Corr catches a bad case of short-term curly-lip. "You didn't do all of your homework, Chawley dear."

AK fakes a yawn of his own. He gives Corr a cocky wave of his hand. "See ya."

The man leaves the café.

"Of course he left. He had no choice." Corr spits at the door.

Welf comes quickly to her table. "You ok, Corr?" He waits, ready for anything, beside her chair.

"Yeah-yeah." Corr flaps her hands in front of her a few times. She is still glaring at the door. "You were right. He's trouble. And he's a liar. I wouldn't trust a single thing he said."

"What was he up to?"

"Haven't the faintest. The question that interests me more at the moment, though, is who sent him. The words *Judy Blue* keep popping up. But the picture-making machine points to Lawlady...and way off over somewhere to Vogs." To all outward indications, Corr has switched to thinking-out-loud and is no longer aware that Welf is standing beside her. "But Judy Blue wanted those missing paintings *bad*—the paintings that Lawlady knew had gone missing a second time maybe even before I knew it."

Welf looks lost. "Judy Blue?" He scratches his scalp. "Do I know her."

"Oh." Corr realizes Welf is still there. She folds and unfolds her hands as she glances up at his face. "She and I talked to each other in here, a couple of times. You probably don't remember her."

"She's not the woman who you said lives with that guy I was seeing you with for a while?"

"Wow, Welf! Do you remember every single person who comes in here?"

"I remember every single person *you* have talked with in here."

"Ooo! That's real nice and real scary at the same time. You don't, I hope, keep a picture of me in your bathroom at home."

"Just calm yourself down, Corr. If you even just see that guy a block away, let me know right away."

"Aye aye, Captain Captain."

(36) +

"That was two bad boys quick in a row. Yep. And a bad neighbor. And a missing friend. And a very dead friend. And a slimy couple. And a dressy man with a bat up his butt. And a turning man behind the wheel of someone else's truck. And a duo of gallery flakes. And an anonymous global-memory freak stationed out on the street corner with a paper bag over its head. And a sidewalk sitter who's out there, too, forever dialoguing in mono. And an empty house. And an empty beach. And a blue *bicche*. And a spooky painter who talks to herself. And Vogs' *Endlessness* who calls herself Char Wrig and who taught me the word *bicche* and who gave me the address of the *unpopulated* house and, later, a green set of clothes. And—"

"Corr? Can I come in?"

Corr gulps and whispers, "That's Char Wrig's voice! How do I do that? I just said her name, and she promptly called out to me."

It's midmorning, and Corr still has on her robe, her only robe, the blue terrycloth whose many large white spots have darker blue spots at their centers. She stares down at the spots. "And I have on this robe again."

Sounding agitated, irritated, worried, and just plain upset, Corr tells herself, "Yes, I guess my having on this robe is entirely fitting for the next scene to-be. But where be where are the greens? I have to say they probably won't be on Char Wrig's body this time—not the exact same green clothes anyway!" Corr actually checks under her robe. There's nothing but skin and hair and the slightest sweet musk under there. "I took them off in a rush the day that Lise dropped by to tell me about Judy Blue being dangerous to me. What did I do with them?" Corr glances around the studio. "No, I took them off upstairs. So they're probably still up there somewhere."

A brief, memory-refreshing timeline: The preceding absentminded discussion of the whereabouts of the greens immediately followed Corr's noticing that she still had on her robe. The noticing of the robe followed Corr's hearing Char Wrig's voice calling to her from out on the sidewalk. And "Vogs' Endlessness" had hailed Corr Cor from out there in the sunlight just one tiny moment after Corr had reached and magnified Char's name on a disorderly list of atypical personalities who have stepped into and/or passed out of Corr's arena fairly recently.

Fine. That much is easily known. But just prior to Corr's arriving at Char's name on the list, was Char herself approaching Corr's door thinking she was going to just walk on into the studio uninvited and unannounced, the way she did the first time she came to see Corr? (And would that also be just like Char did the day she secretly laid the greens on Corr's bedroom chair? Maybe yes, maybe no on that last question; for it is not actually obvious yet whether Char is the one who left those greens for Corr.) If Char did try the studio's door handle first this morning, she surely found that turning and pushing on the handle did not open the door. The door is locked. Corr has been trying hard to keep her street door always locked, as advised by Welf, since that run-in with Amass King. (Corr chose to not tell Welf about Sly Redder, the self-proclaimed gunman. Welf was also not informed that "that guy I was seeing you with for a while" sometimes carries a gun, too.)

Has Corr taken it into her head that she has no time to run upstairs for a rushed look-around for the greens? It does seem so. She strides to the door and turns the lock. Small and large, her bodily movements have all speeded up. She jerks open the door and turns around and marches away, all in one motion. Zow! When Corr stops and whirls about to face the door, she gets a big hard hit.

"Vogs!"

She shudders and looks down at her hands. "And in walks Vogs." Corr's hands could be squashing an egg between their palms.

She looks up again. "No, it's not Vogs. It sure looks like Vogs, but it's not. It's Char Wrig, dressed in clothes just like the ones Vogs used to wear—exactly like the ones Vogs used to wear, including the umpteen paint stains."

"Ah!" Char looks pleased by Corr's thick, heavy reaction. "Even Corr Cor saw through my disguise. What tipped her off?"

Corr, on the other hand, is looking decidedly displeased. She scowls and grinds her teeth. And her answer? "The head is not big enough. The physical head, that is. The hair's the right color, but it's still not thin enough. And lastly, the facial features are too soft, too female. —But only by a smidgen!"

Grinning like a known and established cat, Char soundlessly closes the street door. Soundlessly? Has Char too been practicing Corr's ghost moves?

Affecting a noble indifference, Corr flops herself down on her padded chair. But the sound of a sudden silly snicker sucks her eyes right back to Char's eyes.

Char says with a simper, "We could always talk again about me pulling your leg, honey."

"Huh?" Corr truly looks befuddled. "What are you talking about now?" Then she realizes that the front of her beltless robe is open.

Then she realizes the fact of the front of her robe being open. She closes her legs, closes her robe, and says with a depreciating gash in her voice, "Have you got another address for me in your pocket?"

"That I do."

Disarmed by Char's prompt and unexpected response, Corr can't say anything back. Her eyes glaze over. She opens her mouth and, eventually, exhales.

Standing tall, confidently loitering, Char just watches Corr. Corr *is* a watchable item.

From a memory ship wa-a-ay out on the ocean, Corr delicately whispers like Necky. "The women change clothes. Char takes up residence in the building, and Corr wanders off down the blocks looking for old or new words of her own."

The smile on Char Wrig's face waxes realer. And then realer yet. Perhaps she is enjoying right now a pleasant remembrance of Corr saying those very words the day that Corr slipped out of that blue-and-white robe as she, Char Wrig, slipped out of her greens—the now missing greens?—right here in this room.

"Boom boom, girl." Corr is off the memory ship and back in the room, her studio. She shakes a finger at Char's eyes.

Char pops back here, too. "Only time will tell."

Corr rotates her head until her face is impossibly horizontal. She then inquires with a sneer that, turned clear sideways, is especially horrible to see, "Is that Char Wrig's habitual response when she finds herself temporarily weaponless?"

"No. That was probably the very first time in Char Wrig's life that she voiced that trite expression." Char is not blushing. Not quite. "Vogs used to say it ever so often and then laugh tumultuously."

Corr reflects for a moment. "I don't remember Vogs ever saying 'only time will tell.' Not once."

"Probably he grew tired of making fun of that aspect of our culture before he got around to you."

"Sounds to me as if he was making fun of *you*, chickipoo. Do you know where he is?"

Falsely Char sighs long and deep. "That is an exceedingly difficult question to answer."

"A yes-or-no question is hard to answer?" Corr rattles her head in disbelief.

"That one is."

"When are you going to give me that new address you brought with you today? Must I disrobe first again?"

"*That* I would not mind at all."

Char pertly strolls over to the overstuffed chair. She locks eyes with Corr and—pip—drops something on Corr's lap. Smiling like Big Old Sun Outside, she leans over Corr and whispers just like Corr had whispered like Necky. "It was nice meeting you again, Corr Cor. I do love your body. Goodbye." Char gaily waves as she exits the building, leaving the door standing partway open again and again.

Corr has not yet looked down at what is on her lap. She picks it up in her hands, yet her eyes remain on the not closed door. "Folded into quarters," she intones, sounding very much as though she is just about to swoon, "the small piece of paper or paper replacement feels indeed nice to the touch." What is Corr doing?

She must have been laboring to focus her memory, because she begins reciting words that Vogs said to her on their last outing, while they were discussing the pictures that Laura had shown him. "...rocks, flowers, grass, trees, cliffs, caves...lots of detail...if the light was from this planet and not merely constructed, it would not be the normal light anywhere on this continent."

Corr's eyes are closed. Corr's eyes are open and looking down at her hands.

"Pretty blue ink," she mutters, machinelike. Clearly Corr is disappointed. "On a sheet of rice paper stationery." Her temper turns to acid. "Four dumb integers and two lousy words!" Corr crushes the paper in her hands.

Shrilly, she shouts at the cracked door, "Why just another *address*? In common blue ink on old-fashioned paper? Why not an otherworldly outdoorsy scene in mysterious gray-scale? No, that would have started hooking things together! Things just might have begun making sense to me!"

The four integers and two words are "5963 Scenic Drive."

(37) +

"Scenic Drive? Where's that? It *must* be around here somewhere." Corr is bent way over in her bedroom closet searching for the greens. "No, I now believe that this is not the place to look." She tosses one last shoe over her shoulder. Is there significance in the fact that this final shoe is a member of the only pair of shoes in the closet that is not forevermore marked with paint? "Little to no chance is there of me finding 5963 Scenic Drive in here. Or of me finding The Ghoulish Greens in here, either, it would seem. Yea, it do does seem someone has stolen the outfit from me. Was it the same person who left that verdant ensemble here in my chambers in the first place?" Corr stands up to exit the closet and—bonk!

"Ooo!" she moans. She banged her forehead against the sharp edge of a sideshelf. Her eyes draw together as they roll upward in a vain attempt to see her forehead. "Am I bleeding?" More mindful now, Corr slips sideways out of the closet and fumbles into the bathroom.

A song from somewhere outside the building can be heard coming in the bathroom's little double-hung window. The lower sash is raised several inches. The song is in the middle of a prolonged high-pitched cry that gradually rolls over and falls into a lamenting male voice. "...I-I-I-I-I-I-I-I touch your hair, and it's not there. I-I-I touch your tit, and it's a pit. I-I-I touch your bun, and it's a hun. I-I-I touch your nape, and it's a cape." —What! What happened? The song just stopped, all at once, coming in the window. Does it always end that abruptly? *No* seems the best answer; for that sudden silence is followed by this loud nasal yell: "Baby Boy! Keep your wits about ya!" And *that* be the end.

"No sign is seen of the defining red." Corr has examined her damaged head in the sink's mirror. Her forehead is not bleeding; it won't suffer any ugly swelling either.

She lays one hand caressingly over her injury and steps to the window. Lowering her butt while keeping her back ultrastraight, she pushes her puckered lips into the open crack to reacquaint the outside world with a garden-variety truism that is ever so easy to forget. "Life is a shallow pond."

Corr rises to her best height and returns to the sink. "*Gainst*." Apparently she has heard that song-from-the-outside before and knows its title. "That's *Against* shortened, I presume. Had it been up to me, I would have called that stinking ragbag *Somugly*, short for *Some Ugly*. Song writing is like tying your shoes one-handed with your eyes closed: some people get good at it, but certainly not everyone does."

Corr suddenly turns her head to blink at herself in the mirror. "Wow! I remember Scenic Drive! Wow!" Her arms shoot out to her sides. "Double wow! Triple wow!" She blinks her eyes at herself several times while her arms metamorphose into glider wings. "Wah-h-h-hatchy-y-y!"

Ten windswept seconds later, Corr interrupts her gliding-without-moving to beam at the mirror. "I even remember 5963 Scenic Drive."

She does not return to her pretend gliding but twirls merrily on that spot before the mirror. Corr is often a twirler. But soon—"Too soon! Too soon!"—her spinning begins to wobble, ominously. "Help! My brain has turned into a quagmire!" She grabs ahold of the sink and barely manages to shut down her off-center twirling without falling to the floor. The porcelain of Corr's bathroom sink is so chipped that most every morning she makes out a different fantastic landscape on its gray and white and black and brown surface.

Corr is unexplainably breathless. "I was going to say that 5963 Scenic Drive is where Vogs' parents live—or lived." Corr turns away from the sink...yet still holds on to the sink with one hand. "But Vogs had no parents! He was raised without a mirror. And even if he did have some parents once—as Lawlady might have been claiming—how would I know where they lived before they died if Vogs didn't even know himself?" Like a lone sheet of toilet tissue dropped from on high, Corr collapses face-first to the floor tiles.

A long, yellow-greeny, uninhabited minute passes silent through the room afore Corr musters the strength (read *motivation*) to raise her chest from the cool floor. She turns over and very slowly sits up on the bathmat. She sits up straight and draws her robe tightly about her. She closes her eyes and crosses her legs on the woven vegetable-fiber mat.

"It is a puzzle like another...it is a puzzle like another...it is a puzzle like another..." Corr is faithfully pronouncing each well-worn word. She stops speaking. She turns her head and opens her eyes to peer out the bathroom door and into her bedroom. "Necky?" Her calling his name does not mean that Corr is thinking she heard Necky approaching. She is probably remembering something, remembering her and him doing something together. She closes her eyes again. "I can see a soft light shining in the night. It's a front porch light. I'm sitting in the dark on the curb across the street from that porch, watching the light. Someone is sitting beside me on the curb. It's

Necky, I think. He's whispering even more whisperingly than he forever whispered. What is it he is saying? I'm not sure. I can't quite hear his words. Why are we here? What are we doing? I am now making out the small silvery shapes under the light on the porch—the numbers 5, 9, 6, 3." Corr's eyes pop open to reveal that she is bouncing back and forth between sharp awareness and a dream state. Her deep, regular breathing may be the only thing preventing her from falling clear away from the world-as-we-all-know-it. Her mouth opens and produces a vibrating sound that is startlingly similar to the warning sent out by the tail of a cottonmouth. Her eyes close, close tightly. "Necky had secrets. Some of them he told me. Some he didn't, like his associating with those two slimes who live down at the beach. Vogs had secrets, too. But his secrets always impressed me as only smiles and gestures from afar. 'Half of this and half of nothing,' as the old saying goes. I could have been wrong about that." Corr drops back flat on the floor with her arms hugged tightly to her sides. Her legs have uncrossed. Her eyes are still closed when she barks up at the ceiling, "Everyone had secrets but me!" Corr's robe has parted, and the front of her body is exposed from her head to her toes, except for her arms.

While Corr did allude to "those two slimes who live down at the beach," her mention of them might prove to have been insignificant. Her bid to forget Calo Colm and Stiff Wind forever has been mostly successful up until now, and Corr may never think of those two again.

Suddenly Corr jerks her head savagely to the side. "What was that sound?" She forces her ear against the floor. "I locked that door—so there can't be anyone downstairs!" Her eyes flip open. "Ho! Why am I not understanding that not everyone can be stopped with locks? Didn't I just lose the entire, priceless contents of a well locked storage room?" She snaps her head this way and that. "Or *did* I lock the door downstairs? Did I even close that door after Char Wrig wiggled herself through it and out into her pear-son-all chaos?"

BIGUM BOXSE.

The door to the street is not only not locked; it's wide open and a big man is standing in the doorway, staring into Corr's studio. The man all but fills that good-sized doorway. On the front of this oversize man's pullover shirt is BIGUM BOXSE, spelled out in squarish red letters that are individually outlined with dark blue. The shirt itself is, of course, white. He speaks. "Suit yourself, missy; but I don't think it is safe to just leave your door hanging open, even in the daytime."

Stopped, nervously waiting on the bottom step of her staircase, clutching her closed robe with one hand, patently not sure what to do next, Corr takes the offensive. "So what's that to you?"

"Nothing. Nothing at all. Just trying to be helpful."

"What prompts you to call me *missy* when you're no older than I am?"

The man snorts good-naturedly. "I'm much bigger than you."

Corr catches the involuntary giggle before it bubbles up out of her throat. She takes a few tentative steps toward the door. "You certainly are that, yes. Is that your name on your shirt? *Big Box.*"

"Wish it were." The man grabs the tent-sized shirt to pull it out from his body and gaze down at it. "BIGUM BOXSE would make a good name for me." Out of his mouth comes a high, faraway laugh. He hasn't budged from the doorway. "But it's the name of the company I work for."

"Humm." Corr purses her lips and nods her head. "Oakydoaky. If you don't slip up and tell me your real name, peewee guy, I think I can call you BIGUM BOXSE. I'd be happy to do so. And it will always be in all-caps. Now tell me what you are doing standing there halfway into my home."

The man in the doorway throws a thick thumb over his shoulder. "The truck out there."

Corr tries to see around him. Glimpsing just enough painted metal to make a positive identification, she says, "Yes. There is a truck outside." Somehow she made that simple and flatly delivered retort of hers sound both wondrously clever and deathly cutting, with just a little I'm-your-buddy mixed in, too.

"I have a whole bunch of tall, wide, skinny boxes for you."

Corr scratches her temple with one fingernail. "Tall…wide…skinny boxes?"

"You know, like mirror boxes. But it's not glass inside these boxes."

(38) +

"Who sent them?"

"Don't know. My assignment sheet said to load the boxes and deliver them to Corr Cor at this address. Are you Corr Cor?"

Corr flaps her hand to tell the man to move aside. He does so, and she strides on by him and out to the rear of the truck. The door is up. Corr looks in and sees tall-wide-skinny boxes queued belly-to-back for the entire length of the cargo space, while several even taller and wider boxes stand strapped against the other long sidewall.

"Behold! What's this?" Below the delivery info on the label of the closest box—and only on that first box, as far as Corr can see—is a little pencil drawing of a horse head. Corr stands motionless at the tail of the truck with her hands dangling at her sides. She is staring long at the box label.

BIGUM BOXSE had stopped six feet behind Corr and is waiting there quietly. He apparently figured out in time that he had best not break in on her thoughts.

Time is passing. Empty, borderless time. All movement in the local world has ceased.

Corr suddenly reaches out and covers the drawing with her hand. "It's not believable. No. Someone wants me to believe that it's true, but it is not! G.J. Horsey Fatts did not draw that horse head. The pencil lines are stupidly wrong. Yes, Horsey knew that I had them: he walked right into that upstairs room before I started keeping its door locked. But Horsey did not tell Judy Blue, accidentally or otherwise, where I was keeping them. And Judy Blue did not then come here and steal them. And Horsey did not grab them away from Blue and return them to me here today."

BIGUM steps to Corr's side. He is more than a foot taller than she and a couple of feet wider. He lowers his mouth nearer to her ear and gently confides. "I heard what you said, but I don't understand any of it. Should I start unloading, or should I take the boxes back to the warehouse?"

Corr glances over her shoulder at the neighboring building, *Pepin et al.* A quality similar to but not the sound of sadness resonates in her voice. "I'm just trying to put two things of equal reality on the same spot at the same time, BIGUM. Don't worry about it. There's nothing to understand. Yes, let's unload them."

"You're going to help me unload?"

Corr perks up. "Why not, big boy? I have carried these very same contents into this very same building and up those stairs before. And that time I was all by myself." Corr pushes up the sleeve of her robe to show BIGUM the glowing flexor muscle of her upper arm. "See this?"

A happy child is laughing. BIGUM pretends he is much too scared of Corr's muscle to touch it.

39

Corr yawns and snuggles up to BIGUM with a meow of sleepy satisfaction. "Tell me a story," she says like a lazy, old, deep-rooted tree sighing in the wind.

The eternal bed sure looks smaller than it has ever looked before, almost certainly because BIGUM does not wholly fit on it. The bed's lack of supernormal size is all but counterbalanced, however, by the bed's being extra attractive today. It has been made with nearly new crimson sheets; and one of the pillows—the one that Corr is using—is wearing a fresh, newish, yellow-on-pink case.

BIGUM carefully turns over onto his back. Already he has told Corr about the man he knows who builds doors and door frames out of steel, and now she wants a bedtime story. BIGUM gathers up his extra-large hands and puts them under his head on what used to be Vogs' pillow. *This* pillow will never ever have its case changed, not as long as Corr is calling the shots. BIGUM's head on Vogs' pillow? Vogs had a big head, but it wouldn't compare to BIGUM's. Welf Aceicou is "not a small man," but BIGUM is *real* big. "Well…ok. This is a story that my mother told me every night as she tucked me into bed."

Corr and BIGUM worked well as an unloading team. All the boxes are up in that room. They are not unpacked, though. Corr didn't want BIGUM to see what was in the boxes. For his own good, Corr didn't want BIGUM to know what is in the boxes.

"I memorized every word of Mom's story, and I repeat it to myself—now that she's dead—every night when I go to bed, just before I go to sleep."

"'When the mind temporarily escapes the prison it has made for itself.'"

"Huh?" BIGUM is real surprised by what Corr just said. "You must be a mind reader, Corr. That's what my story is about."

"Going to sleep?"

"No, not that!"

"The mind escaping the body?"

"Yeah! Exactly."

"Tell me it, BIGUM. Please."

"Remember, Corr, these are Mom's words, not mine. And remember, too, that I will fall asleep immediately after I finish the story."

BIGUM prepares to tell the story. And to go to sleep.

"A man asks, 'If the mind creates its physical body from day one, how is it that after the mind escapes at death, the body is still lying there?' A second man—a wiser man?—answers, 'Ah! It seems to me that you are presenting two viewing points as if they were one. The body that the mind created *does not* continue to exist after the mind has departed. The body that does continue to lie there after its death has been created by the perceiver, which is another mind, a mind that is still associated with a body of its own.'"

A profound hush holds the room. Dead quiet are the two occupants of the bed. Neither so much as twitches a nose.

Until Corr explodes. Air explodes from Corr's mouth.

She's happy. She's nearly laughing. She says, "You did a great job of telling the story, BIGUM! I must say, however, that was one very strange choice for a bedtime tale." Corr props herself up on an elbow. "Tell me, please, about your mother."

But BIGUM, having done his daily duty and more, is sound asleep.

40

True, BIGUM cannot stretch out fully and still have his body altogether on Corr's bed. But when he's lying on his back with his hands up under his head, as he is now, there is more than ample room left on the bed for two people of Corr's size. These two people would have to lie real close alongside BIGUM's body, one under each of his arms.

Corr is soon fast asleep in the slender *7* on BIGUM's left. She is dreaming another zigzag dream out loud. Listen to her.

"I have said this before... No! Hold it! Welf was there! I was sitting at my table in the café, and Welf was standing beside me thinking I was talking to him when I said that Amass King's lie about his having a mental-picture machine pointed me directly at 'Lawlady...and way off over somewhere to Vogs.' But I'm thinking now not of Lawlady and Vogs but of Lawlady and her fabled clients, the would-be parents of Vogs. Likewise, the theft of Vogs and Necky's paintings from my upstairs room points right at Lawlady and her newly acquired man, Mr. Gunman, alias Sly Redder. Poor poor Judy Blue. She so wanted those *missing* paintings, yet someone beat her to the punch. But—say hey!—the paintings are now back in my building and darling JuBu has 'nother chance at them. Oops! There it is again. Several times lately it has suddenly occurred to me that *passion* has too many definitions. The most scrumptious definition, *sexual desire*, my personal favorite of all the definitions, is always way down near the bottom of any list. *Who? Who? Who?* The flashing question at the moment is *who* boxed up the paintings and shipped them back to me. It is a puzzle like another. And I must soon go in search of 5963 Scenic Drive. If and when I find the house, I'll saunter up onto its porch to closely examine the four small silver numbers— while I'm knocking on the door. And a very old couple who both look exactly like Vogs will answer the door. I'll gasp. And they will say to me, 'Won't you come in, dear? Vogs is upstairs waiting for you. He caught his little dog in the wringer, but he's ok now.' I will remain silent. Perfectly quiet, I'll turn away from the two and tiptoe off their porch and float soundlessly down their cobblestone walkway and mindlessly wander away from 5963 Scenic Drive. And where will I go this time? I'll try again to wander on the wandering road, even though every time that I've tried it before, the double wandering made me sick to my stomach. Everyone thinks of themselves as a box of goodies. Everyone *hopes* they are a box of goodies. Everyone thinks they are safe in the world because they are a box of goodies. Me? Meself? I kind of missed out on the world. I'll be lying on my deathbed sneezing and hacking my last gig, and I'll still be waiting for *my* turn."

End of dream.

Did BIGUM wake up to hear any of Corr's curiously snaking dream? No, he slept right through it. "I wake up when I have slept exactly eight hours. And not a minute before," he told Corr the next morning after precisely eight hours of sleep.

BIGUM, while proudly describing this indestructible sleeping habit of his, couldn't take his eyes off the painting of Corr hanging on the wall. It's that painting Horsey did and then gave to Corr.

(41) +

"I'm trying to remember time and space in my infancy. I keep seeing the two as one then. When did they become two separate concepts for me? When did they split off into love-of-space and disdain-for-time?"

Never before has Corr intentionally overheard a conversation from another table in the café. Today, she is sitting quiet and listening attentively to the man who is facing her back from across the next table behind her.

"—I know, I know! I have heard people talk. I have heard them saying under their breath that they have little need of space, that they have a close and quite satisfying rapport with the daily unfurling of time. Their beat-down life is not my concern."

The man is talking about space and time to the woman sitting directly behind Corr, sitting nearly back-to-back with Corr. Why is Corr listening to this man? "His voice surely gives me a chill." Is Corr purposely not remembering that the last person she heard using the phrase *love of space* was Vogs, their last time at the beach?

The woman at the man's table is speaking now. Corr listens hard.

"Curses!" In hushed tones Corr says down at her tea, "Her words were directed away from me; so I didn't catch any of them."

Therefore it is unknown to Corr whether the man will be continuing with what he was saying or whether his next words will be in reply to whatever the woman said.

"If life is a hunt," he proclaims with ringing words, "it is much more agreeable to me to be hunting in space than in time. I'm not talking about outer space, mind you. Space for the hunt can be discovered on mountainsides, on any urban street, in bedroom closets, under a weeping willow, anywhere in all the salty water of the oceans, or at the very bottom of an abandoned mine shaft with a shabby moon shining straight down the rugged shaft at my face."

It's the woman talking again. "Mumble mumble mumble waxing mumble mumble mumble mumble behind mumble."

"She has a sweet voice." Corr smiles in her frustration. "Still, the only words I picked out were 'waxing' and 'behind.'"

"Can you hear me clearly now?"

Corr bounces on her chair in surprise. "What?" She throws her face over her shoulder. The woman is turned around on her chair and staring straight at Corr.

Corr is always tougher-than-thou in the clutch; but today in the café, she is thoroughly humiliated. With her head down, she gathers up her personal stuff, which is next to nothing, and heads for the door. She trips over the man's foot and falls clear to the floor. The woman springs from her chair like a cougar and lands on Corr's back all teeth and claws. The man stands up and starts barbarously kicking Corr's ribcage. Over and over again he kicks Corr. Bones are breaking, muscles are being torn loose, skin is ripping, claws are sinking deep. Dark green blood has begun to trickle from Corr's mouth.

"This is another of the definitions of *passion*, not one of the definitions I particularly care for, but one that I apparently had to remind myself of." Corr wipes the brush clean. "I hope Welf never sees this painting. Violence in his café? Unheard of! Even this made-up scene would upset him, hurt him to the quick, maybe even do him eternal harm."

Corr backs up to her tall steel stool and sits there on it studying the painting. "The scene is not real, though. Look at the faces of the man and woman. Their faces are not ugly, cruel, horrible. Their faces are transparent. Look, it's like the consciousness of the man is out for a break. 'I'll be back shortly,' he says to his body as he departs and leaves his body to its grim, ironfisted task. Or in this case, *ironfooted* task."

Corr's shoulders sink to her hips. "'The scene is not real, though'?" She crosses her wrists. "Yes, I said that. Was I referring only to the scene that I painted? Vogs would, of course, say that all scenes are unreal. But that's not quite what I'm asking myself. How can I-me-this-person-here believe in ugly, cruel, horrible violence? How could I believe in anything but the otherness of the grand plane and the relativity of all things human?"

So suddenly does Corr start laughing that she nearly chokes. She laughs so loud and hard that she all but forgets she is sitting on a stool and leans back. "Surely so! Certainly so! I am laughing at myself, at my pomposity. Certainly so."

Laughing she is, yet a genuine tear or two can be seen in each of her eyes. "Surely so. All I need now is for a bunch of doors to permanently open in my head, like Vogs said a series of doors opened for him. Would they be doorways to that coherent yet inconceivable new world he spoke of? *New world* sounds silly and oldfangled, not at all like something I'd think of as coming out of Vogs' sometimes sage mouth, unless he was joking, of course, which he wasn't at the time, I'm sure. But I do think he used exactly those two words, yes. Lawlady told Vogs he was seeing *his* world. So would I then see a different world, my own new world? Would I—"

Aha! The timing was perfect. Speaking of doors opening, Corr can open a door herself, right now.

"Zingo! That sounded like someone struck my door twice with a knobkerrie. If not with a knobkerrie, then at least with a very heavy wooden fist."

Yes, another *insertion* is going to take place. Three short lines leading from a dim background to the dimmer present will be posted here, next in this paragraph. A couple of days ago, Corr came upon a long-dead woman's line drawing of a primeval knobkerrie. Corr examined this drawing closely and has rendered a rather similar short club herself, in paint, today. It's there, lying alone on the floor behind Corr's mangled body.

Corr does not go to answer the door but vividly clutches and wrings the lapels of whatever she has on. "Don't open the door! Don't invite the killer in. Don't move. Hold your breath. Wait. Wait for your brain to collapse into dust from lack of oxygen."

"Corr! Are you in there? It's me."

Corr stops wringing her clothing and brainlessly drops her hands to her thighs. Softly she asks herself, "How many *me*'s in the world do I know?"

No one could have heard her through the door.

"And why have I, the sole resident of this building, never installed a peeping lens in that door?"

Something in or about Corr is preventing her from shifting to a Plan B. Even without "a peeping lens" built into the door, she could step over to the door right now and press her ear to it. She might then be better able to discern the owner of the voice, if *Me* has anything further to say. But Corr does not even approach the door. Perched unstably on her high stool, she begins humming random snatches from easily remembered musical airs. She is another in a long line of high, thin waterfalls that totally evaporate before they reach the ground below.

Hark, a loud scratching sound. Someone seems to be raking up and down on the outside of Corr's door with a steel spike or maybe a large nail. The bizarre sound grows louder, then fades away, entirely.

Corr has not stopped her humming. Was "the killer" at her door produced by her doubting the reality of violence even after she has seen dead Necky?

Now she stops. Corr will hum no more today. She climbs down from her stool and goes directly over to stand facing her new painting with her knees slightly bent. "On his bed." Corr is speaking with understated force. She reaches out her hand as if to touch her palm to the still damp surface. "Dead." Her hand hovers ever so close to the paint. "Yes, someone *helped* Necky die."

Corr grabs ahold of her floating hand with her other hand. She squeezes one hand, then switches and squeezes her other hand. "Someone has also stolen Vogs from me. Someone also stole Vogs and Necky's paintings from me. And the same as an ant could climb up onto my foot and follow my sweet leg right up into my crotch hair while I'm asleep on my bed, just like that ant, someone comes and goes, giving and taking in my building without my knowledge." That was not her long list, for sure. It is, however, as long a list of her perplexing troubles as Corr is into making at the moment. Just the high points. She grabs the back of her hair with both her hands and staggers about the studio.

"And—believe it!—all this has happened since Laura Pepin pranced into my life. No! I should *not* just go ahead and have filthy sex with Her Highness and get it over with. Her clothes alone are enough to make me puke." There might have been a curl of budding humor in Corr's voice. She may be pulling herself out of her hole— whichever or whatever gross image that string of words provokes. "Or! Maybe I could invite the enchanted Lawlady over to my boudoir and have BIGUM waiting for her. Wouldn't Laur-from-far just love that!"

Corr lets go of her hair to draggle her hands from the back of her head around to cover her eyes. "The way things are going for me, yes, she would love it."

A shout trumpets through the door. "We humans are a decidedly lesser form of life!" The doorhandle rattles forcefully. "Let me in!" Apparently *Me* hasn't given up yet. "I'll huff and I'll puff and I'll croak right out here on your doorstep!"

"You know, that does sound exactly like Horsey. What could he want?"

Click. Click.

"What's that? Is someone unlocking my door? Oh no, no, no!"

Corr runs to the door to prevent the lock from unlocking. She's too late. The door has already opened a crack before Corr throws her weight against it.

Through the narrow opening, which Corr is vigorously preventing from growing any wider, a voice that sounds very much like Horsey's says, "Just let me see an identifiable inch of you so that I'll know you are all right. P-l-e-a-s-e, Corr."

"Where'd you get a key to my door?" Corr is hot (angry).

"I made a copy of your key. While you were sleeping one day. Just in case I might need it. Like I just did."

"What makes you think you *just* needed it?" Corr's face is fuming like molten steel right before the incredible mush bursts into flame.

"You have been screaming and hollering for hours, Corr. Your window over there is wide open. Everyone's been hearing you. They were worried."

Corr whispers to herself from high up in the back of her throat, "Horsey doesn't live around here. So who?" She beats her head against the door, just one time. "I remember! Yes! Laura knew Horsey's name to spit it in my face. I'm sure those two were having some kind of thing for a while there. Oh, such a sicky, ugly thought! I'm going to have to gurk up my toenails this very minute."

Corr gets ahold of herself (to a limited extent) and whispers snidely out the crack, "Did the bitch next door bid you come and minister to my failing flesh?"

"She asked if I would check on you. She thought you might hurt yourself somehow."

That had to be exactly what Corr had expected to hear from Horsey; even so, his answer throws her dangerously deeper into a dither. She tears open her shirt and furiously pushes one of her nipples into the skinny opening of the door. "You can think about sucking on this while you're getting your vastly overgrown ass out of here. Go! Go! Away, dark splat on my memory!"

(42) +

When she sighs. When she *seriously* sighs, several heads jerk, as if to turn, as if to glance at that woman, the artist, sitting all alone over there at Her Table. *That woman, the artist,* opens her mouth again, not to repeat her sigh but to speak affirmatively in a strong voice. "Yes, it's me!"

The woman in question had declared her identity quite loudly enough that all three of her words could have been and probably were heard everywhere in the café. But this time not one head jerked as if to turn her way. Even so, the room has become significantly quieter. And who is *me* this time? For obvious reasons, *me* cannot be Horsey again. But it can be and is the very same party who, while Horsey waited most impatiently outside her door, had asked herself out loud, "How many *me*'s in the world do I know?"

Shifting her shoulders on a horizontal line to her left until she is sitting on *Her Chair* at *Her Table* at a forty degree slant, Corr C0r sniffs her nose and then, in the deepest Vogs-iest voice available to her, re-declares, "Yes, it's me." To this she adds without pausing first, "And here I am again, Necky, staring right down the throat of Onerously Severe Perpetuity Uphill Just A Bit From The Sea." She sits up straight, stops speaking in her wannabe deep voice, and waits.

Staring up into a corner of the room, Corr's eyeballs move with the tiniest jerks, as eyeballs might if they were examining themselves in a mirror mounted high in that corner. Or, as it might soon seem, is she seeing herself up in that corner looking down into the room at Her Body sitting on Her Chair at Her Table?

"A previously unknown, nearly life-size sculpture of The Lone Artist has been mysteriously placed on the seat of the artist's chair at her table in the café." Corr has lowered her voice to a whisper. She could be imitating Necky here, but she is not talking to him right now. "And it appears that the figurine can move; for, rather abruptly, it assumes The Thinker pose."

The Thinker pose? Is that a roundabout way of *not* thinking out loud? Will Corr be thinking in a classic mode for a moment?

Tick-tock. Twas a short moment as moments go. Willfully or not, Corr used that little puddle of time to line up the first letters of the last ten words she had said in her Vogs-voice.

Those ten words were "Onerously Severe Perpetuity Uphill Just A Bit From The Sea." She now pronounces the aligned first-letters as if they had formed a single, sayable word: "OSPUJABFTS." Could she be searching for a name for her new painting?

"But aren't five plus five words way too long for an illustrious title?"

Although that last sentence had started out in the same Vogs-like voice that Corr had used to address Necky a short while ago, Corr has still not gone back to talking to her phantomized friend, Necky. And by the time Corr had reached the second *five* in her latest question, her voice had risen from the deep to its everyday sardonic level. She was asking *herself*.

Presto she answers herself, "Ten terms are obviously too many, yo'dull dingbat. Except perhaps in the case of one All-Blue painting."

That woman, the artist, flings up her very bare arms and shamelessly presses the outsides of her index fingers together high up above her head. Eagerly she says/shouts, "The very mention of an all blue non-existent painting inspires a short shout-poem: *Ho, hue! Innumerable shades of blue!*"

Corr lowers her arms and sighs. It's a silent sigh this time. She almost frowns. She rubs her chin while fingering the handle of her teacup. "I have two hands, you know. I might just as well make use of both of them."

From that singularly contextual remark, Corr's thoughts shift to the man who poured this tea. "Welf must be in the know, too. Isn't he over there eyeing me this very moment? Why wasn't he the one to come knocking at my door to see if I was all right? Like he did that other time." Corr takes a long-drawn-out breath with her mouth closed tightly. "But isn't Welf always eyeing me? So, I guess, that doesn't mean a thing. Maybe he was all tied up at the time. Literally, all tied up."

Instead of slyly chuckling at whatever image she has of Welf all tied up, Corr-of-many-pigments soberly shakes her head.

"Actually, I was not in any kind of trouble this morning. I just got myself thoroughly involved in the execution of a violent painting. I'm surprised Horsey didn't recognize that at once and tell old Laura to buzzle off."

Using old Laura as a pivot, Corr's thoughts shift from Welf and Horsey to the two known business associates of Laura Pepin. "At least LP didn't send either or both of her but-misters over to my place. Gett Resu and Sly Redder." Has Corr also shifted her attitude, from *shallowly earnest* to *deeply flip*? "I called those two flunkies 'but-misters' just now because one of the more workable definitions of *mister* is 'a man without a formal title,' and neither of those guys are anywhere close to being worthy of a title like *Her Highness*." Corr snickers viley and laughs gleefully. "Ho-ti-ho!"

She must know she is laughing too loudly. She tries to stop, kind of tries to stop.

People are openly looking at her. So she stands up and raucously informs the crowded room, "Those two are not even worthy of the much homier title of *Lawlady*. GR&SR are mere but-misters! Whoa! Wait! Could they also be butt-misters? Right, they could. Maybe they are. That would explain a few things or two." Corr plops heavily back down on her chair, seemingly absolutely delighted with herself.

"What are you going to call your new painting, Corr?"

Corr's mouth slams shut. What is going on? Welf Aceicou never talks to her about her work. He never discussed painting with Vogs either. Nor with Necky. But Welf just walked right up to Corr and asked her what she is going to call the painting. Needless to say, Corr is more than surprised. "What painting is that, Welf?"

A tad jumpy yet smiling hugely, he says, "The one you just finished."

Curiosity is calming that woman, the artist who is no longer completely alone at Her Table. "What makes you think I just finished a painting, Welf?"

"The same old signs." Smile, smile.

Corr is interested. "Pray tell me about 'the same old signs.'"

Welf clasps his hands together and presses his wrists against his stomach. "Many a time I have glanced out that window over there and noticed that the building across the street is sort of quivering." He is paying meticulous attention to what he's saying. "Then, wow, that whole building starts shimmying and shaking as if it were about to rise above the ground. And a couple of hours later or the next day or a week later or whatever, you come in here all aglow from what is still working in your brain. Well, your building did its magic dance most of the morning, and this afternoon you are in here looking like a bouncing flame. I thought it safe to assume you have finished a new painting. Is that the case?"

Corr is a touch stunned. "That is the case." Is she realizing again that Welf is much more aware of her life than she is of his?

Or was she overwhelmed by his using so many well-chosen words in one string? He no doubt rehearsed that poetic, detailed statement of his a good number of times. "You could have used *buoying flame* instead," says Corr cautiously. "You know, *flamboyance*. But your 'bouncing flame' image was nice, Welf, and in the end probably more visual." Corr rolls her eyes well away from Welf and secretly reactivates her cynicism. She had just looked longer than ever before into his eyes. "In the end though, I am not and was not thinking the thoughts of a bouncing flame while sitting here. I have an ugly mind."

Welf jumps into what is for him very deep water. "Don't we all?"

Corr nods her head in damp agreement.

"But looking from the other end," softer she says, "maybe I am that flame. Maybe even right now. It was a good painting session. It burned deep into every part of me. In time I will undoubtedly see the painting as a marvelous accomplishment for me. And you shared that accomplishment with me from afar."

"From just across the street, Corr."

"Did you know that Necky's lustrous black chest hair had all been shaved off?"

Welf doesn't flinch. Nor, in fact, does he move in any other way. "Hmm." He then risks a glance around his café. No one is looking at him or at Corr. "I think I had better get back to work. Do you want me to bring you some more tea? Or something to eat, Corr?"

"I think maybe I'd like…a raisin knobkerrie. If you're coming back this way any time soon."

(43) +

"Are you seeing me? Do you see me in the universe? Do you see me in the universe at its thoroughly irritating present stage of development? Do you see me in the night? Are you seeing me flying low thru the city? I am, I am flying in the dark just above the stone carpet of the hive— What! I say, did something move over there just now? Did I barely catch sight of a streak of gray slipping nearly unnoticed through tonight's night? —Shore-nuff! For there it is again. —Yikes! Where did it go? Where did that streak go now? And what was it? Ah! There it is again. Oh! I know now! Yes! It's most unbelievable! It's The Shadow! What more can I say. Famous for centuries, though seldom seen, The Shadow pulses in and out of sight, silently, fleetly gliding down the dark avenues and up the alleys and around corners."

All three—The Shadow, she who threw The Shadow, and she who caught sight of The Shadow—are none other than Corr Cor. The Celebrated Explorer of the Exotic, as Corr christened herself at the outset of this latest trip, is out on a hunt for 5963 Scenic Drive. "It has been and will be a much more far-reaching search than was in any way conceivable up in my bedroom closet." Right now Corr is clipping along a dim, sporadically lit city sidewalk at goddess speed.

"Look!" Not skipping a pulse, Corr points a good finger across the street. "That window." She grins like a child getting her picture taken. "Oops! Now it's gone.

"Double-oops!" Corr sidesteps a kidney-shaped puddle of something unidentifiable on the sidewalk.

When next, after only the briefest pause, she says, "I must be clear past it by now," she is not referring to the grisly puddle. No, her eyes have shot back across the street to look for "that window."

"For but a second, a reflecting storefront over there displayed for me not The Shadow but The Filament, an ephemeral, alien body whose transverse dimensions are negligible compared to its length. An outlander of some lesser fame than The Shadow, The Filament is built for speed. Vertical speed. Yet for the duration of that one quick flick over there, the filamentary body showed great agility on this horizontal plane."

Corr laughs and funnels her lips. "Would I be a whisp of a slip or a slip of a whip? Or a—"

Yes, she sees it. Corr stops her flight through the night (and her silly-upon-silly narration of that flight) and steps prudently to the dark curb to stare down into the storm drain.

"A faint, slightly greenish light. Below the grate. Down in the drain. Phosphorescence? Certainly there is not a bulb of the *incandescent lamp* type lit down there. Perhaps the glow is the result of some newly designed food decaying in the presence of the always strange street-stuff."

"Speaking of always strange street-stuff…"

Corr freezes, instantly, totally. That last *street-stuff* bit was not her speaking.

Corr Cor can maybe move like a ghost; she can maybe see better than most people in the dark; but she cannot yet see out the back of her head. Will she or won't she just dare the danger and turn around to see who is behind her?

Corr whispers her *won't* very softly. "Don't look back! Don't say anything to the killer."

The voice, the flawless male voice, says, "Ah, 5963 Scenic Drive is not a quaint little house. It's not a house, either quaint or conventional."

Corr's body immediately starts shaking uncontrollably. Who could know she is out looking for 5963 Scenic Drive? She told no one where she was going. Woe, who is behind Corr in the dark?

As if in answer, that voice says, "And then you travel to the next neighborhood, and you look around. And it's the same as the last neighborhood. That's why I talk like this to myself all day and night."

As Corr spins about, two bright shimmering silver stars splurt from her mouth. "Jonny Facemoral!" She is suddenly smiling gigantically.

It's Jonny all right. He is sitting on the sidewalk barely three feet from where Corr is standing. His deeply set eyes are not quite visible in the dim light. He says, "I don't think Jonny is actually seeing us or even hearing us, love. I think he's all mind."

Corr is mortified by Jonny's words. Instantly and totally mortified. She has not a clue what to do now with her immense smile. She had said those very words herself; she had said them to Vogs while thinking that Jonny would not be understanding her.

"She is just getting past the chilling fear for her life," intones Jonny, "when she takes a strong blow to her solar plexus."

"I'm sorry, Jonny." Corr's face is all puckered up in embarassment. "I didn't know."

Fast she adds, "And I *still* don't know."

Suddenly Jonny's eyes are clearly seeable. They are fixed on Corr's eyes. "Heavenly person, your friend is lost in the eternal night. There is no moon."

Thoroughly confused now, Corr hurries to ask, "Are you talking about Vogs?"

"Good night."

Something forces Corr, against her strong will, to look away. When she is able to look back again, Jonny Facemoral is gone. There is nothing there on the sidewalk but unidentifiable darkness.

Corr turns around, completely around, twice, peering into the night. She wails. "What am I to think? What am I to think?"

Slapping a hand against her thigh, she wanders off in the direction that she was fast-walking before she stopped to gape down into the drain. "Maybe he meant that Dead Necky is lost in the dark of death or something. I can't imagine Vogs getting lost anywhere." No longer is the consciousness called Corr being borne through time by a quick alien filamentary body of great agility. The pace of the present body of Corr is slow, clumsy, self-absorbed. "If 5963 Scenic Drive is not a house, like Jonny said that it's not, is it the moonless eternal night in which a 'friend' of mine is allegedly lost?" In the chilling last second before Corr would have run smack-dab into it, she becomes conscious enough again of the city around her to notice the *big black pole*! She has zero time to stop either her talking or her walking; but she does veer madly to the right and barely avoids a second collision with a post, assuming again that a pole can be called a post and vice versa. Her talking-walking continues as if nothing had occurred. "I can clearly remember remembering seeing a front porch light shining in a dark much like tonight's." What else is Corr remembering? Is she or is she not also remembering that the other time like this time, when she actually ran into a post, knocking herself cuckoo, Jonny Facemoral was conveniently sitting nearby? "I'm across the street from that porch, sitting on the curb beside someone, probably Necky. The numbers 5, 9, 6, 3? Did I construct them myself during the remembering process that I'm remembering right now?" Totally introverted and, hence, completely unaware of what is about to happen to her, Corr steps off the end of the high sidewalk to drop almost a foot to the street. She stumbles and falls to one knee. Yet she remains oblivious to the night and its impedimenta. She's seeing only the numbers in her head. "These numbers—or should I treat them as one number?—could be of little matter when I'm dead." The knee of her pants is torn. She pays it absolutely no heed. She stands up and blindly walks on. "It is important to me that I said '...*could* be of little matter....' Which brings up another matter. I wouldn't want to die while I was cold and shivering and lonely. Neither would I want to die while I was hot and sweating and intimate. I want to be already in transit when I die. So! So I should keep myself always in transit. Right! But would that be like keeping my blunderbuss cocked all the while or like remaining in meditation endlessly?"

After nearly thwacking her head up against a pole and then actually taking a nasty fall off the end of the sidewalk shortly thereafter, what is next for Corr? Where is The Shadow? Where is the nimble alien filament? Where is her ever trusty ghost aspect? Have they all abandoned her? Corr's shoulders are drooping, and she has slowed to taking one step at a time. Every one of her men have left her, too.

Corr tugs on the sleeve of her garment and looks sorrowfully about her. She raises her poor face to a patch of the night sky. Her sad voice is soft like velvet. "This whole city might just as well be empty." She puffs up her cheeks, repeatedly, as if she were trying to inflate a thick-skinned balloon. Her voice has changed from quiet to coarse when she bellows, "For I have glimpsed the secret: All others are my dream!" She sweeps her hand in a grave gesture to include all the others, though there is not a one around to be seen or heard. "They are my dream of life, my dream of my life, my dream of how life would look to me if anyone else were alive, or my dream of how life *could* look to me if I were alive. I am alone."

Please stand by for a moment, a surprise is forthcoming. Corr all of a sudden giggles and slaps her face. Yes, that was the surprise.

"But if I am alone, I must be indeed grotesquely talented to have made all this ugly up. —Hey, girl! Stop that! You're beginning to sound as if you're trying to grow up to be another Vogs. You just misquoted him misquoting someone else. Be your own person!" Corr is laughing now. "Imitations are necessarily second-rate. And faulty. And incorrect. And inaccurate. And disgusting. And pathetic. And enough said."

Watch out!

Whew! Corr just about ran into someone. Maybe she mistook the person for a post.

Corr screeches to a halt to say she is sorry; but whoever the individual be, he or she has scurried on by and vanished in the night before Corr gets out one word.

Corr blindly swallows the half-assembled apology and spits out instead, "Disjointed!"

Looking yet after the evanescent individual, Corr witnesses the proof of the person: the super-thin radiant outline of a human. This ghost-before-her-eyes ultimately disappears into the black, too; yet Corr stares on and on, deep into the darkness, the darkness that just swallowed her chance at having someone to talk to. "I am not alone. I am merely a run-on sentence. I am endlessness."

Corr is both startled and awed by her pronouncement. "It just jumped out of my mouth!"

She cradles her head between her hands and forces her head to rock from side to side. "Is that what I just said? *I am endlessness*? I did, I did all right. Does that make me Char Wrig, the Gal-in-Green? Or am I *just one of Vogs' oft used words*? And how about Nalaen Figg's question about whether endlessness is the reality of my life? Did he see something that I didn't? Something sweet and eternally beautiful hidden in the back of Vogs' brain? And how can I turn this mishmash of unanswerable questions into a painting? Perhaps I should come up with a title first, to use as a guide while I'm creating this exquisite hodgepodge painting. It would have to be a half-witted, artless title. Something like, Life Is Different At Night. Or I could use one of those gargantuan, totally stupid titles: Life Is Different At Night / You Don't Have To Read All The Signs / You Don't Have To Relate To The Jumble Of Colors. Or what about a thoroughly insipid title? Something completely empty, like, My Messy Medley."

Corr emphatically frees her head from her hands and takes a big breath. "Well, I hope you're done with that, my little chickenwicken. 'Something completely empty…'? Indeed, the empty one here is Corr Cor."

Totally disoriented, Corr the hawkeye gawks in every direction, including straight up. "So where am I? And how long have I been standing here spewing forth like a melting fool?" It was Welf who called her chickenwicken.

(44) +

Welf laughed recklessly at Corr's sudden seriousness, a seriousness that bordered on solemnity. He slapped the wall and said, "You are certainly an odd person, my little chickenwicken." No, Welf did not curl up and die right then and there that day, that being the day that Dirty Bird flew into and out of Welf's café. And less than sixty of Welf's seconds later in that same day, after he had safely tiptoed around the corner and escaped from Corr's sight, he said with some pride, "Danger is as danger does." Being a kind man, Welf paid no sorry price for that sliver of trust in himself. But neither did he end up in Corr's bed.

Nor is he out here beating the streets with her tonight.

"Steps! Big steps! Giant steps! Ba-ba steps!"

Yes, Corr's body has started moving through space again. "Only time will tell. Only time will tell. Only time will tell. Only time will rid me of this dingdong dingdong dingdong motto that's ringing round in my head. If I hadn't opened the door for Char Wrig that second time she came to my studio, I would not be stuck now with this pulpy plastic platitude that she said she said that day for the first time—*nor* would I be reeling along like a moron-without-a-map, looking for 5963 Scenic Drive!"

True, Corr does appear to be rambling rather aimlessly now.

"Then where would I be?"

The artiste nods her head with gusto, for she knows and knows the answer. "Home in bed!"

Her neck disappears as her head sinks between her shoulders. "But with whom?"

She covers her ears with her hands as if that could possibly prevent her from hearing her next question. "Or would I be all alone again in my bed?"

Corr uncovers her ears, covers them again, uncovers them and drops her useless hands to her sides.

"That other address…832 FOX…" Corr rambles on in desultory contact with her surroundings. "The Greens materialized on my body as if from out of nowhere immediately after I had checked out that place, Char's first address-gift to me." Is Corr off now on a different Char-based track? "So I'm wondering about the Vogs-like getup that Char was wearing the second time, the last time she came to my studio. Will a painted-every-which-way outfit like that be hanging over my bedroom chair if and when I return to my building? No… Maybe… I might have to actually find 5963 Scenic Drive and go inside, like I did 832 FOX. Which could pose a problem if 5963 Scenic Drive is not a building. No, Jonny said it is not a *house*! So it could still be some other kind of building." Corr blinks her eyes self-mockingly. "Should I then keep my eyeballs peeled for a black building with an unlit sign that alludes to there being an eternal night cooped inside?" Corr presses the tip of a finger against the tip of her nose, for just one second. "Actually that sounds to me like an incredibly unwise course of action. *Unwise* as in *daft*."

She agrees with herself, also self-mockingly, and suggests another first-procedure. "Perhaps I should sit myself down on the sidewalk like Jonny does. He seems to know things that are impossible for him to know. Could his secret have anything to do with his having a larger contact-surface with the concrete? Or maybe he leans way forward and puts his ear to the ground and hears voices from the eternal night. And the voices tell him things, like why Corr Cor is out here staggering around like a dying deer."

How does Corr know how an expiring deer might stagger? Does she have an untold history outside the city?

"How do I know how a damaged deer does or does not stagger?" Corr crosses her eyes, pretending to gaze deep into her brain in search of the answer.

"Eureka!"

What has she found in there?

"My possessing such classified knowledge does not pose a *National Security Threat* after all, not a serious one anyway. What seems arcane is actually lucid. There are billions of ways accessible for everyone to pick up images, both static images and images that change meaningfully with time. And as I have said myself, many times, any manufactured or found image in any medium can be translated partially or wholly into 'a real thing.' Vogs and Necky and I had many, *innumerable* discussions about images turning physical. We talked about if, how, when, and why they turn physical. For example, very early one morning we as a threesome were pantingly deep in passion when Vogs all at once broke free and sat up and sang to Necky and me, 'What about the images that are created entirely in the mind and are never let out, not ever?' Vogs, of course, promptly sang us an answer to his question. 'They turn, too. In fact, mental-only images turning physical is probably *the way* the world is/was made.' His bursting into song like that, his suddenly saying things like that to promote an elevating conversation was the best of reasons to adore Vogs."

Shiny tears fall out of Corr's eyes. She just might turn back now and head for home. But does she know the way to go to get to her building? Or will she need to figure out her return course on the fly? Surely her fine nose will tell her in which direction the unflat sea lies. Will that be enough to start with?

"Words. Words written in unsullied mercury are now materializing one after one before my inappropriately damp eyes. I recognize the words and remember the sentence they are constructing. The sentence is from a discarded freebie seen lying on the ground a long time ago. Years ago. As I passed by the crumpled publication, I furtively glanced down at it and my eyes caught one statement. I didn't understand the line at the time, yet it stuck in my head."

Corr will read the first three words very softly. And once the third word is said, Corr's voice will gradually rise to its normal speaking level. "'Even her dreams are haunted by the longing to know what has happened and to hear some good news.'"

Corr may or may not have had in mind Dead Necky and Adorable Vogs as she recited that short passage from the past. Her eyes have changed their focus; so probably she is not *seeing* the words any longer. Yet she repeats the quotation again and again, carefully, slowly, breathing more and more easily and more and more completely.

"Zuk! Just when finally I'm about to pop into Understanding, a truly nauseating little vision fills my brain." Corr pushes her fists not against her temples but against her jawbone.

"I'm down on the beach. Two hundred pelicans on a death cruise are circling lower and lower above three men standing as a triangle not far from me. One man, obviously distraught, is staring at the skin of my stomach and is saying, 'Looks like I'm gonna have to punch me some holes in that material.' Staring at that first man, the second man is soberly saying, 'Naw! That's what I like about working on a man: you can't just accidentally hammer the wrong hole.' The third man is not staring at the second man, nor at the first man. He is watching the flight of the birds above and is saying, 'I'm a holy man with no organizational affiliation.' End of vision!"

Corr impersonates a dog barfing and does it so well she actually brings up a large portion of the contents of her stomach. Corr has always been unceasingly vigilant about her diet, tea being her only excess; therefore—therefore?—these contents do not glow slightly greenish.

(45) +

These contents do glow, however. The sidewalk that Corr has just personally decorated lies long in a section of town where most every vertical structure is big and tall and, hence, where most of the sky is blocked from sight from the sidewalk, day or night. Nevertheless, the few stars that are not concealed by the towering buildings tonight shine directly on Corr's spew.

Corr takes a moment to study the results of her heaving-canine portrayal. "My curving line of regurgitated matter looks amazingly like a glorious snow-covered sierra as seen from way high in the sky above. This is a sight straight out of the readings of my grade school years. I can all but make out tiny bucolic villages nestling in valleys far below. What I cannot see down on that mountain range, though, is 5963 Scenic Drive. Yah!"

With a slick and a slack, Corr salutes her latest creation and strikes off again. Walking, walking, walking. Is she still looking for that address or is she going on home? She rolls left round a square corner and has drifted on by a lofty building or two when she glances up. She immediately stops walking. With her head thrown back so far that it's all but pressing against her back, Corr gawks up at a huge sign hanging down over the sidewalk. The sign is not lit. Not at all.

"The sign is old…old and so dark a gray that impulsively I tag the lack of color on the sign's surface with a title straight out of those same grade school years: 'The Deep Gray-To-Black Of The Ancient Night-Worshipers.'"

Corr takes a half-step back to better see the sign. "With determined effort, three words can be made out: DEATH WALKS QUICK." She bobs her head, just once. "That sounds strangely familiar. 'Death walks quick'? I wonder what it means. Why would anyone attach a very large but barely readable sign to the side of a building to hang out over the sidewalk if the sign only says 'DEATH WALKS QUICK'?"

Corr drops her eyes from the sign, straightens up her head, levels her line of sight, and stands very still a few seconds, looking at nothing.

Her head moves. Corr turns her head to the side to study the dark, silent building beside her. "Hmm. As best I can see, tall as it is, this building has no windows on this side. Neither is there a door." Corr is so troubled by the lack of door and windows she shakes her head. "This *is* a spooky looking place." She hugs herself as if she is now feeling cold. "Am I scared? That's not likely. What is there to be afraid of? If this edifice is the home of the eternal night—ha!—with no door and no windows it's not exactly inviting me inside."

Grinning toothily, Corr takes one medium step toward the building. She reaches out her hand in the dark to touch the wall. "Feels like a building."

Corr takes another step, a small step. She leans forward, and softly touches her forehead to the building. "Feels like a building."

Corr hoists the waist of her flowing blouse and balloons out her stomach. Yes, she presses the bared skin of her stomach—not yet punched full of holes—against the building. "Feels like a building."

Corr rotates a full semicircle to face the street. Dropping the hem of her blouse, she holds her arms loosely out away from her sides and gently falls back against the building. Leaning quite comfortably against the dusky wall, she crosses her legs. "If it feels like a building and feels like a building and feels like a building, then I would say that if it is not a building, it must be as different from a building as my hand is from the air."

"Well said."

Fast, as fast as she can, Corr swings her head left to right. That was *not* the "flawless male voice" again. Corr sees no one. No Jonny. No one. She starts to speak, hesitates, then speaks. "There's no one here except me. Who said that?"

"There is not a single place in the universe where one can be alone for long."

Corr cautiously uncrosses her legs and shoves her back away from the wall to stand squarely on her feet. She looks around again, more carefully this time. "Sidewalk to the left…street…across the street…more street…sidewalk to the right." Moving her head and keen eyes in a slow half of a circle, she spots no one.

She confesses in her full voice, "I have always been afraid to say what you just said, that '…not a single place in the universe…' thing. What if it is not true and I have already said that it is?"

"It is true."

"So saidest the enthusiast."

"That too was well said."

"All these compliments!" Corr gets tricky "How might I repay thee?"

"You might kiss my thumb."

"Show yourself then."

"You must turn around again if you wish to see me."

"No!" Corr doesn't believe that. "You're *not* the building."

"Either I am or I am as different from the building as your hand is. You will awaken soon."

"I'm not asleep."

"Would you speak to a building that's behind you, if you were awake?"

As was so recently suggested that she do, Corr turns around. From the ground to well above her head and for ten feet in either direction, she searches the dim surface of the building. "There you are!" Corr hops a couple of feet to her right. She has discovered a thin delivery slot built into the wall only inches below her eye level.

But it is even darker inside the slot than it is outside on the sidewalk.

"All right, you have discovered me. Would you like to come inside?"

Corr does not answer the question. She was moving her ear closer to the slot. For sure, the words are coming out of the hole. Still, they don't really and truly sound as if they are. And if Corr was troubled a short while ago by the absence of a door and windows on this whole side of the building, she must be asking herself now—she is silent but her lips are moving—why is there a little delivery hole on this big blank wall.

"Ah, you have turned quiet out there. If by any chance you are not speaking to me because you are fully occupied at the moment with considering whether you should come on in here, you should hear this first: this is not 'the home of the eternal night.'"

Corr purses her lips. "You heard everything I said?"

"Probably. I picked you up while you were tagging the lack of color on that sign out there."

Corr takes no pleasure in nodding her head. "You most likely got it all then."

Foolishly yet sincerely she asks, "Are you dangerous?"

"Silly question."

"Can you see me out here."

"Not really."

Corr scratches the side of her nose. How does the answer "not really" fit with the recommendation made just a

short while ago that she turn back around to face the building?
"Why are you inside there?"

"I work in here."

"At this time of night?"

"You got it. Just walk to your right to the edge of the building, turn into the passageway there, and take the first door on your left. I'll go unlock it."

(46) +

She yanks on what looks in the dark to be the stout handle for the forbidding door. Nothing happens. She gets the same result when she pushes on the handle. "Try turning it," she tells herself. Corr cannot turn the handle. "Well, Girl-O, whatcha gonna do now?" She glares malevolently at the massive, steel-clad door as if she were attempting to stare her way through it. Wait. A pint-size puff of air has forced its way out between Corr's pursed lips. This wee bit of invisible medium turns (again, the way a leaf *turns* in the fall) tawny yellow. In two blinks of Corr's eye, the yellowish puff has expanded into a mighty, miles-wide duststorm blowing over the desert and ripping the roof off Jerome's cabin. But the storm, if it truly exists, is far removed from here. It too does Corr no good in her battle with the door. Next? She issues herself a sharp order: "Feel around on the surface of the cursed thing." Above the handle and more toward the even darker center of the door, Corr finds a little nob. "Could this be it?" She turns the tiny doorknob and gives it just a little shove. The heavy door smoothly pivots on bearings into the building. Corr steps in out of the night, and the thick, armored door closes by itself behind her.

She, Corr, is standing at one end of a long, narrow, well-lit hallway. Unmarked doors line both sides of the hall. The doors are beige, the carpet is a slightly darker rendition of beige, and everything else is cream. All the doors are closed. Corr is quite alone.

She waits, allowing her eyes time to fully adjust to the brightness of the light.

She starts to take a step but, no, decides to wait where she is. At that same moment, a good stroll down the hallway, one of the doors opens.

Will Corr assume that the person who just came out into the hall is the same someone as the voice who talked to her when she was outside? She cocks her head and says in a raised voice, "You must have really run to get down here and unlock this door and then to get all the way back there and close the door after yourself."

The tall, white-haired person dressed in faded black does not walk down the hall to welcome Corr. He doesn't move at all.

So Corr doesn't move either. Her head is still tilted. She only turns an alert ear more toward that other person.

"You are mistaken, dear. I am not the one you were talking to."

Corr whispers, "The voice is different all right. This one is more pensive."

She raises her voice again. "Then where might I find that person?"

"You cannot."

Corr is perplexed and the slightest bit annoyed. "Then why was the door unlocked to let me in?"

"A coincidental oversight."

Corr wrinkles her nose. She raises herself up onto her toes. Her hands squirm at her sides.

She drops back down to stand flatfooted. She has forcefully fisted her hands to quiet their agitation. "Why is that DEATH WALKS QUICK sign out there?"

"If you must know, the sign is a mystery to us all. You are perhaps aware that you were at the rear of the building. The main doors are on the opposite side of the block from the sign.

There are many groups working out of this building, and not one of them knows why the sign is back there. It is an unsolved puzzle."

"Why can't I see who I was talking to?"

"Come to the main entrance midmorning tomorrow and ask your question at the information counter. Good night."

Corr quivers like clouds do sometimes. But she does not yet turn to leave. Earlier in the night Jonny Facemoral had dismissed her with the same farewell. "Good night," said Jonny and something beyond Corr's comprehension had forced her to look away. "Good night," says Corr with a faint tip of her head and a clever swoop of her hand for the unyielding figure still standing hand-on-door way on down the hall. Cruelly she adds, "Me thinks the sign is meant for you."

(47) +

Outside again, in the dark again, Corr, for maybe ten long, sour seconds, lingers menacingly within an arm's reach of the utterly obnoxious door. She is shifting her weight from one foot to the other and quickly back again. She abruptly turns and swiftly and stiffly strides right back around the corner of the building to *the rear of the building*, where she stops and stands, bone-hard and ready, facing the slot. She does indeed look just like that age-old drawing of one of the known wrathful deities peering powerfully into a small, silent opening. A thin whistle-like sound sneaks out between Corr's lips. No doubt she's trying to keep her anger under control.

Alone again out on the sidewalk in the night air, Corr Cor pops a question at the slot, a question with the bark of a command. "Can you hear me?"

Apparently not? Not a peep comes from the slot.

Corr waits. Corr waits.

Corr can't wait any longer. "What did you expect, you acerbic heap you?" No, she was not addressing the slot again; she has turned on herself, to scold herself. She does not slap herself, however, as she did earlier on while giggling. She is far from giggling now. —And some time ago, didn't she slap her face in her great sadness and make Jerome's eyes blink in disbelief?

"Really!" Deep loathing dyes dark each and every word as Corr proceeds to tongue-lash herself. "I know you! You were not counting on hearing the voice-from-the-hole-in-the-wall turned tiny and clandestine and answering you by woefully pleading, 'Help me! I'm being held prisoner in a mail closet!'" Corr bows her head as if she is now a humbled person—ha!—and covers her eyes with the palms of her hands. "Nor were you anticipating a fuzzy, patronizing voice that would mumble-grumble to you, 'At least you got out with your life, my child.'" Corr pounds her foot on the unseen sidewalk, pounds it hard, like a pile driver driving its message into stony ground. "What you were actually wanting to hear, my dear-aah, was a scheming voice, fairly dripping comic intrigue, *hissing*, 'The sign's being up there is why I'm pretending to work in here. In reality I'm an investigator for the…'" Again Corr pounds down her foot. "Righto! *That's* our Loco Lacuna!" Her recent brief reception just barely inside the skin of this building must have been a big disappointment for Corr. Or a terrible affront.

She stands motionless with her shoulders hunched. Aye, the hands are still covering the eyes.

Stamp! She stamps her other foot and grumbles theatrically, "Deprived of purpose, of hope, of enthusiasm I am."

She uncovers her eyes but then stands quite motionless again.

Her mouth opens.

"To remain utterly still." Corr is speaking in a low tone as if she were hinting to someone offstage. "To remain utterly still and transparent for an eternal moment."

Suddenly she begins to spring about, supposedly dancing. And while she is performing this sharp, savage dance, she says in that low-and-aside tone, "To re-materialize in an eternal instant, to force the not pliant body to dance a lively jig in triple time to loosen that body and clear the mind."

She stops her dance. Her body may be looser and her mind clearer, but she sounds no less discouraged and irritated with herself when, next, she speaks up and tries to explain away the voice-from-the-wall phenomenon.

"It was probably just some weird maintenance employee getting five minutes of deviant amusement from an unsuspecting passerby during the graveyard-shift's lunch hour."

Corr starts to huff off into the distance but stops short. "So what was the address?" She scratches behind her ear like many a dog has done. "Me does think I will just have to scoot around to the front of the building and see."

She skips back to the corner of the building, zips left around the corner, and skips blindly on by *the bad door* to the next corner. There's a bit more light here on this corner of the building than there was on the sidewalk at the rear of the building. The black-on-white signs high on their skinny pole read "Scenic Drive" and "Jurnor Mandst Way."

Corr backs her fine tailbone up against the sign post to stand erect with her hands hanging slackly at her sides. What is she doing now? Evidently she is performing a mental approximation—no easy feat in the dim—of the distance from the corner that she is standing on to the entrance of *that* building. Having completed her estimation—or whatever else it was she was working on—she closes one eye and then the other. She's not using her hands to cover her eyes this time. Keeping both eyes tightly closed, she proceeds to walk easily and unerringly down Scenic Drive to the front-center of that building, where she comes to a halt, pivots exactly ninety degrees, and opens her eyes. The address is right in front of her: *5963 Scenic Drive.*

"Gotcha!"

With its wide, shallow, heavily tiled roof being supported by four granite columns that stand on a polished marble porch that serves more than one elegant door, the entrance structure for 5963 Scenic Drive would more than likely be labeled by the guardians of historical and architectural name usage as a portico. But who knows. Each and all of the six tall doors (three sets of two, minimally shown off by tiny floods set into the marble) are a symmetrical mix of gleaming yellow metal and squares of thick, faceted glass.

Corr tries the doors, the six of them. "Locked."

She spins around to face Scenic Drive. "Drat the workaday world! I will have to wait until midmorning. Which is *hours* from now!"

She leans back her head. "Good night." This sweet goodnight was directed up at those same few stars that illuminated her vomit but which are now shining down on Corr's radiant face.

"Corr's divinely *beautiful* face!"

(48) +

"It's Leaking! / The System Is Leaking! / From Out Of The Old System A New Way Is Born!"

Corr walked around drowsily in the dark for a while, looking for a pigeon-proof place to nap awhile, and ended up out in front of Deathstacks, Horsey's gallery, where she found, facing out at her from the inside surface of the lit window glass just to the right of the front door, a large poster bearing the above three lines of text centered over a wildly bombastic and outrageously colored drawing of a golden egg with artists of every stripe breaking out through its shell. What are Corr's comments on the composition? "Yick yuk!" She's mussing her nose at the poster. "A hatching egg is *not* a leaking system. Get it straight, guys!"

The nodding painter turns away from the window and is about to leave the gallery behind in her search for a place to doze when a patch of blacker black somehow catches her weary eyes. She investigates. In the corner where the sidewalk in front of Deathstacks meets a protruding wall of the building next door, Corr discovers a low, cave-like space just big enough for her. She curls up in that hidden, very dark corner and surrenders to sleep.

Night is fading. Daybreak is near. The gallery's guard is making his rounds. Trudging along his routine circuit, bored to the bovine bone, the guard SUDDENLY spots someone encamped where they are NOT SUPPOSED TO BE. He resolutely stomps over to that closed corner to confront the trespasser, who, he finds, is sound asleep. Seconds into his rough rousting of the vagrant, the guard suddenly stops, backs off, and mutters something.

Sleepy-eyed Corr was just about to punch him a good one. Or, rather, since she is out of her cave now but still on her knees, she would have at least *tried* to punch the guard. She springs to her feet to stand face-to-face with him. She snaps at him, "What you say?"

"You were in a painting." The guard is grinning so hard his lips are white in the half-light from the night-lights inside the gallery. "On *that* wall in there."

While this man has not been acting exactly well-witted, his recognizing Corr from a painting that most people would regard as "anything but realistic" definitely says something positive about his mind. And he even recognized her before she stood up.

Corr prods. "It must have been a while now since you saw this painting."

"Yes, it has…been a while. —But I remember the painting was an *awesome* thing to look at." Had the guard stood there night after night staring at the painting of Corr?

"Who was the painter of this painting?"

The guard stares off into the rising light across the street. "I remember the name—it's a long name—but I don't recall if it was a man or a woman."

"The name?"

"G.J. Horsey Fatts."

"Very good. I will shake your hand."

The man rushes out his hand but quickly retracts it. He's blushing now. He must have figured out that Corr's statement was facetious. She is still up on her toes with her bold face on.

"Why were you sleeping out here?" The guard has jerked back to being *the guard*, although his tone now is far less overbearing and insolent than what one might expect from someone with the audacity to assume such a position, that position being *the lawful interrogator*.

Corr drops down on her heels and smiles without meaning to. "I have an appointment near here this morning that I did not have the time to go all the way home and then come back here to."

"Oh." The guard looks confused.

Not for long though. His face cheers way up, and he asks Corr if she would like to come inside and join him in having something warm and stimulating to drink. "In the staff lounge on the second floor."

Having already checked out Deathstack's current show from outside the glass and having deemed it not of interest, Corr keeps her eyes on the run-down heels of the man's shoes as she follows him in through the door, across the shiny wood floor, and up the stairs. Halfway up the stairs, she Neckys (whispers) to herself, "I dub thee Mean Lips."

Surprised and then tickled by the obtrusively large, red-on-white sign on the door, a sign that states in no uncertain terms: "STAFF ONLY LOUNGE," Corr guffaws softly. Mean Lips looks back questioningly at her. She merely shakes her head and follows him in through this second door.

She glances around the untidy room. "Very nicely rigged out, I must say, sir. Where's the restroom?"

Once she is safely inside the WOMEN ONLY room—with the door meticulously closed behind her—Corr finishes her throwing-up, producing just one round mountain in the sink this time, not an entire sierra on the sidewalk. "Another man with a gun. Just what I need."

She rinses out her mouth and splashes her face and armpits with cold water. "But I could and could and could use a bright cup of tea right now. And that softy couch looked real yummy. But…da da ta da! How about the guy? That guy out there. Yes, another yo-yo packing the troublesome two: the heater that hangs inside the pants and the de-heater strapped on the outside of the pants." Corr is watching herself in the mirror. "Enough now. No more watching me in the mirror." She wipes her eyes with her finger-fingers and turns away from the sink. "I think I'm pretty sure that Mr. Mean Lips is probably not one of those gents who maybe all of a sudden might turn out to have a weird idea or two. That I'm pretty sure of."

(49) +

The granite-gray entrance structure for 5963 Scenic Drive, as described above, looms large before Corr like a terrible purple dream. "I can smell it in my broken and bruised love-bones: this is not going to be a walkabout like 832 FOX."

Corr had set her course for the middle pair of brass-and-glass doors, but somehow she got herself stopped on the first low step of the stone porch. While the entire entrance is bathed in bright daylight, the sun itself has not yet made its way down into the canyon, if it ever will. "Suddenly I fix on Jerome. The lower floors of some of these buildings around here may have never actually seen the sun. And gruesome particulars like that are exactly what made Necky's brother dislike the city so much."

Someone inside the building is looking out at her. Corr nervously waves. The person inside waves curtly back at her, then turns away and disappears in the reflections on the glass.

"Muster your resources, bab-by!" Corr is mustering her resources. "Tote your tough ass on up there! Haul it in the door and right over to 'the information counter' and *say the words*.

Before Corr even ascends to the next stone step, however, someone comes out the left set of doors, walks right by Corr, doesn't speak or even glance at her.

"A regular looking person, a downtown person, a regular downtown person." Corr turns her knob a bit to watch the person walking away.

She yaps a little louder but certainly not loudly enough to be heard by the passerby, who is already shrinking into the distance. "If you put on a certain kind of clothes, I take it, you don't even have to nod to the people you pass." Corr pretends to push a finger up her nostril.

"Just wait one second now! Was that person of the male or female or whatever or whichever or of *any* persuasion?" She pretends to wipe that finger up and down her blouse. "You know, I didn't notice. There is not all that much difference with downtown habitués. Not as far as I can see. They obviously see themselves otherwise—yeah yeah—but doesn't everyone."

Say the words.

"Why can't I see who I was talking to?" Corr rests her wrists on the chest-high edge of the white counter and smiles like a king of old.

The pretty person on the other side of the floating cabinet/counter appears to be standing on a surface several inches higher than the floor on which Corr is standing. That higher person looks at Corr, holds Corr's eyes for just one moment, then returns her own eyes to what she was already doing. *Her, she?* Yes, probably. A tag fastened to the lapel of the black-ash suit says "HELGA."

Corr leans her head over the afore mentioned edge of the counter to more easily read the tag, better known as a badge by the people who use them or require them. Under the big "HELGA," smaller letters say "Helga Helms, receptionist." There is also a line of numbers and wily whatnot along the bottom edge of the badge.

Despite Corr's persistence, Helga Helms does not look up at Corr a second time. The receptionist does speak, though. She says one word and briefly pauses before she says a dozen-and-a-half more words. She has—to say the minimum—a very *noticeable* voice. "You…are the unauthorized person who entered the building last night. Please go to the seventh floor, Room 741."

Such a dense admixture of iron-blue pigment in the voice of an otherwise uncommonly attractive person caused Corr's eyebrows to arch, twice. Even so, she, Corr does not then humble herself and allow her own voice to whine while she is saying back to the woman, "Will I meet there who I was talking to?"

Corr had barely completed her question when all that iron-blue pigment—Zap!—sucked up into one mass and—Zap!—hardened into a glistening blued-steel shaft. So armed, the woman unambiguously instructs Corr, "You are being directed to Room 741 to have your *first* question answered."

But Helga's face remains truly expressionless. And her eyes have not drifted one inch from the countertop since their brief lead-off inspection of Corr's eyes.

Far below the gaze of either woman, Corr's right sandal is rising from the floor.

The dark, dusty sandal lifts itself high and presses its sole to the inside of Corr's left thigh. (It was the right knee of her pants that Corr tore when she fell from the dim sidewalk last night.) What does this rising-and-pressing portend? (*Portend* was used there the same as it will now be used in this slightly crooked fabrication: "That *whop-whop* from Vogs on the beach *portended* serious trouble for Corr.")

Corr curly-lips (used as a verb this time) and grins at the same time. "How might I repay you for your courtesy and humanity, Helga Helms?"

"You can repay me by turning around without making a sound and leaving, either by crawling out one of the doors over there or by slithering on up to the seventh floor. Makes no difference to me which you choose."

Corr stares. Corr stares quite stupidly at the woman whose badge states that she is the receptionist.

Still, Helga's eyes refuse to rise from the flat, sloping, glass-covered surface that separates the two women.

Swallowing what little be left of the convoluted sneer on her face, Corr softly pronounces, "You'll have to excuse my gawking, please. But I didn't realize that anyone in this part of town had a mouth like that."

Even now Helga does not look up. "The mealymouthedness of us folk is a stereotype held on to dearly by the city's riff-raff. You will suffer untold other rude-awakenings if you remain 'in this part of town.' So you might just as well make a rushed decision and leave the building *and* the neighborhood right now."

Corr hears Helga.

Corr did indeed hear Helga. Corr turns away and takes one slow step toward the doors. She takes another such step, pauses briefly, then pivots counterclockwise a quarter turn to address the great empty space of the all-white foyer in a mighty woman's voice. "She may have been a knock-down-jump-on'er beauty at one time, but look at what life in a booth has done to her!" Booth? What booth? Corr thrusts a hand at the high ceiling and keeps that hand way up as she twirls in place. She twirls and twirls and absurdly twirls *in situ*, ultimately coming to a stop more or less facing the info counter. She throws her other hand at the ceiling. "Who is the holder of the wisdom vessel?" Corr's two-hands-up delivery is both powerful and eloquent. "Who is the wisdom vessel itself? And who is nothing but a mad dog on a short chain?" Corr stares tenaciously at her make-believe audience. "In answer to question number three, I offer to you—to all of you over there—Helga Helms, receptionist."

Oops! Helga has a de-heater, too!

While Corr was answering her own hard-coated question, HH had simply bent her knees behind the cabinet/counter, then smoothly straightened back up and quietly laid the latest thing in pistolas on the narrow level strip that runs along the upper edge of the countertop, all without looking at Corr.

Corr sees the powerful shooting iron but shows absolutely no fear of it. "Built in a rage she was! Helga Helms, receptionist!"

Corr may not be showing all that many *smarts* right now, either. It does appear that Helga has a low tolerance for rowdies.

Someone is heard approaching from Corr's right—click, click, click—walking smoothly and precisely toward her. "I'll take it from here on, Helga," says this person in a pleasant, calming voice.

Corr turns unwaveringly away from Helga and says to the beautiful silver man, "Organizations that don't disband immediately after completing that one first chore are a different class of beings."

"I am very *very* happy to meet you, Corr Cor." The silver-haired man, dressed in a silver three-piece and silver shirt and shoes, has stopped before Corr and put out his hand to her.

"You know my name." Corr grins wickedly and puts out her hand to him. "Are you Room 741?"

"That I am." The man reaches his hand out a little farther to close the gap that Corr deliberately left between their hands. Cordially he shakes her hand. "And I would immensely appreciate your coming upstairs with me."

Corr tips her head to the side. "Right now?"

The man tips his head to the side. "When else is there?"

"Hmm. That must be today's point-to-keep-in-mind. Yes, Corr Cor will toddle up the stairs with you."

(50) +

"Were you sounding surprised that I knew your name down in the lobby?"

Corr ignores the question. The man points his open hand to a chair for her to take.

"Because you entered the building through the backdoor last night, we were unable at that time to identify you, Corr. But when you walked through one of our front doors this morning, we were promptly provided with a big part of your admirable history." The man tactfully waits while Corr steps over to the indicated chair before he attempts his leadoff question once again, in a slightly different getup this time. "Were you not aware of this already, even before I said your name?"

Corr dismisses this second version of the question too. She painstakingly checks out the lightweight chair before she sits down on it facing the man, who has sat down on a different kind of chair behind a see-through desk. The stark clarity of the transparent desk leaves the silver man nearly as visible to Corr as she is to him.

Corr sits so silently on her chair she might not be breathing. She is breathing, very softly. Her lips start moving. They're moving the same way they did out by the delivery slot last night. Her whisper is nearly as soft as her breath. Her hand floats before her mouth as if to prevent her lips from being read. "This is certainly the quietest building of this size I've ever been in before. It's hushed as a tomb in here."

The man is quietly watching her.

Corr drops her hand from before her face. To test the acoustics of the room, she zooms an unwhispered reply in the form of a generalizing question at the splendorous man. "Are all of the buildings around here geared up like that?"

The man smiles at her test. He is smiling with his mouth open a crack. "Many of them, Corr. Not all. Some hardcore individualists have held out. Deathstacks, for instance."

The jerky bounce of Corr's eyes tells that she understands perfectly what the man's Deathstacks example meant. She doesn't say so out loud, of course; she says falsetto, "Do tell."

She changes the subject. "Am I to continue to address you as Room 741?"

"That probably won't be necessary. Why don't you just call me Room?"

The man titters at his own pale/frail joke. He watches Corr's eyes.

Why is Corr waiting? Why this delay? Why hasn't she already replied to the man's nonsense? It's not like her to take so long selecting something disgusting to slap back.

The man owns up. "Actually, Reon Stars Renvoi is who I am."

"Pippity pip!" Corr is much quicker to speak this time. "Boy! That's a handle!"

"And it's mine."

Corr casts her eyes all over the man's chest. "I would have known your name right off, as well as your assigned duty, if only you had been wearing your price tag today, Reon Stars Renvoi."

"You must be making fun of the name badges. In this building, badges are worn only by the staffers who normally have intercourse with people from the outside."

"Ahh, I am maybe beginning to understand. These badges replace the sweet looks and smiles and helpful words of yesterday?"

"Only occasionally, Corr."

"Why can't I see who I was talking to?"

"Hmm. That must be today's question-to-keep-in-mind."

Corr harrumphs. "Does that mean that it's going to take me all day to get an answer?"

"Why is this absolutely marvelous painter really here today in my humble office?"

"Well, really, Reon, I came expressly to learn why you dress up like a tinsel ornament. But I've changed my mind. I don't want to know. So why can't I see who I was talking to last night?"

The man laughs effortlessly and draws his eyes away from Corr. "You seem very attached to that question."

"No, I am not attached to the question. I'm trying to get an answer to attach to."

Mr. Silver appears to be busy with something on his desk. But there is nothing on his desk, as far as Corr can see. He asks without looking up. "Corr?"

Corr's face inexplicably brightens. Her smile is odd but delightful. "Yes, Reon Stars Renvoi?" From her toes to her crown, a soft white aura emanates from the body of this "absolutely marvelous painter."

The man does not witness this marvel. His eyes are yet down on his desk. He asks, "Do you see life as an aging process, bodily speaking?"

Corr's sublime radiance vanishes, instantly, completely. She just sits there, looking strange and eerie and very much out of place on the skinny chair. *Strange Face.* Corr's present facial expression harks back to the only face in a painting that she did in two days when she was eight, her "first real painting." *Strange Face* is/was its title, that being the sole comment of the first person, besides Corr, to see the painting. Today, that painting stands on a shelf inside Corr's closet, behind a stack of folded, seldom-used, nice clothes. Corr's mouth opens. It opens much wider than it would if she were about to say something. Her mouth closes as her eyes float away from the man. This will be the first time since she entered Room 741 that Corr answers without open mockery in her voice.

"No. I tend to look upon life as a time for the draining off of all the nasty habits that I've accumulated. If I were watching my body, I wouldn't have a choice: it would just get older and older. But since I am watching my mind, I have a clear choice: either I am happily emptying the dark pool, the pool of my revolting habits; or I am stupidly filling it even deeper."

The man has looked up at her. Tersely he says, "Yes, I recognize those words. You knew Vogs well, didn't you?"

Good thing Corr was sitting down. She is thoroughly taken aback at the man's question.

She musters her resources. Still, it is in a faraway voice that she says, "Did Vogs say that? Those were his words?"

The effect of her mustering finally snaps in, and Corr tightens her attack. "And how would you know?"

"He did and they were. Vogs was way ahead of you there, Corr."

"I'll repeat myself. And how would you know?"

As if he had not heard Corr, the man says, "The question about whether you see life as an aging process was a test."

Recognizing that repeating herself again would serve no productive purpose, Corr gnarls, "Did I give the correct answer, teacher?"

"Your answer was fine. I would, however, have preferred it not to have been a quote. You are said to possess an original mind. I would like a taste of that mind, to better appreciate the nature of its originality."

The tigress purrs. "My mind is not the only thing about me that is original."

"I am aware of your legendary sexual prowess, madam. Your ingenuity in bed—or *wherever* you find yourself—is one of the few remaining *collective wishes* of our times." Could this man be speaking candidly? Probably he is not. Probably he is taking sick pleasure in rubbing Corr's face in her own dirty ego. "Nevertheless," he goes on to say, "you needn't waste your time trying to scare me with the *unparalleled* talents of your body. I have lived longer than my compulsion for diddling."

That was an unexpected turn. There is a pause in the conversation.

Corr is not as thwarted by Reon's disclosure as he may have hoped. By opening her heart to the stranger, she shoots him in the groin. "You're not going to start bawling on me now, are you, sweetie? I'll take off my blouse if that will make you feel any better."

Now it is Reon who is not as wounded as Corr may have hoped. He shakes his silver-topped head many times, yet he's grinning sagaciously. "And I thought Helga had a bad mouth. She was no doubt right: she would have needed that pet gun of hers to top you, Corr."

Corr snaps back, "She could have had *two* pet guns and I still wouldn't let her get on top of me."

Before Reon can reply, a wry sliver of a smile slips onto Corr's face. "And you don't have even one gun, Reon from the stars."

This unmitigatedly personal assault apparently does Reon no more damage than Corr's preceding barbed thrusts. Still grinning—with sick pleasure?—he cleverly remains silent.

"You've given me a little test." Corr folds down one finger at a time on her raised right hand. "You've informed me that you don't need my body. You've made it clear that you know everything about my past and that I have no privacy whatsoever in the present. So why can't I see who I was talking to last night?"

Again, Reon ignores *the question*. He merely says, "Char Wrig."

A squirrel will jerk her head erect when she's caught off guard by an unexpected sound. "Do you know Char Wrig?"

"I have her picture in my wallet, Corr."

"I'll ask again. Do you know Char Wrig?"

Why is Corr sounding so surprised? Who was it that pertly dropped the address of this very building into Corr's lap in Corr's studio?

Or has a wrong assumption been made? Maybe those minuscule whirls and lurches in Corr's voice were *not* indicators of surprise. The dizzy unevenness of Corr's speech could have been produced by something else altogether. What? *Impending understanding* flashing like a million mica flakes from behind her words? Perhaps Corr noticed something vaguely familiar about Reon when she first saw him downstairs, something that all but snapped into place for her up here when he said Char's name.

"She's my daughter."

Corr takes her sweet time mulling over that thin-but-tasty slice of information. It is her turn now to remain cleverly silent.

But Reon outwaits her without even trying. It is out of the worldly side of her mouth that Corr asks, "Is it Reon Stars Renvoi Wrig? Or is it Char Wrig Renvoi?"

"Neither. We do not share any of our names."

"Do you keep her locked in a cage somewhere on the premises?"

"Yes. And I have only let her out twice, the two times that she visited you, Corr. Would you like to see her?"

That didn't sound like a real offer. Is this another of Reon's tests?

"Sure. Why not, Mr. Renvoi. —Whoa!"

Corr catches her breath. In a big rusty voice she exclaims, "Who-o-oa indeed! I can't believe I didn't see it right off. Char Wrig and Vogs lived together for a while. *That's* why you know of Vogs."

"That is how I first heard of Vogs, yes."

"Bing!" Corr pushes the tip of her index finger to her temple. "And obviously that explains why you already knew of me long before your front door identified me—long before that door conveyed to you a big part of my admirable history."

"True enough."

"And long before I first ever laid eyes on Char Wrig?"

"Yes. That's true, too." Reon lays both of his hands palms up on the desktop and spreads his fingers. "I am seeing your deductive mind. I hope to witness your *original mind*."

"Not all women are role models."

"Perhaps that's true, perhaps not. What is your point, Corr?"

"Am I a painting put on display for you?"

"Yes. That is exactly why Char gave you this address."

"What about 832 FOX, *Reon*?"

"That was another 'little test.' We have been able to make do with such simple tests in our examining of you because you are so oral, so verbal. While most people prefer to each build their own individual world in solitary conversations with their self, you build yours pretty much right out in the open. You externalize so many of your thoughts and feelings that we have experienced no need for the normal complexity in testing."

Corr pushes her tongue against the inside of her cheek. "Who is this *we* you speak of?"

"We who work at 5963 Scenic Drive."

"Everyone in this gigantic building?"

"Every last person."

Corr narrows her nostrils. "Including Char? Or does 'every last person' only include white- and silver-haired men and Helga the hellion?"

"Yes, Char works here, too. She is one of us."

Corr's face snaps hard to the left. Had she caught a glimpse of a fleet movement off to that side?

Corr gazes steadily to her left. Why? At what is she looking? No, she has not spotted The Shadow again: the light in this room is much too bright, uniform, and omnidirectional for a return appearance of The Shadow. The one thing to gaze left at from her chair is a white, undecorated wall, which has been standing quite still, right there all the while.

"First it was Not All Women Are Mothers Or Mothers-To-Be." Corr is probably not talking to the wall. She sounds as if she is addressing someone or something off in the distance, a much greater distance than the wall permits. "Then it was Not All Women Are Women. Next it was Not All Women Are Men. And now it's back around to Not All Women Are."

Reon squints at the right profile of Corr's face. "I don't think I completely understood that list or your purpose in reciting it, Corr. But your tidy slate sounded as if it reduces to bitterness. There is absolutely no need here for you to feel bitter."

Corr's eyes leave the wall or whatever and drop to her hands in her lap. She will begin a sentence shortly, but the weak light at the start of that statement will dim and go out before she reaches the subject for the sentence.

"If all of the parts don't work together…"

Reon's eyes dart from Corr's mouth to her throat, to her left ear, to her waist, to her scalp, to her other ear. His eyes then fix on Corr's dropped eyes, and he nods decisively and does not wait for her to pick up from where she had left off. "Is this the beginning of a demo of your original mind?"

"I have learned something here today, Reon." Corr's voice is still pale. She keeps her eyes down.

"What is that?"

Corr decides it is all right to tell him. "I now understand why people carry guns with them everywhere they go. They just might run into someone like you."

Reon blasts into loud laughter. Does he think that Corr was kidding him? Yes or no, he is thoroughly enjoying himself. "Ok. Ok. I'll drop a tiny crumb in Corr Cor's mouth."

"I'm waiting, master." Oh so tart were those words spinning slowly out Corr Cor's mouth. Her icy eyes rise to meet Reon's jolly eyes.

"You cannot see who you were talking to last night because you were talking to a constructed being." Reon pauses to watch for Corr's reaction. She doesn't even blink. Reon continues. "Inside that slot under the DEATH WALKS QUICK sign is just a workroom, the workroom of the man you spoke with in the bottom hall when you stepped into the building last night. Other than that man, whose name is Octal, there is no one in that room. Octal's Being—that's our nickname for it—is always in flux. It never has the same voice, never has the same apparent mind. The only *personal* contact that Octal's Being has with the world outside that room is through the fake delivery slot in the dark of night. The slot is its only portal to the world."

"In the dark of every night, master?"

What was that sharpness in Corr's voice? Was it the mark of sudden interest or of growing hostility?

"No. Not every night. Not hardly. OB's nights-out occur quite irregularly. And nearly never is there anyone outside on the sidewalk."

Corr thinks, silently. She flicks at her lips with her finger. "That's quite a crumb. Thank you."

Tis true. That was indeed an unloaded thank-you from Corr.

This remarkable thank-you, Corr's first polite expression of gratitude today, will be taken to mean, for the time being at least, that her dogged query—"Why can't I see who I was talking to?"—has been finally and satisfactorily answered.

"Reon is now silent," says Reon.

"Corr is now reflecting on the role of landscape architecture in a liberal civilization," says Corr.

Reon laughs, silently. But he will not remain silent much longer.

A *one* and a *two*.

In a genuinely charming and seemingly gracious voice, Reon asks, "I have in stock some of the same tea that Welf prepares for you. Huh?"

One third or more of Corr is surprised by Reon's offer. "That would be nice…" The other third or more of Corr most likely didn't even hear the offer. For Corr is just reaching a point in her thinking where she can ask a question that most likely has been bothering her for some time.

"Who is Jonny Facemoral?"

"Nice jump, Corr. Jonny Facemoral is your protector."

Corr smiles.

Believe it. She did *not* flare up faster than the speed of sound upon hearing Reon's revelation. She smiled.

And she is smiling sweetly even now. With not a trace of scorching indignation detectable in her voice, Corr says, "So he *is* there when I get the feeling he's somewhere around but I can't actually see him." Her smile is as sincere as was that memorably unloaded thank-you.

"Yes, more than likely he is there. Jonny keeps you from harm." Reon is up from his chair. "Real harm. Not like running head first into a post." He steps gingerly to the wall, opens a magic panel, pulls out a fully prepared tea tray and a tiny tea table. He sets up the steaming tea station next to Corr, carefully not touching her. He then returns in a silver flash to his chair behind his desk.

Corr is not finished with the subject, Jonny Facemoral. "I talked briefly with Jonny last night—but you undoubtedly already knew that."

Reon nods.

"He said to me that a friend of mine is lost in the eternal night. And there is no moon."

"Yes. Jonny was not supposed to tell you that. He is, however, a free agent; he calls his own shots. He deserves a sizable portion of the credit for getting you here."

Corr shrewdly brushes aside Reon's last sentence. "What does what he told me mean?"

Reon gives it to her straight, no chaser. "It means that Vogs skipped a step and ended up in the realm between life and death."

Corr is not going to accept that. No. NOT!

But before she can *verbally* fill the room with an expression of her strong disbelief, her eyes shoot off to a place where there is no need for such a space.

"Oh my!" Corr's hand zooms out in front of her to the very end of her arm. She trains her eyes on the man's face and points a long brush-worker's finger at his nose. "That means that Lawlady works here, too."

Reon easily ignores the finger that's pointed at him and has even less trouble with translating the word *Lawlady*. "Yes, Laura Pepin works in and out of the building. She was the Vogs operative."

Reon had not gotten the word *operative* completely out of his mouth when Corr started a question. "Were the pictures that she showed him one of your tests?"

Reon laughs under his breath. "In a way. The pictures were used to see if his was a suitable mind to take the tests."

"So why did Lawlady move into Vogs' building after he was gone to wherever she took him?"

"She moved in *next to you*, Corr. You were her next project. She was your assigned operative for a while, but we changed her role when it became totally clear to us that you can't stand her. Char, known to be our most subtle operative, took over your case. As far as you are concerned now, Laura Pepin is merely keeping 5963 Scenic Drive posted on your condition. She is at the same time working on another case."

"My condition…" Corr quivers and shakes in disgust.

To calm herself, she sips her tea. "Where did she take Vogs?"

"She brought him here."

"Who is this *other case*?"

"Not a chance, Corr."

"Who is Amass King?"

Reon grins as if with pride. "Good assuming, Corr."

He rolls his eyes to the ceiling. "Amass King was a novice when you met him. He was being tried out as a field operative." Reon grins naughtily at Corr. "You broke him in two. He's back in the building behind a desk now."

Next on Corr's check-off list is the fancy dressed man. "Gett Resu?"

"Gett Resu is a real, actual lawyer. He was hired to give *Pepin et al* a legitimate look.

Before Corr utters the next name on her list, the name of the sweet but secretive whisperer who lost in one night both his breath and his chest hair, she tenderly closes her eyes, holds them closed, then slowly reopens them. "Necky Watershighagain was murdered the night of the day that Laura Pepin turned up in his life."

"A coincidence, Corr."

Corr all but spits on the floor. "That white-haired man down in the hall last night, Octal, used that word, too. It clanks in my mind. Your group—or groups—don't sound like people who would believe in coincidence."

"*If...* If I am talking to you right now, Corr, the world must operate on at least two fronts, making coincidence not only possible but necessary."

Corr sneers at that pat definition yet explores further. "Mr. Gunman?"

"Are you referring to Sly Redder? If so, he is a flunky for Jonny."

Corr minimally shakes her head. Her eyes are two thin slits. "And that dark sign out back?"

"Octal told you the only truth we know. The sign is a mystery to us all. It was here when we commandeered the building."

And then, as predicted by Octal's Being, Corr wakes up.

She is stretched out on the couch in Deathstacks. Mean Lips is not in the room.

And then she wakes up in her building, in her own bed. Horsey is sound asleep beside her.

And then she wakes up in Vogs' bed in Vogs and
Necky's building. Vogs and Necky are both asleep, one on either
side of her.

Now she is crying.

(51) +

Standing close by, so close in fact that the toes of both of
his scuffed black shoes are actually under the plastic couch, the
gallery guard stares down at Corr with an anxious look on his
face. He opens his mouth to ask a question, and his words tumble
pell-mell over each other. "Didn't you say you had an
appointment sometime this morning?" He abruptly rotates his
face, perhaps trying to parallel Corr's sleeping face. "It's almost
noon."

"Oh! Hi! There you are." Corr sits up on the couch and
rubs her sleepy eyes.

She stretches. "Yeah, I said that." She yawns. "But I
decided I would not keep the appointment. I'm not going back
there."

"Well…" Mean Lips stammers, again and again and
again. "I have to tell you…my shift was over a long time ago. I've
stayed for as long as I can…to let you sleep. The gallery is not
going to open today…but you will have to leave now, too."

(52) +

"Hey, Horsey! Judy Blue is outside calling out your name
for everyone to hear."

Horsey jerks up from Corr's bed to support himself on
his fists. "What? What? I don't hear anyone."

(53) +

"What was that you said, Vogsy?"

"Actually I didn't say anything, Corrie. I was just farting out the dust of old fat. I won't be needing it any longer, as far as I can see from this here-and-now. And old Necky over there is certainly not going to have any use for love fat, even in its dehydrated state, since he has no foreseeable future as Necky. I know you don't like to be called Corrie, but do you know what a corrie is? It's a cirque. Do you know what a cirque is? No? Then you ought to look the word up. It's a geology term. Words are important to painters too. I looked up both *corrie* and *cirque* a week or so before the last time we were together, you and I. One of the shared definitions—I think it was the basic definition for both words—impressed me as a nearly perfect picture of you in some of your moods."

(54) +

Sixteen hours after Corr Cor departed in the dark in pursuit of 5963 Scenic Drive, she returns to her building, alone. She stops outside her studio door in the warmth of the afternoon and scans the scene. "The world is a soft blue."

She glances at the café across the street. "I must be hungry."

Spreading her arms, not like a butterfly but like a high flying bird, she cranes her neck to peer down just in front of her feet. "Go around," she sings. "Go around. I've been around." Perhaps Corr's bird is looking down upon Corr's journey, seeing that the completed trip has drawn a jagged, sloping circle.

Go across. Go across. She goes across the street.

She hops from the pavement up onto the sidewalk and confidently strides a beeline for the door of *Welf et al.* Suddenly, mid-step, Corr freezes. Her head cranks around, and she stares back across the street at the building next to hers. "It looks…" She shakes her head. "The place looks empty!" Corr snaps the rest of her body around to face the building in question. "All of the curtains are at their usual *proper* settings…" Corr's antsy hands slide up to rest high on her hips once more. "And the *Pepin et al* sign still hangs out front. Yet the building looks utterly abandoned." Corr did not see Welf pop out the door of his café.

Stepping like a split stick of ice-water crisped celery, Welf stiff-leggedly approaches Corr and stands beside her. He too has got a bit of the jitters showing most noticeably in his hands. "What are we looking at?"

Corr's eyes haven't left the building across the way. "Lawlady's building. It's deserted."

"How can you tell, Corr?" What prompted Welf to come outside? Wasn't it just yesterday that he approached Corr in the café and surprised her by asking what she was going to name her latest painting? Yesterday and today, concern for Corr's welfare may well be what is motivating Welf. "The building looks exactly the same to me."

"It does?" Corr sounds less confident.

Welf, on the other hand, is calming down and is sounding more self-assured. "Look there." He points to an upstairs window.

The back and head of a person can be seen through the window. Then the body parts move away from the window.

"Right!" Corr lovingly slaps Welf's upper arm. "Thank you, sir. This case is now closed!" She sneaks a glance at the side of his face.

"You are certainly welcome, madam. Any time."

Corr then surprises Welf by taking hold of his elbow to steer him around to face the door of his café. She wants him to be gazing directly at that door while she tells him the story of her upcoming entry and his upcoming reentry into the café. "They strode arm in arm in the door. The patrons inside neither exploded into loud applause nor into boisterous cheering. Other than our two, no one knew of the grand rescue of a damsel in distress that had taken place just outside *Welf et al* only a short while before. She takes herself to her silent table as he returns to his quiet work."

Welf is embarrassed to the point he can't speak. Corr can't help laughing at him. She gets behind him and pushes him inside. No one inside lets on that they even notice "our two."

Welf straightens his shirt. "Tea, Corr?"

"Yes! And one of your big, thick sandwiches." Corr pats him lightly on his back and veers away to her silent table. Remembering her manners, she shoots over her shoulder, "Pretty please, sir."

All at once Corr is rushing. She yanks out the drawing pencil that's always in her pants pocket, while her eyes search everywhere. A napkin has been left on her table by the previous occupant. Corr flops down on her chair and on the napkin writes, "I should have asked about the actual process, the actual translation of Vogs, in other words, his being removed to a nontemporal condition without his witnessing death." Will this late thought of Corr's initiate a painting? Under the long wistful sentence she scribbles almost unreadably, "If that is what happened."

The tea is not here yet. Corr is fidgety. She props her chin on her hand. She looks at the ceiling. She looks out the window. Her mouth would have dropped open if she had not been holding it closed. Across the street, someone is up on a ladder taking down the *Pepin et al* sign.

Corr stares. And stares. Is *this case* soon to be declared un-closed?

She is whispering. "A man in white coveralls. A mover? A carpenter? A hanger of new signs?"

The man takes down the old sign and proceeds to hang a new one. Corr is puzzled. "What does the sign say? It is so demurely formal I can't read it."

Welf comes up behind Corr's chair. "I see that you too are checking out the new sign across the street. I can't read it from out here, but from the kitchen I could see it well enough. The sign says," says Welf as he steps around beside Corr, "GETT RESU, ATTORNEY AT LAW."

Welf sets down the tray and downloads Corr's tea and sandwich. And utensils. And a new napkin. "Looks like your 'Lawlady' is indeed leaving us."

With the greatest show of assurance in the world Corr replies, "She is already gone."

(55) +

"So…. So our rather tall, slightly slim, abundantly ego-ed, golden haired vixen in exclusive clothes is working on another case. Could her next someone be someone I know? Probably not. —No, hold on there, Miss Pickle Rickle. Why not? It could well be someone who I know. Her Highness could be working a chain, with each link known personally by the link that proceeded it. First Vogs and then me and then…who? Welf? Negative! I do not think Welf has the type of mind they are looking for. — Better backtrack a bit, CC! Our Vogs would not necessarily have been the first link in the local chain. Who could have been before him? Necky? Necky *did* have secrets. He might have failed their 'tests' and ended up dead. Nix, that is not very likely. I don't think these people are into cut-em-up violence. —I could be seriously wrong about that, however!"

Corr is still in the café. She has eaten her sandwich, drunk her tea, and turned down a refill on the tea. "Stop and think a sec or two, Corr. You have not in fact been inside yon building of yours since you returned from your fun overnighter." Corr raises her ever frisky hand to play at mopping her brow as if she's suffering a sudden sickening suspense. "Laura Pepin just might be planning to keep 5963 Scenic Drive posted on my condition by moving in with me. She may be over there in my bed this very minute. If so, I'm going to have to go on over and kick the slam flam ruggle out'a the ex-lawlady."

Corr pushes back her hair and her chair as she stands up. Welf waves goodbye to her from the table that he's waiting on across the room. The man sitting sideways at that table looks up, gives Corr an ugly scowl.

"He is new to the café. He has never seen Corr Cor before. He is sorry already, and he will be forgiven this time. But if he dares to shoot daggers at me a second time, hideously horrendous olden dreams of blood and broken teeth will haunt him day and night for many months."

Corr raises her nose high and secures a refined exit. She hears the café's door close behind her. "Up and out I was, and across the way to unlock and in my door I go now."

She pulls up her spotted pony just inside her building and quickly looks back over her shoulder at the shutting studio door, to aid her memory. "Yes. Yes, the door was still locked."

Corr spreads her feet, plants her feet, throws both of her arms low behind her, and slowly revolves her head to scrutinize the studio. And she does it again, a second time. Both times, she warily rotated her head from its left stop to its right stop. Her report: "No marked change is observable in the always-changing orchestration down here."

Corr skips over to the foot of the stairs and stares up the incline. "And the stairs, they are clear enough."

Up the staircase she gallops like Horsey. Throwing open the first door on her right, she steps into the room. "Vogs and Necky's paintings, unboxed and hanging in here proudly now."

Down the hall to the bedroom she slides. Under the bed she looks. Into the closet she looks. Into the bathroom she peers.

"Ok. That will serve as a preliminary check. Onward now to the serious investigating."

Corr inspects every space big and small in the whole building, while reciting over and over again an aging memory that is chillingly similar to her present activity. "Corr goes in and walks through the entire building, searching every nook and cranny. There is no one in Vogs' building, no one but her. Has Vogs been killed by Laura and packed away?"

Corr returns to her bedroom. "Hmm. No news. Is that favorable news? Or just no news?"

She pulls her blouse over her head without unbuttoning it. "One bit of news is definitely auspicious, amiga or amigo, as the suit fits. There is still time for a siesta." Having dropped her pants to the floor, Corr leaps high and happy and revolves in the warm afternoon air to land flat on her back on her bed, making nary a sound, which is, of course, not possible.

"To sleep I went. To rest after a difficult night and arduous next morning. But immediately I began to wonder. If Laura Pepin is not really a lawyer, what was her interest in the theft of Vogs and Necky's paintings from my room down the hall? It could well be that she had no interest at all in the theft. She might not have even known about it. I can venture that surmise now because of what I was told by Char Wrig's father. If what Reon the Silver Star said is the truth, Sly Redder was actually Jonny's 'flunky,' not Lawlady's. Mr. Gunman's claiming to be an employee of *Pepin et al* could easily have been a bare-assed lie. A lying gunman? Sounds imminently violent to me. To me. To me."

Need it be said that Corr is asleep and dreaming out loud? It does need to be stated, however, that Jonny Facemoral is standing tall in Corr's bedroom doorway, watching her, listening to her, slowly shaking his head.

No, Vogs is not standing beside him.

(56) +

A wet picture of Necky.
The smell of nasty water.
A dry picture of Welf.

**(end) **

•••••••••••••••••••••••

www.ingramcontent.com/pod-product-compliance
Lightning Source LLC
Chambersburg PA
CBHW031106260626
47172CB00001B/237